BIRTH OF THE MORTOKAI (PART ONE)

THE FIRST CHRONICLE OF DANIEL WELSH

By

D G Palmer

This is a work of fiction. Similarities to real people, places, or events are entirely coincidental.

BIRTH OF THE MORTOKAI

First edition. August 1, 2019.

Copyright © 2019 D G Palmer.

ISBN: 978-1099518171

Written by D G Palmer.

Also by D G Palmer

The Chronicles of Daniel Welsh
Birth of The Mortokai

Standalone
The Choices Of Man

Watch for more at https://www.dgpalmer.com.

To Sugarplum for giving me that final push to get this book over the
line

Prologue

The smoke and vapours from the cauldron rose wistfully into the rafters. Shadows danced on the walls, as the fire it rested on crackled and spat. The flames licked the sides of the silver gilt kettle as its contents violently bubbled away.

The bulbous boiler was exquisitely crafted. An intricately designed gold relief depicted a hunt; wondrous creatures being chased by what looked like men on horseback. It had seen countless use over its long lifetime, a fact supported by the tell-tale marks, the blackening of its underside, and the watermark around the rim, suggesting the many concoctions that had been brewed up within its depths.

The pyre beneath the cauldron was the only source of light within the musty, stone-clad room, which had no windows or doors. The organic nature of the flame, which seemed to give life to the inanimate objects around it, moved and swayed, and the dark shadows it projected cavorted with it.

Suddenly, the very air began to shimmer and a small hole opened in the void. It widened rapidly until the portal was large enough to allow a man clad in dark clothing to step through. He waved a hand nonchalantly and the portal vanished behind him.

Gydion strode purposefully toward his cauldron. His dark grey robes swung back and forth loosely around his arms and legs. In the darkness its hood hid all but his pointed black beard. He looked into the large pot and breathed the distinctive aroma deep into his lungs. Satisfied with the state of the mixture, Gydion opened his robe and from a hidden pocket withdrew three bundles: flowers of oak, flowers of broom, and flowers of meadowsweet. He tossed these final ingredients into the brew and watched as a large plume of white smoke wafted into the air. The acrid smell that had prevailed was quickly replaced by the sweet, fragrant smell of the blossoms, which prompted Gydion to nod his hooded head in approval; it was time.

He pushed the embroidered sleeves of his robes away from his hands, revealing more of his sinewy forearms. Holding his hands out in front of him, his fingers extended as far as they could reach, he began to recite powerful arcane words. Runes appeared, one by one, on the ground around the cauldron and pulsed a brilliant green. His eyes were closed as he concentrated on each word that passed his lips. All he had done before would be for nothing if he made a mistake in casting the spell.

Gydion began to create intricate shapes and patterns with his hands, as the conjuration continued unabated. A light shone from within the cauldron, growing brighter and brighter, as if in tandem with the mage's voice, which became louder and louder, his casting of the spell becoming more insistent.

Without warning, everything stopped. Gydion ceased casting and straightened his sleeves. The runes disappeared. The fire died down and eventually extinguished itself. The only aspect remaining in the room to suggest any sorcery had taken place was the light shining from the cauldron. The light, though dimmer than it had been during the spell cast, was still bright enough to illuminate the chamber.

Suddenly something stirred within the cauldron. Inch by inch, what looked to be an auburn-haired teenage girl rose from the depths of the bulbous pot. When she finally stood fully erect, she opened her green eyes for the first time and looked around, taking in her surroundings. When her gaze finally rested on Gydion, she gave him a warm smile of daughterly affection. His response was to remove his hood and look at her sternly with his dark eyes. They held an unimaginable amount of wisdom, garnered from hundreds of years of study and from seeing the many realms. The wrinkles at the corners of his eyes and the few speckles of grey hair in his beard did little to betray the true age of the mage.

He scrutinised her with an examining look, almost boring into her very being. When he was satisfied with his investigation, Gydion softened his face and gave her a small smile. 'How do you feel?' he asked gently, as he held out his hand for her to take. She did so happily and stepped out of the cauldron.

The solution dripped from her body and she left wet footprints as she padded on the hard stone floor.

'I feel cold,' she replied stoically. 'And wet.'

'Of course,' he stated with a slight chuckle. 'Just a moment.' With that, he held out his hands, palms facing upwards, and quietly recited a spell. As he finished speaking, a delicate, red silken gown appeared and he handed it to the appreciative girl.

'Thank you, Father, it's beautiful.' She smiled as she held up the vestment before slipping it on over her head.

'What do you think of Trinity?' Gydion suddenly asked her.

'What?'

'For a name,' he replied. 'Where we are going, you'll need a name so that you might blend in. I was thinking of Trinity Evergreen.'

She mused over the name. 'Trinity Evergreen?' She said it slowly and then quickly as if trying to get a feel for it. 'Yes, I like it. Where will we be going?'

'Lady Rhiannon has tasked me with finding a deserter who is in a vision she has had. I, however, am tasking you with finding someone else, and we will find these people on the Earth realm. Now, we must go to the library, as there are many things that you will need to learn while we search for our respective missing persons.'

'Yes, Father.' Trinity nodded as she followed Gydion through the portal he had just conjured. Within seconds, they and the portal had vanished.

1

Daniel Welsh was running for his life. That was the feeling he had deep down inside. He could feel his heart pounding rapidly and his blood rushing through his body as it went into survival mode. 'Fight or flight,' that was what it was called; he had seen it on a wildlife programme on *National Geographic.* His mind was a little distracted at that moment, but he was sure it was about the Serengeti, or could it have been the Masai Mara? Either way, it had involved a pride of lions hunting a herd of gazelles. It was how the body reacted to a threat; turn and face it or turn and flee from it. He was more than happy to choose the latter, as he pumped his arms and legs as fast as he could because he knew what the consequence would be if he slowed down. He was not looking to be that gazelle anytime soon.

The 'lion' that was chasing him down right now was Bobby Brinkmeyer, captain of the school rugby team and his two cronies, Jack Thompson and Willis Jeffries. Daniel was astonished at how fast he was for a big guy. If he kept running in a straight line he would be caught in no time. He needed to take some evasive action.

The wind blew into his face as he sprinted down roads, in between people, and past shop fronts. Daniel could feel his sunglasses bouncing up and down on his nose, and they threatened to fly off at any moment. The strings on the hood of his jacket were pulled tight to make sure it was secure during his rigours, just as he always had them when he was out in the sunlight, to protect himself. Doctors had told his parents when he was younger that because of his albinism, he was more susceptible to the sun's ultraviolet light. His skin and hair were as white as ivory. Not only could he burn more easily, but the chances of him developing skin cancer were increased. The sunglasses he wore were to protect his yellow eyes from the photosensitivity they had due to the lack of melanin pigments.

He could understand why they called him Ghost Face, but it did not mean that he had to like it. It had just gotten too much for him, all the teasing, the bullying, being the butt of all the jokes. It had been going on for so long. He thought that when he'd turned sixteen, and left high school for sixth form, that things would be different. But his tormentors had followed him. When Daniel first told his parents all about it, his mother had told him to just ignore them and they would get bored and eventually move on to their next victim. His father, however, had told him that bullies did not like to be confronted and that he would have to stand up to them one day. Today had been that day, but things had not gone as he had hoped.

Daniel's weekday had begun as it always had, with him waiting at the corner of the gates to his sixth form college until the last minute, when everyone else had gone to their classes. He stood against the wall trying as hard as he could to be inconspicuous and invisible. Sometimes he felt that it was actually working, especially when two girls walked right past him without even taking a sideways glance. He wished it could be like that always, with nobody taking any notice of him. Where he would be regarded as normal.

He had one last quick look around the grounds before making his way inside. The halls were empty, as he desired, with just the faint sounds of learning coming from rooms as he passed them; pupils umming and ahhing their way through queries, while tutors droned through text unenthusiastically.

When he reached room 9, he stretched out his hand to open the classroom door, but he hesitated when he heard Bobby's American voice answer a question posed to him by his tutor, Mr. Dram. Daniel was about to walk off and head towards the library, his only true refuge at school, when he heard the hurried footsteps of someone running down the hall towards him. He turned just in time to see Trinity Evergreen rush around the corner and come to a panting halt in front of him.

She had transferred from another school only two weeks ago and from the first time he had seen her, Daniel had been taken by her glistening eyes, which were as green as her name suggested. Her floral aroma wafted past his nose and he couldn't help but inhale it. He didn't think she heard him do it as she flicked her auburn-coloured tresses forward and then back, before sliding an Alice band through her hair to keep it out of her oval-shaped, demure face. He noticed that her English rose cheeks were more flushed than usual, which, he reasoned, was probably due to her run just now. Today she had a small gold hoop in the left side of her nose where usually she had a diamond stud. The white floral maxi skirt she wore flowed around her legs as if she were walking through a meadow on a spring morning, and her gladiator sandals showed off the deep purple, glitzy nail polish she had on her toes.

'Phew!' she exhaled, 'I'm not the only one late.'

Daniel was struck dumb by the fact that she had spoken to him. 'Uh huh,' was all he could reply, his mouth slightly open in a shocked expression.

'Well?' she smiled, as she grabbed his arm. 'Are you going in or not?' She opened the classroom door and literally dragged him stumbling inside.

'Well, well, well,' Mr. Dram said. 'So nice of you to join us, Ms. Evergreen, and you, too, Mr. Welsh. Just because you two are the brightest in the year doesn't mean you can turn up to classes whenever you want.'

Daniel made his way to his usual chair at the back. *It's not that I'm brighter than everyone else,* he thought to himself, *having this photographic memory just means I can retain information indefinitely. Is that true intelligence? The ability to regurgitate facts and figures at will? That's all it takes to pass exams; they're merely a test of how much you can remember throughout the year. Unfortunately for me, I remember everything I've read. Would it be enough in the real world? Probably not, unless I intended to make a career out of participating in general knowledge quizzes.*

Trinity took her seat in the front row. She turned and smiled at Daniel just as he took off his shades and pushed his hood off his head. He briefly smiled shyly back at her before getting down to his work. She shuffled in her chair as she too knuckled down to her assignment.

Time passed and the buzzer finally sounded to signify the end of the lesson. The familiar sound of chairs being pushed back and scraped along the floor could be heard all around the college. It was lunchtime, and everyone was rushing to find out what was on the menu and also to get a good seat for themselves and their friends.

Daniel didn't usually bother with lunch. With all the students in that giant hall at once, any bullying would be under a microscope and, ultimately, intensified. He always compared it with what it must have been like to witness an execution at the Coliseum; bloody, messy, and with all the onlookers baying for more. And then there were all the stares. Hundreds of eyes trained on him, watching every move he made, every mouthful he took. That's why, to avoid the unwanted attention, ordinarily at this time Daniel could be found hiding himself away in a corner of the library with a book and eating a chocolate bar. It was his sanctuary. This all too frequent practice of missing meals was the major contribution to his slim physique. He was glad that physical education was no longer on his curriculum; at least he avoided having to hear the skeleton jibes or have boys trying to play his ribs like a xylophone as he changed into his gym kit.

Daniel broke from his usual routine and ventured into the dining hall for one reason: Trinity Evergreen. He wouldn't describe what they had shared as 'a moment,' but she had spoken to him, and only tutors ever said more than two words to him. She had also spoken with a smile, and the tutors never did that. His expectations weren't high; he just thought it would be a welcome change to have a study partner that actually wanted to study *with* him and not study him.

It had been a while since he had last been in here but things didn't seem to have changed much, including the menu. Daniel picked up a tray and walked along the counter. He took a plate of what looked like Beef Stroganoff with roasted vegetables but smelled like something completely different. After adding a carton of drink and a bowl of dessert, Daniel paid at the till and then turned to look for a seat.

The sea of heads was unnerving to Daniel and the cacophony they were making, as they each raised their voice to be heard, was making it hard for him to hear his own thoughts. He inched his way down the aisle, his head bowed, not wanting to make eye contact with anyone and draw attention to himself. But no one seemed to be taking any notice of him, as if he wasn't even there. Then he had a sense that someone was staring at him and he couldn't help but glance up.

Trinity was smiling at him with an even bigger smile than she had given him in the classroom. He looked back at her and she was all he could see; it was like everything else had faded to grey and she was the only bright spot in the hall. A smile crept across his face.

Slowly Daniel made his way to the table where Trinity sat alone. Thoughts of what he would say to her ran through his mind, but before he had a chance to implement any of his ideas, the New Age girls, who had been walking from the opposite end of the aisle, rushed to fill the empty seats.

The smile that had been on his face vanished and Trinity couldn't hide her look of disappointment as the lonely figure of Daniel walked past. That look quickly turned to one of concern as she saw Bobby creeping down the aisle. Her misgivings were proved right when he shoved Daniel hard in the back, sending the much lighter boy staggering down the walkway as he tried desperately to keep his balance. He might have been successful if someone hadn't stuck out their leg and tripped him.

Daniel lay sprawled out on the floor in his Beef Stroganoff. The howls of laughter were deafening. The only person he imagined not laughing was Trinity. He hoped so anyway. He just got up and ran out as fast as he could without bothering to look back to check.

It wasn't until he had reached the lavatories that he stopped. He could feel the tears burning in his eyes as he sat down in a cubicle. Tears of anger directed at that American oaf and his goons. Tears of frustration at being taunted and ridiculed about something he couldn't change. Tears of embarrassment at being made to look a fool in front of Trinity.

He pulled off some toilet paper and tried to clean himself up the best he could. He had already decided that there was no way he was going to attend afternoon lectures after this.

'Daniel, are you in here?'

The sound of Trinity's soft voice made him freeze. As much as he wanted to, he was just too embarrassed to speak to her right now, so he kept quiet. He heard the banging of the doors to the other cubicles as Trinity started to check them one by one. Finally, she approached the one Daniel was in and sniffed the air. 'You can try and hide all you want. I know you're in there. I can smell you. I can smell that...that stuff on you.'

He looked down at the brown mess on his shirt. 'Great, just great,' he said under his breath, and then he spoke through the door. 'What are you doing here, Trinity?'

'I just wanted to make sure you're okay,' she replied, full of concern.

'What would your clique say about that?'

'I don't care; besides, they're not *my* clique,' Trinity stated as she leant against the door. 'Look, when I started here, they flocked to *me*; it wasn't the other way around. I guess it's because I know a bit about crystals and stuff like that.'

'So, you told them you were coming after me then?' Daniel asked.

She paused as she decided whether to lie or not. 'No, I didn't,' she said truthfully.

'So much for 'I don't care,' huh? You're no different from the rest of them.'

Trinity took offence at the remark and let him know exactly how much, by kicking the door in anger. 'Look, Daniel, I didn't have to come here! If I were like the others, as you say I am, I wouldn't have. I'd be sitting in the hall eating my food and having a good laugh at your expense. But here I am, concerned about you, and if you can't see that I'm different from the rest of them, then I guess I'm wasting my time here!'

Silence reigned supreme as neither of them spoke for what seemed like an age. Eventually, Trinity shook her head and with a disappointed sigh turned and began to make her way back to the dining hall. She really thought she could get through to him. The sound of a cubicle lock being slid open stopped her in her tracks.

'I'm sorry,' Daniel said sheepishly.

'It's okay,' she said as she approached him. 'I'm sorry for what happened to you.'

'It's just another day in the life of Daniel Welsh.'

'But it shouldn't have to be. You're special, Daniel.'

'Special needs, you mean?'

'No. I mean special as in *special*.'

Before Trinity could continue, the door behind them opened and a boy stood in the doorway staring at them. He looked at Daniel then Trinity, then at Daniel and back to Trinity again. A grimace came over his face and he started to hop from foot to foot. Then Trinity remembered where they were.

'I think we should go and talk somewhere else,' she said to Daniel, suddenly becoming sympathetic to the boy's needs. They heard a loud groan of relief as they walked away.

2

It wasn't long before they were sitting in the quiet surrounds of the library, a much more appropriate location for them to meet. The library was a well-stocked place of study. It was laid out over two levels; the upper level housed rooms for quiet study and the reference books, the lower level had all the other books against the walls and in tall shelving along the length of the library, on either side of the rows of desks that ran down the centre.

Mrs. Berry, the school librarian, greeted Daniel and Trinity as warmly as she always did. She believed in the power of the written word and she kept her library in immaculate condition, even though these two were the only students that ever utilised it.

The two classmates sat down opposite each other at a desk at the back. Sunlight streamed through the large arched windows and the rays warmed the wood of the table.

'So,' Daniel dragged the word out for all it was worth, 'here we are.'

'Yes,' Trinity replied, 'here we are.' She absentmindedly played with the shards of light that streamed through the window, casting shadows across the desk; something weighed heavily on her mind. 'Does it bother you?' she asked all of a sudden. 'Not being able to go out in the sun?'

'I *am* out,' he said whilst throwing his arms out in a wide gesture.

'You *know* what I mean, Daniel. Having to cover up like it's winter. Not feeling the sun on your skin, the warmth or its healing energy. Does it get to you?'

He rocked back in his chair and gave some thought to what she was asking. 'It used to,' he replied after a few moments. 'A lot more when I was a kid than now. Now I'm used to it, it's like second nature. I don't even think about it. But back then I'd watch films, mostly Bond, and see Caribbean islands and stuff like that and know that it'd never be me. I thought I'd burst into flames like a vampire nightwalker. No sun, sea, and sand for this dude. I've always wanted to go to Antigua or St. Bart's or Seychelles and the Maldives. Then there's Natal in Brazil; I've read that the coastal waters around there stay at a constant twenty-eight degrees.'

'What if you could go to all of them?'

'Then I'd be gone in a shot. No need to offer me a second time,' he chuckled sombrely. 'Some people's dreams can come true; unfortunately, mine never will.'

'But what if one day they could? Hypothetically speaking, of course. What if they could?' She thought a moment as she still tried to gage Daniel's reaction. 'But you had to take on some sort of, I don't know, let's say some sort of *extra* responsibility, would you?'

Daniel sat there and looked at her with a quizzical face. 'What the heck are you on about?'

'Don't worry about it,' she said with a nonchalant wave of her hand. 'I was just trying to get to know you, especially if we're going to be study partners.'

'Study partners?'

'Yes. That is what you want, right?'

'Yeah! Yeah of course! Actually, that's what I was going to ask you at lunch.'

'I was hoping you would,' she said and smiled that winning smile of hers. 'I actually kind of had a feeling.'

'Oh, then you must be *special* too then,' Daniel stated with a sarcastic smile.

'More than you could imagine.' There was a hint of playful mystery to Trinity's reply.

'I don't know, I could imagine quite a lot.'

'*Star Wars*? You're quoting *Star Wars*?'

'Would you prefer I quoted *Pretty Woman*?'

'Only if you want me to start teasing you too!' she exclaimed in a matter-of-fact way. Then they both burst out laughing. The day was fast becoming Daniel's best one at college. He hadn't laughed and smiled this much in ages, and he knew it was all down to Trinity. Usually, around people, he felt tense and on edge. He was always half expecting people to start whispering and pointing at him. But she seemed to have a calming, relaxing effect on him; around her, he found it easy to open up and be himself. It was a feeling he could learn to get used to.

'So, study buddy, tell me about your parents. What do they do?' she asked after they had both composed themselves.

'Well, my dad's a construction foreman and my mum's a doctor. What about you?'

'It's just my father and me; he's a professor. My mother left when I was still young.'

'I'm sorry.'

'Don't be; you weren't to know.'

'Have you ever thought about trying to find her?'

'No.'

The abruptness of her reply let Daniel know that this subject was a no-go area. 'Your dad being a professor explains your own smarts. You must get lots of homeschooling. Do you feel pressure to succeed because of him?'

'I am who I am because of him. He's a great man; you'll see for yourself one day. I'm sure he'll want to meet you.'

'You know, you still haven't told me what you meant by me being special,' stated Daniel suddenly.

Trinity looked down at her hands. 'Yeah, about that, I shouldn't have said anything to you,' she replied, looking down at her hands with regret.

'But you did.'

'And it wasn't my place to.'

Daniel gave her a confused look. 'Okay, now I'm curious. What's with all the mystery?'

She continued to look at her hands intently, as her eyebrows furrowed and she began biting her lower lip. She gave little nods and slight shakes of her head, plus the occasional shrug of her shoulders. All the while Daniel watched her inquisitively as she had a deep, thoughtful conversation in her head.

'Right!' Trinity shouted as she slammed her hands down on the table, which made Daniel jump in his chair. Mrs. Berry shushed them from her desk. She apologised to the librarian and then huddled closer to Daniel and whispered to him conspiratorially. 'Okay, I'll let you know. I think it's only fair that you should have some foreknowledge because sooner rather than later your life will change.'

'Well, that doesn't sound ominous at all,' he said sarcastically.

'It's supposed to,' she replied with an air of seriousness. 'Magic is not to be trifled with lightly.'

'Wait a minute. You're kidding, right?' Daniel said as he leaned back in his chair with an exasperated look. He was expecting some ground-breaking revelation, not this. 'This is what this is about? David Blaine, Dynamo stuff?'

'Don't be idiotic, Daniel, I'm not talking about card tricks,' she said as she put her hand into her satchel. She brought it back out and held it before her, palm up, so Daniel could see what she held. In her hand lay a multifaceted olive-green rectangular gem. 'I'm talking about *real* magic.'

Trinity stared at the gemstone unblinkingly and Daniel watched her just as intently. Her eyes were mesmerising him once again, and then he noticed that they were beginning to glow brighter. Her lips moved but he could barely hear the words she was speaking; they sounded almost melodic. Then the stone's core started to throb with incandescent light. As it did so, it began to levitate slightly above her hand. As she spoke, he could feel something pulse through his body in time with the light coming from the gem; he likened it to a surge of adrenalin, but this was somehow different.

'You can feel it, can't you, the magic in the air? It's called Essence. It's everywhere, within all the dimensional realms and it courses through our bodies also, some more than others.' Trinity briefly looked at Daniel as she said this to gauge his reaction, then she sat back in her chair, leaving the gem floating above the desk. 'It's what is spent when we cast spells. The more powerful the spell, the more Essence is used up. It's like physical activity in that respect. The more you do, the more stamina you use, the more you tire; Essence works the same way. This spell, for instance, costs practically nothing.'

Daniel looked at the gem in wide-eyed wonder. He couldn't believe what he was seeing. It had to be some sort of trick, he thought, as he edged out a speculative finger towards it, but stopped himself just short of touching it. 'What is it?'

'It's just a peridot crystal. Earth Faeries are closely involved in their for-
mation so they have a strong connection to them.'

'I meant the spell,' Daniel corrected, but then paused a moment as he
processed what Trinity had actually said. 'Wait! What? Faeries? Are you kidding?'

'Yes, Faeries,' she smiled. 'The Fae, the Fair Folk, the Enchanted People,
whatever you want to call them. Dwarfs, Elves, Orcs, Trolls, Ogres. They're
all real, and more besides. If you don't believe me, take the gem, put it to your
eye, and look over there.'

Daniel tentatively plucked the gem out of the air. He treated it as if it
were a delicate piece of archaeology. Once he held it in his hand, however, he
could feel exactly how solid and sturdy it actually was. He slowly brought it
up to his left eye and peered through its centre. Everything appeared in lustrous, iridescent colours.

'Don't look at me, look over there,' Trinity said, pointing to a corner behind Daniel.

He turned in his seat to follow the direction she indicated. There was
something huddled in the corner. What it was he couldn't be sure. All the
rainbow colours he was seeing obscured his vision and made it difficult to
pinpoint anything.

Trinity could see the knot in Daniel's brow as he strained to see what she
could. She knew that she was going to be in trouble for what she had already
told him, so she thought that she might as well make it worthwhile and show
him too. 'What you have to do, Daniel, is rotate the crystal to increase the
focus.'

He turned back to face the corner and manipulated the peridot in front
of his eye. As the lustrous colours faded into the more visually recognisable
colour palette of real life, he was able to make out the sleeping form of what
he thought was a small child snoring in the corner. He moved closer to get a
better look; however, he still couldn't tell what it was. All he could really see
was that the figure had long, black wiry hair and was dressed in a rough green
waistcoat and trousers that may have been white at one time but were now a
dirty grey. Then the figure rolled over in its sleep. The face looked like that of
an old, wizened man with a large warty nose.

'What you staring at, longshanks?' the creature shouted. 'Can't a fella sleep in peace?'

The sight was such a shock to Daniel that he jumped back in his chair with such force that he fell off it and landed on a heap on the floor, which drew another, even more, stern shush from Mrs. Berry and sniggers from Trinity.

Daniel looked at her in confusion as he stood up and dusted himself off. 'What is that...that thing?' he asked.

'It's not a *thing*, it's a Hobthrust,' she corrected.

'Oh right, of course. How could I be so stupid?' said Daniel sarcastically.

'Some call them Hobgoblins, others Kobolds or Brownies. They're House Elves. They keep homes clean and tidy; it's what they do. You never thought the college cleaners did this whole building by themselves, did you? They're good, but they're not that good,' she smiled.

'A Hobthrust?' he mused, as he looked at the apparently empty corner it lay in. 'Why can't I see it without the gem?'

'Why would you?' she asked. 'They disappeared from sight when people as a whole stopped believing in Fae. When they preferred to follow a scientific, so-called logical outlook on life, but they didn't cease to exist. Most returned home but some remained here. Having belief can be a powerful thing, Daniel. It'll help with your magic. What you'll need to do is learn the spells and conjurations, as well as the meditative exercises to increase your Essence control. Look at me; I've been speaking as if you've already made your decision to become an Initiate. It's wrong for me to assume, especially when...'

Before she could finish her sentence, the bell sounded, signalling the end of the lunch break. It was the moment that Daniel had been dreading. Whilst he had been talking to Trinity, nothing else had occupied his mind. He had forgotten all about school, the people, even the mess on his shirt. The only thing that had concerned him was the relaxed atmosphere and the normal conversation he had had with her, or as normal as a conversation about Faeries, Hobthrusts, and magic could ever be. To be honest, he hadn't believed what she was telling him, not at the beginning anyway. Telling him that he was some sort of mage, or rather had the potential to be one, seemed a bit far-fetched, but the floating gem had fascinated him, and he had to admit that he had felt something when she was supposedly casting a spell. But the clincher had been the creature asleep in the corner. He had no rational explanation for it. Trinity, however, did. The question on his mind now was did he believe it all? And the answer he came to, inevitably, was that she had no reason to lie.

3

Trinity and Daniel bid farewell to Mrs. Berry. As they left, the librarian made a comment about being happy at seeing her two favourite students working together. The fact that they were the only students that she saw in any sort of regularity and the only two that she knew well enough to stop and converse with probably helped with her assessment.

The two students headed down the corridor towards their next class. They had talked casually as they walked, covering subjects synonymous with small talk; the weather, new CDs out, latest movie releases. Daniel had even told her about his interest in history and historical items.

As they approached room 101, the location of their next lecture, Daniel determined it was time to make his confession.

'I think this is as far as I go. I've decided not to go to afternoon lectures, Trinity. I've had about all I can take of this muck on me,' he stated.

'You should have said. I wouldn't have dragged you all the way up here otherwise,' she replied, a little disappointed.

'I wanted to come. Trust me, if it wasn't for this stuff I'd stay. I...I've enjoyed your company.' He found it difficult to divulge his feelings. He had put up so many barriers and had been so guarded throughout his life that he had become a virtual emotional recluse. But now he felt himself opening up once again.

'I've enjoyed spending time with you too,' Trinity smiled. 'Okay, if you're going to go, let me show you one last thing.'

She looked into the classroom through the window and saw that only the lecturer was there. She deduced that she still had a few minutes before the class began, so she took Daniel by the hand, felt his slim fingers interlock with her own, and led him to an empty adjacent room. Once inside, she set about rearranging things by pushing two tables together. She persuaded Daniel to lay on them, despite his reluctance.

'What's this all about?'

'Well,' Trinity began, 'I'm not being funny, but you're a little tense and a little stiff too. To make the best use of the meditation exercises that you will be taught, you need to be able to relax, both mentally and physically. Tension is a major barrier between magic and us. What I'm going to teach you now will help you to prepare.'

'Look, Trinity, I still haven't made a decision, but the way you're talking it's almost like I have no real choice in the matter either. I wasn't even sure I believed you at first, to be honest.' He saw the despondent look on her face when he said this. 'But I do now; it's hard not to when you're confronted with a grumpy Hobthrust.'

'I was going to say something to you earlier, before the bell, but didn't get the chance to. Being a mage is difficult. It brings a lot of responsibility and takes a lot of dedication. It opens your mind to new things, some wondrous, some dangerous. You should understand that it is a big decision, and not one to be taken lightly.'

'How is it you know so much?'

'One of the benefits of having a professor for a father, I guess.' She deliberately avoided Daniel's sceptical gaze, as she pushed him back down onto the table. 'Right, let's begin. Close your eyes and focus on your breathing. Now, you should be getting a feeling of warmth growing at the top of your head. This is your Essence. Allow it to flow down your face and neck, taking away all tension as it moves. Feel it pass over your shoulders, arms, hands, and fingers. Now it flows through your torso and finally travels down your legs and feet. How do you feel?'

'I feel totally relaxed and serene. And a sensation of wellbeing and I'm kind of floaty, I guess,' Daniel replied, still laying on the table with his eyes closed.

Suddenly, a purple haze became visible around Daniel. It silently flickered and flared about him like it was made of flames, but it gave off no heat. Trinity stared at it in open-mouthed wonder. She had only seen someone's Essence projected so strongly once before, and her father was hundreds of years old. Just as swiftly as it had appeared, the vapour abruptly vanished. She helped him to sit up and he looked at her with the biggest beaming smile she had ever seen on his face.

'I think we may have overdone the relaxation a little bit. Though that technique is used to relieve tension, it can also be used to replenish your Essence,' Trinity said.

'You smell like oak, broom, and meadowsweet. Like blossoms in a field on a spring day,' Daniel exuded in a euphoric tone.

'Okay, we've definitely overdone it,' she stated with a nervous grin. One of the side effects of having too much Essence than a new Initiate can handle is heightened senses and also a feeling of literally being drunk on power. Luckily for Trinity, this second effect stopped Daniel from divining her true nature.

'I could smell you all day,' he said as he inhaled deeply with pleasure. Then, without warning, he placed his ear to Trinity's chest, making her gasp with surprise. 'And your heartbeat is funny, too.'

'Well, well, well, isn't this cosy,' Bobby Brinkmeyer exclaimed as he burst through the door followed by his two cronies, Jack and Willis. 'Is this a freaks-only party, or can anyone join in?'

'What do you want, Bobby?' His sudden appearance had angered Trinity.

'It's just so nice to see that two people like you, with your obvious afflictions, can find each other in this day and age. I mean who's going to want to be with a ghost-faced skinny wretch like him except a crazy, hippy, tree-hugging freak like you?' he laughed.

'Shut up, Bobby,' Daniel said.

'You're kind of cute,' Bobby stated to Trinity, as he ignored the sobering Daniel. 'If it wasn't for all your nature and crystals madness, I might have been interested in you myself.'

'Shut up, Bobby!'

'I'd let you tag along and cheer me on at my games.' The American again ignored Daniel. 'And if you were a good girl, I'd even let you kiss the captain.' He puckered up his lips and made kissing sounds towards a disgusted Trinity whilst his associates laughed. The laughing suddenly stopped, however, as an angered, frustrated, and slightly woozy Daniel connected a punch on Bobby's outstretched lips, sending him crashing over some desk chairs.

'I think you should run,' Trinity stated, turning to Daniel.

'Run?' he questioned.

She nodded. 'Run.'

He didn't need to be told again and he pushed past the two astonished lackeys and sprinted out of the room.

'What are you two jokers waiting for?' Bobby said as he got to his feet and rubbed his lips. 'Get him!'

The three boys rushed out after Daniel, leaving Trinity alone. She closed the door, so as not to be disturbed, and then went to the window and waited. Within moments she saw the distinctive form of Daniel running across the college grounds, shortly followed by Bobby and his boys. She couldn't help but express a wistful smile as she watched her friend running away. Trinity didn't feel like she was being premature in calling him that. She liked him and she was sure that he felt the same. Daniel wasn't the first potential Initiate that she had found, but he was the first one that she had connected with; she and her father had been searching all over the world for a special Initiate since they first arrived in this realm. Now she was sure she had found him.

Trinity turned from the window and went back to the tables she had joined together. She climbed onto them, sat cross-legged, and opened her bag. Two crystals were taken out and she held one in each hand upon her knees. Her eyes closed and she began to fall into a trance, just as she had taught Daniel. The gems began to glow, an indicator that Trinity had tapped into her Essence as she sent out a telepathic call.

'*Father, I have found him,*' she spoke out in a quiet, dreamy voice. She knew that Gydion wouldn't need to perform the meditation exercises, as she had done – such was his magical ability – and within moments he replied, his voice resounding in her thoughts.

'*Are you positive he is the one?*'

'*Yes. I have seen his Essence. His levels are far higher than anyone his age should be, especially since it is without any training.*'

'*You have seen it?*' Gydion questioned. '*Then that would mean you taught him the technique of Replenishment.*'

'*I did, Father,*' admitted Trinity reluctantly. She was only supposed to identify a boy of potential mage ability and report it to Gydion, so she prepared herself for the angry backlash but was surprised when it didn't come.

'*Very good. I had intended you to be a part of training the child once we had found them and if this is the one, as you say, then he must have some trust in you already. Bring him here so I may speak to him.*'

'*He has already left, but he does have one of my crystals. We should be able to track him easily enough. He seems close to his parents, so he will no doubt be home sooner rather than later.*'

'*Good. I wish to have words with the boy's father. If my suspicions are correct, it would seem that our work here is almost at an end, Trinity. Soon we will be on our way home.*'

Their communication ended and Trinity uncrossed her legs and hopped off the table. As she put her stones away and made her way out of the room, she thought about what her father had just said about going home. *This* was her home; it had been since she was 'born' fifty years ago. She wondered if Ariest could really be called her home, even though she had never been there, just because she was Fae. If she were to go there, being there with Daniel would help; she just hoped that he was willing. She may have told him that he was a mage but she didn't tell him that in order to fulfil his potential, he would have to leave this realm and his family behind him.

4

Although his day *had* begun like any other, Daniel's afternoon had turned into one of new and untried experiences, culminating in him punching Bobby, something that was out of character for him. Teased by Brinkmeyer hundreds of times before, he had never retaliated and now, after just one morning with Trinity, he was getting into fights. Daniel was sure his dad would be pleased with him.

He knew it was wrong – not the punching Bobby part; that had felt good. What was wrong was the reason why he had done it. He hadn't punched him for himself; he had done it for Trinity. For him to be so protective of her already didn't sit right with him. It made him think that he was so desperate for friends he had to latch on to the first person that showed him any sort of compassion. Normally that wasn't the case, but there was no denying that he found it difficult to resist her and, for better or for worse, he realised she was becoming an influence on his life.

He headed down Drake Lane towards the nearby shopping centre, hoping to lose his pursuers in the crowds. Daniel skipped in and out of the shoppers and eventually lost sight of Bobby and his boys, then he slipped into the Next store. Unknown to him, Bobby was on the upper level and saw him enter the store.

Daniel went straight for the changing rooms and sat down, confident that he had eluded his pursuers. He planned to hide out here for a while to give Bobby's short attention span brain enough time to get bored and send him home.

However, Bobby's brain was anything but bored. Right now, from his vantage point, he pointed and directed his cohorts, like a general would his troops, to the place where Daniel had taken refuge. With a cruel smile, he came down and together they began to search the Next store for Daniel.

They systematically worked their way through the shop, checking the racks, checking the aisles until they eventually approached the changing rooms. Just like a hunter stalking its prey, Bobby knew he was closing in on Daniel; there was nowhere else he could be.

What Bobby could not know was that the hunter had become the hunted. The peculiar actions of the three boys had attracted the attention of an undercover store detective, and he now shadowed their every move.

In his makeshift hideaway, Daniel was oblivious to what was happening out in the store's men's department; he wasn't sure if Bobby was still out there or if he had given up the chase already.

After his peculiar day, Daniel, being the introvert that he was, was enjoying having some time to be lost in his own thoughts. The overriding issue in his mind right now was deciding whether to tell his parents about his day entirely. He was relishing the thought of telling his dad about the punch and was looking forward to informing his mum about Trinity, but he remained unsure if he should mention anything about the magic or the fair folk, in particular the Hobthrust.

Eric and Tina Welsh, Daniel's parents, were everyday hard-working people; his dad was in construction, his mum was a doctor. She had told him that they had met at St. Joseph's hospital, where she worked, when one of his work mates had been injured. It had been an instant attraction, and they were married a few years later.

They were what people regarded as open-minded. They were receptive to new ideas, unprejudiced, and unbigoted, but Daniel had to wonder what they would say if he told them that there was a world of magical creatures and that he had seen one. Theirs was a close-knit family, which harboured no lies, so he knew he had no real choice but to tell his parents.

A sudden loud bang woke Daniel from his thoughts. A few moments later there was another bang followed by the squeak of hinges.

'We know you're in here,' announced Bobby. 'There's no point hiding; it'll only get worse for you.'

Another bang, louder this time, as they checked each cubicle systematically, slowly getting closer to the one Daniel hid within. He searched his bag and pockets, desperately trying to find anything to throw at them to give him a chance of escape, no matter how slim that chance.

His backpack had nothing but books – paperbacks, unfortunately – hardbacks would have made much better missiles, he thought. His pockets fared no better in supplying him with ammunition. All he found in his left hand were a few pennies, a paperclip, and some lint. In his right hand, the crystal he had gotten from Trinity stared up at him. He looked deeply into the incandescent light at the stone's core and was certain her could see her green eyes looking back at him.

'Wait, what was it that Trinity said to me?' Daniel anxiously searched his thoughts for anything that could help his situation; he knew time was running out. 'Having belief can be a powerful thing; it'll help with your magic. Being a mage is difficult. It brings a lot of responsibility and takes a lot of dedication. It opens your mind to new things, some wondrous, some dangerous. Tension is a major barrier between magic and us. Okay, so she's told me nothing but theory. Great!'

Again, a cubicle door was kicked open, and the vibrations reverberated through Daniel's hiding place, signifying the close proximity of his tormentors.

'Okay, let me clear my head. I'm supposed to be an intelligent guy; I should be able to come up with some way out of this mess,' Daniel reasoned. As much as he would have loved to believe it, he knew his chances ranged from slim to none at all.

Daniel closed his eyes and started to take deep breaths, just as Trinity had taught him. He could feel the Essence waking up in his body. He hadn't told Trinity that he had experienced these feelings for years. When he was younger, he had just thought it had something to do with his albinism, but he had grown to like it. Just as he felt the Essence wash over his skin, leaving it with a tingly sensation, the door of his stall flexed as it was hit with some force. The bolt which held it locked barely stood up to the assault and it wouldn't be able to take much more of a similar battering.

'I got you now, freak,' Bobby shouted through the door. 'No more hiding for you, no more running. It's time to get what you deserve.'

Daniel watched anxiously as the door contorted each time it was violently struck. When it was hit a third time the bolt finally gave way and the door flew open, revealing Bobby standing in the doorway, staring at Daniel.

'What the...? Where is he?' Bobby asked Jack and Willis incredulously as he looked around the seemingly empty cubicle. Daniel stared at them with wide eyes and wondered why they weren't beating him to a pulp right now.

'Look!' Jack exclaimed as he pointed to the open backpack on the floor. 'He must have been here.'

'That's his all right. He must have climbed over the top when we were checking the cubicles on the other side,' Willis suggested.

'Arrggh! That damn crafty freak!' Bobby shouted as he shook with frustration. 'Come on; let's get out of here. He couldn't have gotten far.'

Bobby and his boys turned to leave the changing rooms and get back on the hunt, but they found their way blocked by the store detective. 'Well, well, well, I hope you fellers wouldn't be trying to head out of here without telling anyone why you were just trying to wreck the place,' the detective said with his hands on his hips and his chest puffed up like he was a sheriff in the Old West. 'I think you guys should come with me to my office and explain yourselves to me and my colleagues.'

With that, the Next store detective led his little trio of vandals off, all the while watched by a baffled and bemused Daniel. He looked down at his hands and pinched his arms; he was still a solid mass and yet none of them had made any acknowledgment of him. He wasn't complaining about it, far from, he was half expecting to be eating out of a straw right about now, so to have that scenario avoided was a bonus, and he wiped his brow in celebration. It wasn't until he had picked up his backpack and decided to leave the store that he discovered, when he walked past a mirror in the changing rooms, the reason they couldn't see him was because he wasn't there.

Daniel stared into the mirror with his mouth wide open. He checked his mouth with his hand just to be sure it *was* open, since all he could see in the mirror was his backpack floating in the air, seemingly unaided. 'I'm invisible,' he said to himself in dumbfounded wonder. 'This is amazing! But how did I do it? I was just doing the relaxation bit while I was trying to think of some way out of this mess and that was it, well, apart from my skin tingling a bit.'

While Daniel had been speaking, he had slowly become more and more visible. Suddenly a member of staff came in to check the stalls.

'Oh, I'm sorry. I thought all the cubicles were empty.'

'That's okay,' Daniel said before leaving the changing rooms. He couldn't help smiling when he left the shopping centre. This whole episode had made two things perfectly clear to him. Firstly, that wasn't party tricks or picking someone's card out of a pack, this was *real* magic. And secondly, he liked the way it had felt.

5

There was one thing that Trinity neglected to tell Daniel about Faerie Folk, Hobthrusts in particular, and that was that they didn't like to be offended. To offend a Hobthrust took no more than to criticize their work or present them with a reward they deemed too generous, such as new clothes. They had a strict protocol and if their rules were not adhered to most would just disappear from the abode, never to return, whilst others would lose their good-natured attitude and become more troublesome and turn into mischievous Boggarts, with their frizzy black hair, crooked yellow teeth, and soured milk smell.

Boggarts love to be a nuisance. Moving things and making people think they've misplaced items is a particular favourite of theirs, but some can be more malevolent than others. Fungal was one such Boggart.

As a Hobthrust in the fourteenth century, Fungal had been unsurpassed in his work in the castle of the Laird of Rum, a small island in the Inner Hebrides. He had been there since the Laird was a boy and had grown to manhood, and become a father himself to a daughter, Agnes.

Fungal was much loved within the Clan, especially by the daughter, and even used his Faerie magic to help Agnes conceive a healthy baby girl, after she had wed, which they named Mary.

When she became four years old and the men folk were away, fighting under the sacred Faerie Flag of the MacLeod's at the Battle of Glendale, Mary, in a moment of childish playfulness, placed a cap on Fungal's head.

The Laird and his daughter Agnes were so attached to Fungal that they both felt a sense of loss at the exact moment that he vanished, even though they were separated by many miles. Fungal himself shed a tear.

When he was reborn as a Boggart, Fungal excelled at thievery, though to him it was no such thing. His thinking was that he was *acquiring* items. If people really wanted their possessions, he thought, they wouldn't leave them lying about, where anybody could just pick them up. Even if these things were in a safe under lock and key made no difference to his argument.

Taking hats was a personal pastime of his, no doubt as some sort of revenge against the headwear that made him into the Boggart he now was. His favourite hat was a bowler he got from a couple of comedy actors he messed with in the early '20s.

Today he sat in his domain, the British Museum station. Closed since 1932, it was one of forty disused Underground stations hidden beneath the bustling streets of London, nicknamed the 'ghost network.' This was Fungal's seat of power.

Boggarts are usually solitary creatures; in fact, all species of House Elves: Boggarts, Boggles, Hobthrusts, Hobgoblins, Brownies, etc. were all solitary, but Fungal had somehow managed to install himself as some sort of Godfather figure or Laird of this realm's Boggarts. Rumour suggested that it was out of respect for the stunts he would pull.

One story about him which had become legend amongst his kind happened when he was still in Scotland – Edinburgh, to be exact. He would transform himself into a cackling old woman, wearing a bonnet and carrying a basket. He would walk out into the streets at night and anyone unlucky enough to chance upon him, if they were foolish enough to look into the bonnet, would find nothing but an empty space and his wizened head laughing up at them from the basket, at which point they would either run away screaming or fall to the ground unconscious.

Though he didn't do as much terrorizing now as he did in his youth, there was one particular person he did like to torment from time to time. His name was Joe Rustin, a descendant of Mary, the girl who had ruined his life.

It was bad enough that Joe had the blood of Mary in his veins, but his cheery disposition really grated on Fungal's nerves. His happy-go-lucky mentality made him a difficult target to get the full pleasure of pulling a trick on. So Fungal had decided that the best thing for him was just to get rid of him altogether. Not by killing him outright – he deemed that action beneath him – but if he were to send him somewhere, say Ariest, he thought to himself, and if Joe were to get himself eaten by a White Toed Murato Puama, then that would be on his own head.

Fungal took out a piece of parchment and gleefully began to scrawl runes of enchantment on it. When the process was complete, the scroll had transformed into a silver train ticket. He weaved some magic over it and it vanished.

With a look of complete satisfaction on his face, Fungal sat back in his throne and waited for his plans to take effect.

Moments after the ticket left Fungal, it reappeared in an envelope addressed to Joe Rustin at his place of employment, Belsize Park station, seconds before he began his shift.

The door of the supervisor's office opened just as the digital clock on the wall displayed 15:00.

'Afternoon, boss,' Joe said as he closed the door behind him.

The supervisor slowly spun around in his swivel chair and eyed Joe with a look of curiosity. 'Still coming in right on time, I see.'

'Are you complaining?'

'No, far from it. I just want to make sure that you remember that you don't get paid extra for it, that's all,' the supervisor chuckled.

'You're a funny guy,' replied Joe as he looked in his pigeonhole. He saw the orange envelope and picked it up. 'What's this?'

'I don't know. I just put the mail in the slots, I don't read it.'

Joe opened the envelope and his eyes lit up when he saw the shimmering silver ticket inside. A Heritage run with a 1933 'John Hampden' locomotive and Q-stock Ashbury 'Bogie' trailers.

'Well, what is it?' asked the supervisor.

Joe showed the ticket to the supervisor and he was just as astonished.

'A Q-stock?'

'With an Ashbury, no less.'

'I didn't know they were part of the Heritage preservation stock. It must be a new addition. They sure kept that quiet,' mused the supervisor.

'I don't even remember ordering a ticket,' Joe confessed.

'Maybe it's from the managers.'

'You know what that would mean, don't you?' Joe asked with a smirk. 'That would mean that you *do* get extra for coming in early.'

'Get out of it!'

Out of the corner of his eye, Joe saw Daniel enter the station. He waved through the large window of the supervisor's office, and then he went out to join him.

The two had become friends several years ago when Joe had interceded in an incident that involved Daniel and his tormentors. Joe had always told him that Bobby would grow out of his bullying ways as he grew up. Daniel was still waiting for that day.

When Joe saw Daniel's shirt, he screwed up his face in confusion. When he was close enough to smell it, he screwed up his nose in disgust.

'Please tell me that's not dog poop.'

'No, it's not dog poop.'

'It sure smells like it,' Joe replied as he covered his nose.

'This is what passes as school dinners these days, and the reason why I don't usually have any.'

'I don't blame you. So, what happened?' asked Joe.

'Bobby Brinkmeyer happened.'

'I should have guessed,' Joe nodded knowingly.

'So much for him growing out of it. It's just so tiresome having to deal with his crap day in day out,' stated Daniel angrily.

Joe could sense the frustration in his young friend. 'What you need is a break away from him to recharge the batteries, even if it's just one day, and I know just the thing to take your mind off of him.'

Even though Joe would have loved to take the ride on the Heritage stock, he could see that Daniel's need was greater than his own. It was obvious he needed cheering up and, given Daniel's interest in history, a ride on a restored 1933 train could be just what the doctor ordered.

Joe took the ticket out of his pocket and handed it to Daniel. 'Enjoy it,' he said with a broad smile as he watched Daniel read what was written on it.

THIS IS AN INVITATION AND RESERVATION
TO EXPERIENCE THE SENSATION OF

The Magical Journey
ADMIT ONE

SINGLE JOURNEY
TRAIN NOW AT ALDGATE

'You're kidding, right? I can't take your ticket, especially for *this* train stock.'

'Take it. I'll just order one for its next run out.' Even though Joe didn't know if there *would* be a next run or even if he would be able to get another ticket, he didn't want to burden Daniel with that knowledge, so he decided not to say anything more about it.

'Thanks, Joe, I don't know how I can repay you.'

'No need, just take lots of pics and enjoy the ride. Anyway, I got to go do my station checks so I'll see you later. Let me know how it goes, okay?'

'Sure thing, Joe, and thanks again.'

The two friends parted ways and headed in their separate directions, both unaware that the simple act of kindness, shown between friends, would soon put into effect events that would change the future of the realms.

6

No. 15 Elizabeth Mews NW3 was the address that the Welsh family called home. Daniel, during a moment of free time, had been able to trace the history of the area all the way back to the fourteenth century, when that particular northern edge of London was little more than open land, in agricultural use, with a few scattered farms and houses. Some five hundred years later, during the late Victorian era, when large villas, with attic and basement space for servants, were being developed, the Mews were built. They originally provided stabling and accommodation for carriage drivers of the wealthy professionals that were targeted by the principal developers.

Because of Belsize Park's long history, architectural detail, and considerable charm, Camden Borough designated it a Conservation Area in 1973, starting with Belsize Park Gardens and Belsize Village, in an effort to preserve its visual appeal. The Conservation Area had been extended on a number of occasions. In 1991 it was extended to include Elizabeth Mews.

Daniel was a supporter of the Council's Preservation Act mainly because of its mandate to protect areas of historic interest, even though it made it difficult to do any renovations. That did not affect him in any way since he lived with his parents and could leave those sorts of problems to the grownups, whilst he enjoyed the architectural time warp of where he lived. Most of the time he would sit in Primrose Gardens and look at the three-storey, red-bricked late Victorian houses and imagine the generations of families that had lived there in the past.

Sometimes he wondered what it would have been like to have lived in another era: eighteenth or seventeenth centuries or maybe even further back to Italy during the Roman Empire to be part of the discussions that would follow a night at the arena. Be in ancient Greece to hear the teachings of Socrates, Plato, and Aristotle. Seen the trial of Phryne, the hetaerae. Seen the Oracle of Delphi at the height of its popularity. Experience the last days of a great civilisation from antiquity such as the Hittites, the Assyrians, or Carthaginians and know what day-to-day life was like for its people before they were wiped from existence.

Daniel's mother had often called him a dreamer, but he didn't mind because that's exactly what he was; he dreamed of a better life. He refused to accept that his lot in life was to be a bullying target forever.

As Daniel walked through the front door, he could hear his parents talking in the kitchen diner. He hung his backpack on the banister and made his way to the back to join them. 'Howdy, parental units,' Daniel smiled as he greeted them.

'Hi, love,' his mum said as she gave him a hug before turning back to the sauce she was stirring on the stove.

'Hey, Dan,' his dad said and slapped him on the shoulder. 'Good day at college?'

'It was...interesting,' came Daniel's elusive reply. He still had not fully decided on how he should tell his parents about the day's events, so he had decided to stall them for as long as possible. Daniel opened the fridge door, desperately trying to hide himself behind it whilst he got a drink. He could feel his parents glaring at him through the door, and when he closed it they were staring right at his face.

'What do you mean *interesting*?' probed his dad.

'You know,' Daniel started as he took a gulp of orange juice, 'same old same old.'

'Same old, same old?' Eric repeated.

'Has that Bobby been hassling you again?' his mum asked.

'Yeah, he did, so I punched him in the face,' Daniel said as nonchalantly as he could and hoped that they would miss his throwaway statement. They did not.

'You did what?' Both his parents made the exclamation at the same time, his mother with a sense shock and his father with admiration.

'I can't believe you, Daniel. After all I've told you.'

'Don't listen to your mum, Dan. I'm proud of you, son.'

'Don't tell him that, Eric. Punching that boy makes him no better than he is.'

'Oh, come on, Mum, it was just one punch,' pleaded Daniel.

'There you go, Tina, it was one punch so hardly a brawl,' Eric said with a grin.

Tina looked at her husband with a stern look. Eric may have been a big burly man, but even he could be cowed by a single look from his wife. 'Why did you do it, love? What did he do to you this time?'

'It's not what he did to me; it's what he did to Trinity.'

'Trinity? Who's Trinity?' Tina asked.

'She's a girl at college.'

'A girl!' both his parents exclaimed.

'Yes, a girl.'

'You kept that one quiet, son,' Eric stated.

'I wish I had kept it quiet longer, to be honest,' murmured Daniel, knowing that his mum was about to turn into an investigator worthy of CSI.

'Tell me about this girl. What's her major? What do her parents do? What's she like? Are you two an item?' enthused Tina. Daniel had never shown any interest in girls or any relationship, so to hear him mention a real, live girl and not a historical character gave her hope of a future wedding and grandchildren.

'Give the boy a break, honey,' Eric said, as he saw the faraway look in her eyes.

'I've been waiting for this day for a long time,' said Tina as she pinched Daniel's cheek. 'So why don't you go upstairs, get changed, and tell us all about her over dinner.'

Daniel was more than happy to take this opportunity to escape up to his room and avoid the incessant questions his mum was bombarding him with. He knew that she meant well, but he did not want her getting her hopes up and blowing this friendship between Trinity and himself into anything more than it actually was.

Whilst Daniel emptied his backpack and changed into his house clothes, downstairs he heard the doorbell ring and moved closer to his slightly opened bedroom door in an effort to hear whom it was.

'I'll get it,' Eric said as he finished setting the table. He opened the door and the smile he had on his face instantly disappeared.

'Hello, Eric.' Gydion stood at the door, leaning on his black oak cane with an expressionless face. A more contemporary outfit had replaced the hooded cloak that Eric was more accustomed to seeing his unexpected visitor draped in. He had on a sharp, tailor-made suit and a full-length black coat finished off with a fedora hat. 'I have been looking for you for a long time,' he continued.

'And I have been running for a long time,' replied Eric despondently, like a man accepting his defeat.

'Well, now it is over. You do not need to run anymore. It is time to come home.'

'This is my home now.'

'Quaint. May I come in?' Eric nodded and ushered his old comrade in.

Daniel peered, unseen, over the banister and tried to see who this unannounced guest was. The man was unknown to him, but he noticed that he moved with a graceful elegance that Daniel couldn't help but be impressed by. Whoever this man was, the youngster knew there was something different about him. He couldn't put his finger on what it was exactly, but he could almost sense a power within the man with every step he took. Daniel sat on the top stair and strained his ears to hear what this intriguing man had to say.

Eric led Gydion to the dining room where Tina was about to dish out dinner, but when she heard their voices she quickly washed her hands and prepared to greet them.

'This is my wife Tina,' introduced Eric, 'Tina, this is Gydion.'

'Pleased to meet you,' Tina said as she shook Gydion's hand. 'We weren't expecting any guests but you're welcome to stay for dinner; there's plenty.'

'I would not want to intrude,' Gydion replied.

'It's okay, she knows where I come from,' Eric said.

'Indeed.' Gydion eyed the woman as if he were trying to peer into her soul. He was more than a little suspicious of a mortal accepting to marry a fey, in this day and age.

'What is it?' The way his eyes seemed to glow, as he looked at her made Tina nervous.

'Nothing, I was just making sure you were who you said you were.' Satisfied with the results of his gentle probe, Gydion turned his attention back to Eric before accepting the drink offered by Tina and taking a seat. 'Well, I must admit that life is a lot easier here now that magic users are no longer being burned at the stake, but if you truly do intend to remain here, Eric, do you not think that you should inform Lady Rhiannon now that she has awoken from her dream weave? Of course, you knew her as the Lady Alina.'

'Rhiannon...' Eric whispered the name as if he had just remembered a long-lost memory.

'Yes, your Queen. I am rather surprised you still remember her, to be honest, considering it has been some fifty years since she awoke and nearer on one hundred since you abandoned her.'

'I didn't abandon her!' Eric fired back at Gydion, before he realized what he had just heard. 'Wait, did you say fifty years? Her dream weaves aren't usually that long.' When the Faerie queen's life force was at an end, she would fall into a deep hibernating sleep to replenish and begin life again, as a new queen. Sometimes, whilst in the sleep, she would have prophetic dreams.

'No, they are not. The Sisters of Calatin have been interpreting her visions.'

'And what have they learned?'

'I do not know. When Lady Rhiannon charged me with finding you, the Sisters were still divining the facets of what they had seen. I, however, believed that you were somehow involved within them, as finding you was the first thing that was on her mind when she opened her eyes. Just imagine her dismay when she learned that her champion was no longer in Ariest.'

'I had to leave,' Eric stated distantly as the emotions that accompanied the recurring memories took their toll on him. 'The wars, constantly defending our borders against the Frell...it became too much. That much bloodshed is bound to leave scars. She could induce her dream weave to overcome the battle weariness, but what did I have?'

'What did any of us have?'

'The blood I've spilt runs deep, Gydion.'

'We all shed blood; none of us escaped that task.'

'But none of you killed your own son.' Eric fixed Gydion with a steely glare.

Tina's mouth opened in astonishment and outside, in the hall, on the top step the eavesdropper replicated the silent exclamation.

'I did not know you had a child,' Gydion confessed.

'I didn't know myself. The mother never told me. She was a Mulenaar.'

Gydion saw the look of a woman that was privy to a conversation that was far beyond her knowledge etched across Tina's face. 'The Mulenaari are a mostly subterranean race that are neutral, luckily for us,' he explained to Tina. 'Powerful both mentally and physically, their shamans are held in high regard.'

'As are their warriors...which she was,' added Eric distractedly. 'Her name was Aloena. We met during the peacetime, before The Second Great War, when she was on her wanderlust.'

'Ah, the legendary Mulenaari wanderlust. Tina, my dear, travelling with a Mulenaar during this time can be special,' he enthused. 'It is a period in their lives when they roam the surface before they decide whether to stay or return to the subterranean colonies.' Tina nodded her thanks to Gydion for his explanation then Eric continued his story.

'Aloena was travelling from village to village, challenging anyone to duel and defeating them all. She told me it was to test her prowess against surface dwellers. When I heard about her, I sought her out. How could I miss this opportunity to test my *own* skills?'

'As I recall, you lived for the thrill of battle.'

'I was younger then. We fought day and night for three days until we threw down our weapons and made a different kind of combat where our blood and sweat mingled.'

Tina felt a slight uneasiness at the analogy. She knew it would have happened long before they ever met, but it still gave her a twinge inside to hear her husband talk about another woman with such passion.

Lost in his past and with a distant look on his face, Eric continued. 'We made camp there and stayed together in the open air for several days before she decided she was leaving to return to her colony. When we parted, I gave her my father's ring to remember me by. I never saw her again.

'You gave her the Bloodstone Ring? Lust makes you do idiotic things,' Gydion exasperated with a shake of his head. 'And that idyllic pairing produced a progeny,' he further deduced.

'Yes, but I didn't discover that until it was too late.'

'Go on, what happened next?' Tina could see the pain in Eric's eyes as she urged him on. This was something that he had kept bottled up for many years and she knew that wasn't good for him.

'After the war ended, I was patrolling the borders of Cuthala with a small armed unit, dispatching any Frell that had been left behind. We came upon a young lone stranger blocking our progress who refused to allow us passage unless one of our number defeated him in single combat.

I took up the challenge eagerly, my blood still raised from the long-fought war. He refused to give his name, going against the customs of a duel, and in response I refused to give mine.'

'And why should you have to? You are the great Eric Mondragon; every-one should know your name, hmmm?' Gydion mockingly said.

Eric shot the Archmage a steely look. 'I'll admit, I *was* brash and arrogant then, but no longer; that arrogance drove me to kill my own son!' After his outburst, Eric paused and quickly calmed himself before he resumed his tale. 'We fought on and I could feel his frustration building because he couldn't get the better of me. I could have finished the contest at any time, disarmed him when I pleased, but I didn't I – I mocked him. My men jeered and laughed. He started to go for killing strikes, drew blood a few times. It en-raged me. Then I returned the favour.' Eric didn't need to say anymore as he solemnly took a sip from his glass. Both Gydion and Tina could guess that his attack had struck true and ended the battle permanently.

Though she was learning things about her husband for the first time, these revelations didn't change the fact that Tina loved him dearly. She reached out her hand and, taking hold of his, squeezed it reassuringly. She smiled gently into his face when he looked up. 'How did you find out who he was?'

'He had the ring I gave to Aloena and with his own dying breath he said his mother had given it to him. I – I was shell-shocked, numb all over. The man I was died in that field next to my son. I ordered my men to go on and, once they were out of sight, I grieved as I buried my boy. Once I had finished, I stripped off my armour and buried it along with my sword. Then I left Ari-est, forever.'

'Forever is a long time.'

'I'm not going back, Gydion. Nothing you say can make me.'

'We both know that's not entirely true, Eric.'

'I'd jump over this table and break your fingers before you could finish casting any spell.'

'Maybe, but I think you have lost your edge; besides, you are not as young as you used to be.'

The tension in the air was at a palpable level but Tina was surprised, and more than happy, when the sudden raucous laughter of the two men broke the silence. Theirs seemed to be a complicated friendship, but Tina could see that it was definitely one built on a deep mutual respect.

'So, who wants a top up?' Tina got out of her chair to get the bottle of sherry they had been drinking from; it was only then that she saw Daniel standing in the doorway. The tension suddenly returned, tenfold.

7

'Hi sweetheart, are you ready to eat?' Tina didn't know how long he had been standing there, or how much of the conversation he had heard, but the surprise on Eric's face revealed that he was also taken aback by the sudden appearance of their son. However, if a member of the Welsh family had chanced a glance at Gydion, they would have seen a knowing smile on his face.

'No thanks. I lost my appetite when I heard my dad say he killed a brother I never knew I had,' Daniel said in a matter-of-fact manner.

'Daniel!' exclaimed Tina.

'What? I thought this was a family where we didn't hide things from each other...no lies?'

'It is; nothing's changed,' Tina defensively replied.

'Are you serious? Everything's changed! He killed his own son and never told anyone – never told us!' Daniel angrily pointed at Eric as he shouted.

'He's still your father,' stated Tina. She had never seen her son so fired up before. Was this the sort of rage that was within her husband all those years ago? If so, could Daniel be pushed to the same extremes?

'And you're no better! You *knew* he was different but you hid it! Were you ever going to tell me?' Daniel's question was met with silence. 'Is this why I *look* like this? Because my dad's not quite human?'

'That's enough, Daniel,' Eric whispered as he held his head down, as if the weight of the world weighed on his shoulders.

'I've been bullied all my life because of *you!*'

'I said that's enough, Daniel.' Though he didn't shout, there was an underlying power resonating in the tone of Eric's voice. Only Tina felt this low-level force, due to her human physiology, and took a step back to avoid it.

'How could it ever be enough? Everything I've endured is your fault.'

'You're right, Daniel,' Eric accepted. 'I'm sorry; I never meant to hurt you or your mother. All I wanted was to start afresh, leave the past behind.'

'You mean live a lie,' Daniel spat.

'I mean become a new man,' replied Eric.

'What happened in the Faerie world was an accident,' Tina said, trying desperately to defuse the situation, 'an unfortunate mistake. There's no denying that, Daniel, but you know your father.'

'Do I?'

'He hasn't changed; he is still the same man you've known all your life.'

Gydion finally spoke for the first time, and his voice delivered in an unthreatening level as if he were a psychologist. He kept his eyes focused on the steeple he formed with his hands. 'What is it that you are angry about, Daniel? Are you angry with your father because he killed someone that could have been your brother? Surely not, for if that unfortunate event did not happen then you, as a result, would not have happened. He would have had no need to leave Ariest and the union between him and your mother would never have happened, and as a result, no Daniel.'

The Welshes looked on, each of them knowing that what the venerable man was saying had a significant weight of truth behind it. A truth which none of them wished to face due to the macabre fact that their own happiness, and in the case of Daniel, his entire existence, had come from the death of someone else.

'Maybe you are angry because your parents hid your true heritage from you, but this would be a waste of time, not to mention rather hypocritical. A waste of time because had you known earlier; you would have done nothing different than what you are doing now. Knowing should be more important to you than *when* you know. In fact, it should not matter to you at all, Daniel, since you have known for some time, have you not? That would be the hypocritical part.'

Daniel's parents turned to look at him. 'How did you know?' Tina asked.

'I didn't know for sure until today,' Daniel admitted. 'Things have been revealed to me piece by piece, like a puzzle, all day. I didn't want to believe it at first. I guess that burst of anger was me trying to reject it. It was too much to accept that I was even more different from everyone else than I already was.'

'You *are* different, Daniel,' said Gydion as he stood to face the youngster. 'You are different because you have a father who is a legendary hero and a mother who is kind, open hearted, understanding, and, above all else, human. You should be proud of them and you have the capacity to equal them both, with a little guidance, of course.'

One hundred years may have passed since Eric was last in the company of Gydion, but it would take more than just a century for him to forget the Machiavellian schemes this man used to weave, and now he was beginning to suspect the mage of subtler plotting. 'You know something? The more time I spend with you, the more I remember how you conduct your business, Gydion. The use of misdirection and crafty and devious tactics weren't beneath you.'

'And your point is?'

'My point is that you seem more interested in my son than you are in persuading me to return with you.'

'Well, I remember how bull-headed you can be; moreover, my daughter told me that Daniel was a 'special friend,' so I thought I would see for myself.'

'Trinity's your daughter?' asked Daniel incredulously.

'Yes, and she was quite right about you, Daniel. You should embrace who and what you are. It will open your mind and you will see how different the realms can look from our eyes.'

'I – I *have* seen things,' Daniel admitted. 'It was like a river of shimmering colours flowing through the air and around things, people too.'

Gydion smiled proudly at the young man's confession. 'That, my boy, is Magical Essence. We Mages can control it and shape it to our wills.'

'This was never about me, was it?' Eric questioned firmly.

'Of course it was,' responded Gydion without turning to face his accuser. 'Lady Rhiannon does want you back; it's just her reasons for wanting me here and my own agenda do not meet.'

'And what *is* your agenda?'

Gydion didn't say a word but continued to look at Daniel as if he had just discovered a prize possession.

8

'You're not taking my son!' cried Tina.

'I would not think of doing such a thing, Tina, but if he were to come of his own volition, well...'

'I think it's time for you to leave, Gydion,' Eric said as he rose from his chair. 'You've overstayed your welcome.'

'Perhaps I have,' the venerable mage agreed. 'Before I go, let me give you all a little something to ponder. Tina, your son has each foot in two completely different cultures. Is it not right that he should be able to experience both as anyone with a dual heritage would? Daniel, Trinity told me of your thirst for knowledge; if you become a mage, you would gain access to knowledge from the past, present, and future of all the realms...how could you resist that? And, finally, you, Eric, you know the power mages can wield. Do you not think that it would be dangerous and irresponsible to leave such power in the hands of a person who does not know how to control it completely? With that I shall take my leave.'

He looked at the three members of the family; none of them returned his gaze as each of them contemplated his words. With no farewell bidden or received, Gydion slowly strode out of No. 15 Elizabeth Mews, and into the night.

A silence descended upon the Welsh household. Revelations that had been aired tonight played through the minds of Daniel and his parents. None of them knew how it would affect the family unit, a family that had, up until now, prided itself on being open and sharing secrets with each other. To have that quality suddenly stripped away left them in an unknown quandary.

'I assume no one's feeling hungry right now, huh?' Tina said to no one in particular as she began to pack away the food into plastic containers and store them in the fridge. 'At least we won't need to cook tomorrow.'

Daniel watched his mum collecting the unused crockery from the table and wished he had some similar distraction so he couldn't feel his father's gaze boring into the side of his head.

'So, how long have you been doing magic?' Eric asked.

'I haven't...well not consciously anyway. Things would just happen sometimes, usually whilst trying to avoid Brinkmeyer. It wasn't until I spoke to Trinity that I found out it was magic and that I could influence things and consciously make things happen. Today, for instance, I turned myself invisible.' Daniel heard his mother's gasp emanate from the kitchen.

'That sounds like it was possibly personal Essence energies you used.'

Intrigued by what his father said, Daniel took a seat opposite him. It was an exciting moment for the teenager but also one that brought a lot of confusion with it. Usually if Daniel was confronted by a subject he knew little about he would pick up a book, skim read it, and he would have all the knowledge he needed but, as Trinity had said, this was real magic and it wasn't part of any curriculum Daniel knew of, not in this realm anyway. 'Do you know a lot about magic?' he asked his dad.

'Ariest is full of magic. I don't know the workings of it like Gydion, but I know that there are three sources of Essence that magic users draw upon: personal, planetary, and realmic.'

'Have you tried anything else?' Tina asked as she joined her husband and son at the table.

'No, I haven't.'

'I don't think you should. Gydion was right about the dangers an untrained mage can cause,' warned Eric.

'I don't know about that Gydion,' Tina stated, revealing her suspicions. 'Trying to manipulate us into giving him what he wants and I bet that Trinity girl played her part in it too.'

'You don't know that,' Daniel protested, but no matter how much he didn't want to believe it, in his mind, he couldn't help but come to the same conclusions.

'Neither do you, son. And since she is his daughter, it's more than likely.

'I don't want you to speak to her anymore,' his mum ordered.

'Are you serious? I'm not a kid anymore.'

'Maybe not, but she obviously has some hold over you.' Tina didn't take any notice of her son's visibly reddening face and continued. 'She'll just poison your mind and try to convince you to go.' The emotion in Tina rose as she thought about the prospect of that happening.

'Come on, honey, that's a bit harsh,' Eric said as he tried to calm her.

'I'm not losing my son, Eric! I won't let it happen and neither should you.'

'I wouldn't if I didn't think it was the right thing to do.'

Eric's confession hit Tina like a knife in the back. 'You what?'

'I think we should let Daniel go. You accepted that he'll be going off to Cambridge next year; this is no different.'

'No different? It's completely different! It's not like I can just jump on a train and visit him,' Tina shouted sarcastically as she waved her arms about for added emphasis.

'Well, actually you can,' corrected Eric with a shrug. 'How do you think I got here? The Faerie sidhe links between realms have almost completely vanished as more and more people stop believing in magic but there are still one or two about.'

'Look, Mum, this discussion is a moot point at the moment because I haven't even decided if I want to go or not.' Daniel didn't know if his mother believed him or not, but he could see how upset she was, and he wanted to give her some reassurance until he knew how to break it to her. 'It's been a mad kind of day so I'm going up. Night, Mum, Dad.'

'Okay, son. We'll talk more tomorrow.' Eric watched Daniel go upstairs and when he heard his son's bedroom door close he turned to Tina.

'Don't look at me like that, Eric.'

'We've always said that we wanted Daniel to reach his full potential, Tina.'

'Yes, but we've also said that we'd do what's best for him and I just get this strange feeling about this whole thing. It's just a little odd that after all these years they would try and split up my family, now. Call it my human intuition.'

'Don't worry, honey,' Eric said gently as he held Tina's hand in his, 'I'll always be here with you.'

9

The next morning Daniel awoke refreshed and fully energised. The bright spring sun mirrored his upbeat disposition as it filtered through his partially closed drapes. It was like the events of yesterday were a distant memory as he rolled out of bed and, with a yawn, threw his curtains fully open. He closed his eyes and basked in the sun's rays, allowing it to warm his skin momentarily. Looking down at his slim, bare arms, Daniel wondered how long it would take before they'd show the signs of sunburn, but before he could harm himself he retreated to the shade.

After getting ready to face the day, Daniel made his way downstairs to have breakfast. His parents had already left for work, which he was more than a little pleased about, because he knew that the first thing they would ask him, especially his mum, was if he had decided to go with Gydion or not. The fact of the matter was that he had no real choice but to do it. He had always felt like he was missing out on something and this must surely be what it was, and he intended to take his opportunity with both hands.

He took out the silver Heritage ticket he had gotten from Joe just to make sure that the pickup point was Aldgate Station. He read the gold embossed writing once more.

**THIS IS AN INVITATION AND RESERVATION
TO EXPERIENCE THE SENSATION OF**

The Magical Journey
ADMIT ONE
SINGLE JOURNEY

TRAIN NOW LEAVING LIVERPOOL STREET STATION

'Liverpool Street?' exclaimed Daniel with confusion. 'I could have sworn it was Aldgate. No problem, it just means less travelling time, I guess.'

Daniel made his way to Belsize Park Station and had a quick look for Joe, to thank him again, but assumed he hadn't started his shift yet when he didn't see him. Two minutes later he was on the southbound Northern Line.

It was after the peak period so he didn't have any trouble finding a seat, but he still received the customary glances from people over the top of their Metro newspapers as he sat down. The commuters on the train at this time were the ones that had agreements with their employers to 'start late and finish late,' all so they could avoid the madness of rush hour. It didn't change the fact that in Daniel's mind he was nothing but a curiosity to them.

Within fifteen minutes, Daniel was disembarking at Moorgate Station to get his connection to Liverpool Street. As he walked toward the Metropolitan Line, he could see a bright red train with a big white 5 on its front sitting on the platform, in the distance. He thought it looked like a 'Hampden' with Q23 cars, but it shouldn't be stopping here. Daniel knew that Heritage Tours usually went from one end of the line to the other without stops.

He neared the train and his first thoughts were confirmed: it was a 'John Hampden.' They must be running more than one train, Daniel thought as he slowly approached it and marvelled at its size. He had read that it had the largest engines to ever run on the Underground and he could imagine it did as he stood on tiptoe to see into the empty driver's cab. It was in immaculate condition, like it was brand new and had never been used.

As he walked beside the carriages, he saw that they were empty and the doors were closed. Peering through the windows, he smiled at the interior; the wooden floors and window frames sat in harmony with the metal of the air-operated doors and the frames of the seats.

Daniel turned and was about to go to the opposite platform, to take the train to Liverpool Street, when a high-pitched, high-speed voice suddenly stopped him in his tracks.

'And-where-do-you-think-you're-going?'

The voice came from the carriage that a moment ago had been empty; now Daniel looked back over his shoulder and found its doors open. A tall, thin man with a long face, large bushy white moustache, which hid his mouth, and dressed in what looked like a vintage London Underground uniform stood there looking back at him.

'You mean me?' a startled Daniel asked.

'Do-I-mean-you?' the guard repeated with a speed Daniel was having trouble following. 'Do-I-mean-you? Of-course-I-mean-you. Do-you-see-anyone-else-standing-here? I-don't-see-anyone-else-standing-here. Unless-you-have-someone-in-your-pocket-of-course. I-had-someone-in-my-pocket-once. Then-I-forgot-and-washed-my-coat.'

'Right...' Daniel said with a puzzled look as he turned left then right and realized for the first time that he was indeed the only person on the platform. 'No, I guess I don't see anyone, but my ticket says I should get on at Liverpool Street.'

'Really? I-suppose-this-is-your-first-time. Right? -Right? -Right? Let-me-see-the-ticket.'

As Daniel was putting the ticket in the man's outstretched hand, he caught a glimpse of the gold print and was surprised to see that the writing on the ticket had changed the last line specifically.

TRAIN NOW WAITING IMPATIENTLY AT MOORGATE STATION.

'Are-you-getting-on?' the tall guard asked as he took the ticket.

Every time the guard spoke it reminded Daniel of machinegun fire, but the youngster accepted the invitation by gingerly stepping aboard the train.

He watched the guard feed his ticket into the bottom of a brightly coloured box that was attached just beside the carriage's entrance doors. A brief flash of shimmering gold light came from the machine and it ejected the ticket. The guard took it and handed it back to Daniel. Once again, the writing had changed.

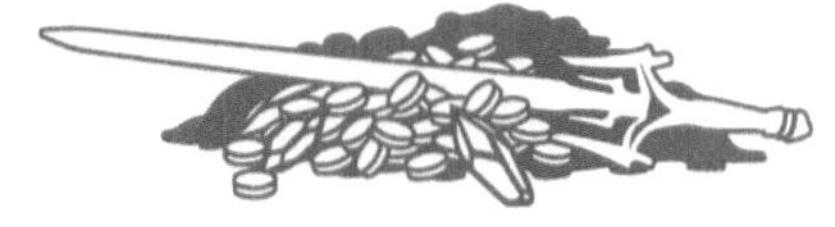

**THIS INVITATION AND RESERVATION
TO EXPERIENCE THE SENSATION OF**

The Magical Journey

Has been redeemed

SINGLE JOURNEY

TRAIN NOW LEAVING MOORGATE STATION

'MY-NAME-IS-WALDO-AND-welcome-aboard,' the guard said as he tipped his hat. 'Okay-Gertrude-we're-finally-ready-to-go!'

Daniel looked around to see who he was talking to, and assumed it was the driver, via intercom, as the door suddenly slid close and the train began to move. 'I was expecting more passengers to be aboard.'

'They-probably-took-an-earlier-train.   It-is-Beltane-Festival-after-all. You-had-better-take-a-seat-young-man.'

As Daniel took a step towards the seats, the train suddenly picked up speed. 'Beltane Festival? What's thaaaaa?' Faster and faster it went, like a jet firing its afterburners. He barely got his fingers around a handrail as the ferocious acceleration of the locomotive threatened to take his feet from under him. And that's exactly what happened as the train accelerated again, popping Daniel's ears in the process and disorientating him with a kaleidoscope lightshow.

His legs flapped in the air as he fought against the Gs and tried to put his other hand on the rail. Before he could, however, the train took a dive, straight down, which forced Daniel to relinquish his grip and slammed him painfully into the back of the seats behind him.

He desperately scrambled to gain a seat. Closer and closer his hand came to reaching its goal, but then the train changed direction again and he was sent tumbling head over heels down the aisle as the locomotive shot straight up. Daniel hadn't even had time to acknowledge how impossible his journey had been so far, before it became even more so as the vehicle suddenly began to corkscrew whilst performing a loop which threw Daniel all around the carriage.

Waldo, the guard, looked on from his seat with amusement and exasperation on his face, completely unaffected by the train's violent movements. Just as it looked like the journey was about to take its toll on his unsecured companion's stomach, he stretched out and dragged him down onto the seat opposite.

Daniel's head and stomach continued to spin for a few moments whilst he gained his bearings. When his symptoms of nausea cleared, he noticed Waldo staring at him intently whilst stroking his voluminous moustache.

'So-what's-your-name-slim?' he asked.

'Daniel,' was the reply, 'Daniel Welsh.'

'Welsh? Welsh,' pondered Waldo. 'Can't-say-I-know-any-Welshes.'

Daniel smiled thinly. 'So what is this?'

'You-really-should-get-out-more-It's-called-a-train.'

'This isn't like any train I've been on before. That acceleration was nuts! I think I must have hit my head pretty hard because I could have sworn we were sideways at one point. I thought we'd derailed.'

'Good-thing-we're-not-on-rails-then,' Waldo said as he looked out the window. Daniel followed his gaze and his jaw dropped in astonishment when he saw that their train was speeding along underwater. He almost jumped out of his seat but Waldo stopped him.

'I-wouldn't-do-that-if-I-were-you.   Unless-you-want-another-trip-around-the-carriage.'

'I must be dreaming,' Daniel said in disbelief.

'Good-grief! -I-hope-not. You're-in-trouble-if-a-young-man-like-you-only-has-enough-imagination-to-come-up-with-a-man-like-me.'

There was a silence, and then they both burst out laughing. When the pair had calmed down and Waldo had wiped the tears from his eyes, he leaned forward in his seat and spoke conspiratorially to the young passenger. 'So, who are you, Daniel Welsh? I've seen humans on old Gertrude before and, even sitting in these enchanted seats, they have trouble keeping their insides on the inside, if you catch my meaning.'

Daniel leaned forward equally conspiratorially, 'So, Waldo, what's happened to your speech?'

Before Waldo could utter a word, the train began to slow down to a stop just as quickly as it had accelerated to top speed. 'Well, it looks like we're here,' he said, and with a clap of his hands he stood up and walked to the doors.

An exhalation of air signalled their opening as Daniel joined the guard. The fragrant, familiar scents of flowers, coupled the unmistakable tranquil sounds of the sea, pervaded Daniel's sense of smell and hearing. His brow, however, creased when his eyesight was confronted with the unbelievable vision of what Daniel perceived to be dual suns, one light blue, the other a shade of lilac, both resting high in a pale pink sky.

'And *where* exactly is *here*?' a dumbfounded Daniel asked.

'*Where*? Its Ariest, of course,' Waldo replied gleefully.

10

Trinity waited patiently outside the college gates. She had her long auburn hair styled in an over-the-shoulder braid and she absentmindedly played with it as she looked up and down the street. It was almost time for lectures to begin and it seemed to her that almost all the students had filed past her, but there was still no sign of Daniel.

Her father had described the previous night's events to her and she felt sorry that Daniel found out about his heritage the way he did. When Gydion had told her that she would be involved with his training, she had hoped that she would be the one to tell Daniel that he was part Fey, simply because she felt her father lacked certain social skills and carried himself with an air of haughty superiority, which was understandable, considering he was close to one thousand years old. She loved him dearly but she also knew that it was hard for people to adhere to him and his ways. And that is why she was waiting here now, to apologise to her friend Daniel and to smooth things over with him.

An hour later and Daniel was still to make an appearance. After checking the library to make sure he hadn't entered the college by the back entrance, Trinity had the idea of trying to use her magic to tap into the peridot crystal she had given him.

Though magic had diminished on Earth, there were still places that held immense power. Places where nature still ruled, places where ley lines flowed, believed to be the paths of subtle magical energy running through the Earth.

Trinity made her way to the nearby park. Though she had never communed with the nature spirits, the dryads, Gydion had educated her on the process and procedures. She knew the great importance trees held within the realms. They are the lungs of the planet; they can provide transport, fire, furniture, food, medicine, and homes for man and creature alike. Their importance can be traced back to the to the dawn of time; in Eden it was a tree that held the knowledge of good and evil; Buddha found enlightenment beneath a tree. Some call them the standing people, signifying a belief that they are wise, living, individual beings, which they indeed were.

She knew that each tree had its own dryad spirit and could confer different gifts upon those that honoured them. The tree she sought now was Hazel, a provider of knowledge, inspiration, and insight.

Soon Trinity found her prize standing tall within a clearing. She walked slowly towards it with her hands held out in front of her. She felt a slight resistance, a cushion of air, signifying the tree's aura. Trinity pushed on through until her hands lay on the trunk of the tree. She allowed its vitality to flow along her arms until it completely surrounded her, whereupon she dipped her head in reverence and spoke in hushed tones.

'I humbly ask for the spirit of the hazel tree to aid me in my search.'

Trinity didn't have to wait long before her pleas were answered and her astral form left her body and entered the spiritual plane. Everything around her vanished; there was nothing in the empty white void except for her translucent form, floating in the nether, and the hazel tree standing before her.

An opening at the base of the tree appeared and grew in size until it was large enough for Trinity to enter. Inside she was confronted by a wooden spiral staircase, which protruded from the bark-covered walls, each step covered in a lush green moss. Even in her astral form she could still smell the scent of a dew-covered meadow as she descended into the depths of the tree.

At the bottom, Trinity found herself in a cavernous hall. The bark walls continued here, as did the moss carpeting the ground. She marvelled at its immense size, and though there was no obvious light source, the hall was bathed in warm sunlight and a feeling of serenity overwhelmed her. The tranquil silence was suddenly interrupted by the soft, comforting tone of a female voice that resonated throughout the hall.

'I am Hazel, the dryad of this tree. What is it you seek?'

Trinity's vision was drawn to a section of the bark wall as, out of the corner of her eye, it converged and pulled away to create a feminine form that strode reverently towards her.

'I seek a friend and wish to use nature's Essence to aid me in this endeavour.'

'Your friend is the one called Daniel? The one they call Ghost Face?'

Trinity replied firmly, 'His name is just Daniel.'

'I will aid you, for I am compelled to do so, but you should leave him be. The dreams of the Lady Rhiannon have been read and the sisters have spoken.'

'And what's that got to do with Daniel?' a confused Trinity asked.

'"The progeny of the champion shall bring death and destruction. The ghost of the dragon shall change Ariest forever. The Mortokai has come." So again I say leave him be, for the good of all.'

'You're wrong! How could you know what was said by the Sisters of Calatin?' Trinity stated, unconvinced by the dryad's recital. 'Besides, the Lady Rhiannon must have many champions.'

'But one above all others, Eric Mondragon. All trees in all the realms are linked to the Great All Father, The Green Man; we know what he knows.'

'Then he is wrong!'

Hazel was taken aback by Trinity's sleight against her deity. 'Rhiannon did not know the details of her Dreamweave when she awoke, but even she knew, instinctively, that they pertained to Eric. Is that not what Gydion told you all those years ago? You were to find him and bring him back to her so she could keep him near. But she does not know it is too late. She does not know how long he has been gone from Ariest. She does not know that the champion's progeny is now a man. She does not know about Daniel.'

'Daniel is kind and gentle, it's not him, he's not the one.'

'Daniel is a Faerie with a soul; he is dangerous!'

'What do you mean?'

'If certain individuals learn of his existence, it could bring about a return to the dark days. Now leave and heed my words.'

'The dark days? I don't understand!'

'Leave!' With that, the hazel dryad's form retreated back into the wall and disappeared.

Once more alone, Trinity pulled her astral projection back to her physical body and left the spiritual plane. She had gone there with one question and left there feeling like she had many more.

She removed her hands from the tree trunk and a piece of the bark, about the size of a sheet of paper, fell away. The tree instantly healed as Trinity inspected the scroll-like bark and saw what appeared to be a map on its reverse side. A three-dimensional image rose out of the bark and she could see a red pulsing dot in the map's representation of the park, which she assumed to be her. A blue dot gently throbbed on the map somewhere in Belsize Park. *I guess that must be the gem*, she thought.

Trinity creased her nose in disdain as she examined the map. This wasn't the magical assistance she was expecting, considering she could have conjured up a similar map herself.

She sighed as she placed her finger on her dot and then traced a route to the blue one. Just as her finger touched the pulsating dot, she felt her body impossibly squash down to the ground and then stretch like she was a rubber band. At breaking point, she vanished and a second later the process was reversed as she reappeared in an unfamiliar bedroom.

'That was awesome!' Trinity exclaimed before she slapped her hand over her mouth, not wanting to draw attention to her presence.

Trinity walked around the room investigating her surroundings, randomly picking up papers to read their contents. She suspected it to be Daniel's room – why else would the dryad's map send her here? – and she knew for sure when she saw his familiar backpack sitting in the corner. Wherever Daniel was, he may not have his bag, but she hoped he still had the crystal with him. She searched its pockets, and unfortunately found the multifaceted olive-green rectangular gem safely stored away. *Well, that puts a damper on me finding you*, she thought. *Cheers, Daniel.*

Trinity continued her inspection of Daniel's room more out of curiosity than anything else. The bedroom was immaculate and clean. Everything seemed to be in its own place. Books on the shelves were in alphabetical order by subject and then by author. She pulled out a book about the battles of Alexander; it looked brand new like it had never been read, but she knew that wouldn't be the case. There weren't as many books as she was expecting, but it sort of made sense, she thought. If you remember everything you've ever read, even if it's just once, then you have no need to be a collector.

These must be his favourite books, she thought, as she relished discovering more and more about the home life of her friend. 'He must have a membership with the London Library, judging by these history books. How could he not; it would be like a treasure trove to him.' Trinity shook her head as she pondered what the dryad had told her. 'This is the bedroom of a person who has a passion for knowledge and learning, not death and destruction like Hazel suggested...but where is he? And what is the Mortokai?'

11

With her curiosity sated, Trinity decided it was time to let Gydion know the situation regarding Daniel. She knew he would probably say it was nothing, that he had no doubt gone to reflect on the past night's revelations, but she couldn't ignore the anxious feeling she had about her troubled friend.

Finding her father turned out to be a far less arduous task than locating Daniel, and it wasn't long before father and daughter were reunited atop the Shard building in London Bridge.

Gydion stood imperiously as he looked out at the sprawling city 300m below him. The wind whipped his coat this way and that, but he stood firm and strong, leaning on his cane, unmoved by the gales.

'The world has changed exponentially since I was last here,' Gydion said as he felt the sudden presence of Trinity beside him. 'I remember when there was but one bridge across this great river and this spot we stand on was grassland. In fact, outside the old city walls the majority of London was fields; Spitalfields, for instance, *was* actually a field. Some of the place names today harken back to those old times. Aldgate, Bishopsgate, Moorgate and Ludgate were all actual gates to the walled city; now they are places where the banking elite reside.'

'I can't imagine London being that small.'

'It was a burgeoning city back then. You should go back and experience it, maybe take Daniel with you once his studies have advanced a bit.'

'And once we've found him.'

'What do you mean?' he asked as he turned to his daughter.

'Well, I wanted to apologize to him for your actions...'

'Unnecessary, but go on.'

'...But he didn't turn up at college, then I asked for help from a dryad.'

'And still no sign of him?'

'None. She also tried to warn me off finding him, said something about the dream interpretation being complete and that it foretells that Daniel will bring death and destruction and change Ariest.'

'Change is not always a bad thing.'

'She mentioned that he could bring back the dark days as well, and something about the Mortokai. What does that even mean?'

Gydion was silent for a moment and appeared not to react, but Trinity knew him to well. 'The dark days? The dark days...are a blot on Faerie history, just as slavery is on human history. It happened centuries ago, before Rhiannon, before even Alina came to the throne. The old Fey had different rules of morality and proof of that is in Faerie tales. Look at the prince who refused shelter to the old woman who was Fey; she cursed him and turned him into a beast until someone would love him despite his appearance, thus learning a valuable lesson.'

'I still don't get it.'

'That is because I have not finished. There are other tales that hide more sinister secrets; Cinderella, for instance.'

'What? Where's the sinister part in that?'

'It's the part that's not in the story, the part before she ended up being with the wealthy family. Cinderella, you see, was Fey.'

'O...kay...'

'You know that when Faerie die they return to their base element; water Faerie to water, earth to earth, and so forth. The old Faerie discovered that humans had an immortal soul that lived on after death. They thought it was something you obtained from living in Earth realm, so they began to switch the bodies of human babies with their own.'

'That's terrible. What happened to the human children?'

'They ended up in Almedia, which has since become a human province. All those Faerie Godmothers in the tales are really Faerie Mothers looking after their children. After all, what mother wouldn't want their daughter growing up to marry a prince?'

'But that must mean there are human/Faerie offspring here.'

'There are, but to my knowledge they have so far been born wholly human or wholly fey.'

'Except Daniel. You don't seriously believe it's him, do you? In the Lady Rhiannon's dreamweave, I mean.'

'What I believe is of no consequence, but it would be better for us if we knew where the boy was.'

'So how do we find him?'

'By tracking *him*, not the gem you gave him, but his actual Essence. We know that he has a high level and he will be leaving a trail of Essence, because he has not been taught to control it, which is why he can do things unintentionally. So, you will focus on that with a magic detection spell.'

'What do you mean *me*?'

'Why not you? You have seen it, you have power enough to do it, contrary to what you may believe, and you have the theory in your head...you just need to try the practical application. You *do* remember the incantation, of course?'

'Of course,' Trinity replied as she flexed and wiggled her fingers.

'Good, then let us begin. Firstly, we should get a bit more height to widen our field of vision.' As he finished, Gydion tapped his cane and an opaque bubble suddenly surrounded the pair. He then raised his palm into the air and the bubble, containing father and daughter, slowly floated into the air and came to a halt hundreds of metres above the towering Shard building.

Trinity closed her eyes as she spoke the magical words in hushed tones and her fingers repeated the necessary movements. She finished the short spell and opened her eyes; they had completely become a metallic jade colour. 'I can see so many colours. Are they all magic users?'

'No, but do not forget that Essence is in everything and everywhere, even in those that cannot manipulate it. What you must do now is focus, filter out the people with low-level Essence, the dim colours, and concentrate on the bright ones; amongst them you should recognise Daniel's. The trails you can see are their movement; the more intense it is, the more recent they were there.'

'There's still a lot more than I would have expected.'

'Why do you think it took us so long to find him in the first place?'

'So, these are the remnants of the dark days. Will they ever be told about their origins, what they are?'

'I do not know, but it is a moral question I am not about to touch, and to be honest, neither is the Faerie hierarchy. It never gets mentioned; it is like the dirty little Faerie secret. They all but ignore the human province, Almedia, except to take the ones with above-average Essence when they are discovered.'

'You're not really painting this place in a good light, you know.'

'It is like any place in any realm. You have the good standing hand in hand with the bad to create the whole.'

'Wait – I think I see Daniel's trail.'

'Good, where?'

'It's somewhere in Central London. Bring us down a bit so I can pinpoint it. Okay, I can see it leading North London to Moorgate. It looks like it's underground, but where the trail of his Essence ends isn't that intense. So, what does that mean? That he just came here and – and vanished?'

'Exactly.'

'How is that possible? Teleportation is a pretty big spell to pull off accidentally.'

'It was not necessarily a spell. One of the few remaining links to Ariest is by an Underground Train.'

'Really? That must be pretty cool. But how would Daniel know about it? And, furthermore, where would you get a ticket?'

'How he knew, I do not know, but there is only one place to get a ticket; the Hobthrust Laird, Fungal.'

12

'A riest?' an astonished Daniel exclaimed. 'But I was supposed to be on a
Metropolitan Line heritage train!'

'Really?' Waldo replied, totally uninterested in what his fellow passenger
had to say, as he stepped off the train and took a deep breath of sea air. 'It's
good to be home.'

'So how do I get back to Liverpool Street? Will this train be reversing
back?'

'Yes, it will, eventually.'

'Good! When?'

'In a week.'

'What?' Daniel's jaw almost hit the floor.

'It's Beltane! Faerie holiday time. No more trains. If you haven't gotten
where you need to be by now, then you aren't going to get there.'

'Seven days? How am I supposed to survive seven days here? I have no
place to stay, no money; I don't even know what the currency is here.'

'Gold doubloons, silver ingots, and copper geldings.'

Daniel slapped his forehead in exasperation. 'I don't have any of that
stuff! I'm so screwed.'

'Look, if you head that way, southeast, you'll eventually get to Almedia.
I'm sure you'll get some help there.'

'I-I have a condition. I can't be out in the sun too long.'

'Is that why your skin is that fascinating snow colour? I thought you
might have been Mulenaari when I first saw you, but they are supposedly
greyer in skin tone,' Waldo mused. 'Anyway, don't worry about the weather

here; it's not like your Earth realm weather. Haven't you noticed my speech impediment has gone? Something in the Earth air does it.'

To be honest, Daniel had actually noticed, but before he could think further on it, the train suddenly rolled onto its side and tipped him out before closing its doors.

'That's what happens when you delay a Faerie from its holiday time. I'll see you next week, Gertrude. Have fun!'

With a blast of its whistle, the train rose up into the air and in a serpentine way flew off into the distance; all the while Daniel watched with his mouth wide open.

'Well, it was nice meeting you, Daniel Welsh, but I think it's time to say goodbye and return to my family.'

Daniel stood up and brushed himself down before he spun around to face Waldo with the intention of thanking him for his help. When he turned, however, he saw a large walrus standing there in the guard's uniform.

'What the hell!' Daniel exclaimed.

'Ahhhh, you don't know how good it feels to be in my own skin again,' sighed Waldo with a stretch.

'What the hell!' Daniel repeated.

'What's the matter with you? Anyone would think that you've never seen a Selkie before. Anyway, enjoy your stay and I'll probably see you in a week. Oh, and by the way, happy Beltane!'

'And a happy thingy to you too,' said Daniel as Waldo waddled off toward the sea, humming a cheerful tune to himself through his bristling moustache.

Daniel was alone in a strange world. He looked up at the unfamiliar sky with its dual suns and wondered if what Waldo had said about the weather being different was true.

He closed his eyes and could feel the warmth of the sun and the gentle sea breeze on his face. He didn't feel anxious as he would if he was doing the same back home; it felt more meditative and, in a moment of repose, he pushed his hood off.

Daniel realised that he had no real choice but to trust in the guard's revelation about the suns. His mind had reasoned and come to the conclusion that he didn't know how far this Almedia was, so if Waldo was wrong either way, him standing here or walking made no difference because he would get burnt and there would be nothing he could do about it. At least there were some trees in the distance if worst came to worst.

As he set off in the direction indicated to him, Daniel began to think about how he had gotten into this situation. Surely it couldn't be a coincidence that he found himself in the same place that Gydion wanted to bring him. It must be him, he thought; he didn't want to wait for any decision to be made so he decided to resort to kidnapping. As far as Daniel was concerned, the buck stopped firmly with Gydion; but how involved in it all was Trinity, he pondered.

Admittedly this is what he had wanted, to strike out on his own, to gain a little independence, to leave the bullies behind, and to live his life to the fullest. He had already decided to tell his parents of his intentions but being all but press-ganged into coming here changed things in his mind, made him wonder if he could really trust this Gydion. After all, his father hadn't been overly pleased to have him there.

Time rolled by as Daniel trudged along the well-beaten path, hoping that he was making good time. His head swivelled this way and that as he marvelled at the strange and interesting foliage and the unusual creatures. One in particular looked like a cross between an antelope and a hyena. At the front, it had a long aquiline head shape, long withers, long spiral horns, though it had a smaller third horn between its eyes. Its back sloped down to shorter hindquarters, similar to those of a canine. The creature's tail was almost twice as long as its body with a sharp tip and was also prehensile as Daniel watched the animal use it to grab strange-coloured fruit from the nearby trees and pull them down to feed. He noticed that they seemed to be travelling in small family groups, like a herd, and one thing he knew about herds of herbivores is that they were usually prey to the more dangerous carnivore.

This thought instantly put Daniel on edge. The idea of travelling God knows how many miles only to be eaten by some animal he wouldn't know the name of didn't appeal to him.

As Ariest's latest visitor, Daniel was beginning to feel like he was on a rambling holiday. He wasn't sure how long he'd been walking. He wasn't feeling particularly tired, but as he noticed for the first time that the two suns were beginning to lower in the sky, he felt the first pangs of hunger.

He saw rows of the trees with the turquoise-coloured fruits the antelope-like creatures had been eating and thought he would try a sample. He was a little apprehensive, to say the least; eating an unidentified fruit wasn't ideal and went against his better judgement, or rather the judgement he learnt from reading Bear Grylls.

Daniel recalled the UET, universal edibility test, to his mind and hoped that it was still applicable in this Faerie world. The first test was to see if his skin reacted to the fruit. He pulled a couple of the large grapefruit-sized fruit off of the tree; he thought the skin felt similar to apples as he stuffed them into his pockets. He then pulled down a third and started to rub the skin off on the tree's bark until he exposed the flesh of the fruit. It was strangely opaque and had no scent, but Daniel knew he was in no position to turn his nose up at it.

Rolling up his sleeve, Daniel rubbed the strange fruit onto his exposed flesh, leaving a trail of its juice on his skin; within minutes he'd know if he was allergic to it depending on if his skin reacted or not.

Daniel was about to step back onto the path and continue on his way when he was suddenly startled by an incredibly loud vociferous voice.

'**Hey, watch where you're stepping!**' the voice bellowed, as a blue-coloured fox pulled up next to Daniel's foot. On closer inspection, he saw that, though the creature resembled the red and grey foxes that he was familiar with, this one had three tails! Then he noticed the little people, no more than six inches in height, that were riding on its back. It seemed like a whole family; the father, at the reins, sat in a seat between the fox's shoulder blades and a harness across its midsection held grandmother and mother, in special basket-encased seats on one side, and daughter and son on the other in an identical basket.

'**Poppa, why are his clothes so funny-looking?**' shouted the young girl.

'**Now, now, Nisset,**' replied the father in an even louder voice. '**What have I told you about whispering in front of people?**'

'**I'm sorry, Poppa,**' she said in her sweet but loud voice.

'**That's okay, dear,**' her Poppa replied with a shout before he addressed Daniel in the same volume. '**My daughter would like to know why your clothes are so strange for a mortal. If you are a mortal, that is.**'

'**Well, apparently I'm only half mortal, and the other half is Faerie.**'

'**Fascinating! I've never seen one before,**' he shouted with his eyes wide open in wonder, and even the fox's ears pricked up at Daniels revelation.

'**What did he say?**' the grandmother yelled as she cupped her ear and strained to hear.

'**He said he's half mortal and half Faerie,**' the mother shouted back.

'**Oooooo,**' the grandmother cooed. '**Well, he's a damn sight better looking than the ones I've seen. Gnarled, twisted creatures they were. Ripped right out of their mothers' wombs, they would...**'

'**Mother!**'

'**Why do you talk so loudly?**' Daniel asked.

'**We are Bellowers; it's what we do. My name's Dilbert Mudd and this is my wife, Felma, and her mother and these are our kids, Nisset and the boy Kanda. And this,**' Dilbert yelled as he patted the head of his mount, 'is Toshi.'

'Pleased to make your acquaintance,' Toshi said.

'Your fox talks?' Daniel exclaimed.

'Fox? I'm no fox! I'm vastly superior to your Earth realm creatures.'

'**Don't get on your high horse, Toshi. You see there?**' Dilbert shouted, pointing to Toshi's tails. '**He's a Kitsune. They grow an extra tail every hundred years; they can grow up to ten of them. Toshi hasn't even started growing his fourth yet,**' he chuckled loudly.

'**So, are you here for Beltane?**' asked Felma.

'I'm here by mistake, and there's no train back to my home until next week. So, I guess I have no choice about this Beltane, whatever it is.'

'**It's a great fire festival,**' Kanda shouted excitedly.

'**We're on our way to Almedia to see the festivities,**' continued Nisset.

Daniel, who by this time had resorted to putting his fingers in his ears to stop them ringing, brightened up at this news. 'This *is* the right way to Almedia then?'

'**Sure,**' Dilbert replied loudly, '**but you'll be hard pushed to make it there by nightfall on foot. We'd better be making a move ourselves. Wish we could give you a ride but maybe we'll meet again in town.**'

After the Mudds had said their loud goodbyes, Dilbert geed up Toshi and the three tailed Kitsune bounded away, leaving a trail of dust behind them.

Once the Bellowers were out of sight, Daniel investigated the patch of skin he had smeared with the juice of the fruit. He was glad to see that there had been no reaction to it because he felt that his rumbling belly could match the decibel levels of the Mudds.

Daniel took a small, tentative bite of the fruit. His mouth was instantly filled with a taste sensation. At first, he was sure he could taste fresh ripe strawberries, then passion fruit, then a moment later it was oranges. Another larger bite of the juicy fruit and he likened it to kiwi before his taste buds were invaded by the flavour of grapes.

As he happily chomped into another bite of the mystery fruit, his ears suddenly pricked up at the sound of faint splashes. Daniel couldn't help but feel a little curious in this strange new world; he just hoped that curiosity didn't necessarily have the same outcome for the cat here as it did on Earth.

Slowly he edged his way through the foliage, as quietly as he could, not wanting to startle whatever was making the sound. Then he heard the snort and neighing of a horse and finally saw that it had come from a black stallion.

It must have been swimming, Daniel assumed, as he looked closer at the beast and saw that it seemed to be wet with bits of seaweed twisted in its mane. At that moment Daniel had a brainwave. He thought about what Dilbert Mudd had said about Almedia, that he'd be hard pushed to make it there by nightfall, but what if he were riding a horse? Admittedly he hadn't ridden a horse before, but how hard could it be to point it in the right direction and get it to move forward?

Slowly he moved towards the animal. He held out one of the fruits, intending to feed it to the horse to show it that he was no threat. Its head rose as it regarded Daniel for the first time. It snorted as it pawed at the ground momentarily, causing Daniel to tense up. Then the horse began to slowly walk forward until it was close enough to sniff at the fruit in Daniel's hand before it ate it out of his open palm.

Daniel put a couple more pieces of fruit down on the ground for the horse to eat, as he patted and stroked its neck. While it ate, Daniel took the opportunity to try and mount the animal. To his surprise the horse dropped to its foreknees to aid Daniel in climbing up. He wasn't about to look the proverbial gift horse in the mouth, and within moments Daniel was sitting on the animal's back with a big grin on his face, knowing that he didn't have to worry about not getting to Almedia before nightfall after all.

The ease at which a complete novice like Daniel was able to get the horse to do his bidding made him think that it might actually have been tame. Maybe it had escaped from a nearby stable, or maybe the owner had had an accident and fallen off, Daniel thought, but with no bridal, saddle, or stirrups, that idea would have been hard to prove.

They trotted peacefully along the beach before Daniel thought that it would be a good plan to get back onto the path so that he could be sure that they were still on the right track to Almedia. He tried to direct the horse that way, but it wouldn't respond and carried on its way. *Perhaps it would follow the fruit if I held one and led it back to the pathway, then I could jump back on and be on my way*, Daniel reasoned, but when he tried to get off he couldn't budge an inch. His hands and legs were stuck to the horse by some kind of resin, which he saw oozing from the animal's skin.

Daniel began to panic and with all his strength tried to pull himself free, but to no avail. The horse suddenly reared up on its hind legs, let out a thunderous neigh, and took off at a high speed towards the sea. Still Daniel strained to get free and as he did so the horse's head turned a full 180 degrees to face him. Its eyes, once glistening black but now blood-red, stared at him intently. Its mouth, hideously stretched and elongated, tried to bite him time and again with its row upon row of shark-like serrated teeth.

It took all the energy Daniel had to avoid the horse's mouth, and then he thought it had all been for nothing as it plunged them headlong into the sea and they disappeared beneath the waves.

13

It wasn't the fact that Gydion had taken Trinity onto the London Underground to find this Laird named Fungal that puzzled her. She *had* been hoping that he would show her the portal spell again, but, as always, he had given her the 'just because we can, doesn't mean that we should' mantra. What really puzzled her was that they took a train from Moorgate to Farringdon, even though her father had told her that the Hobthrust they were after lived in the tunnels of the disused British Museum Station.

She discussed this with him as they walked along Farringdon Road before turning into Phoenix Place.

'The reason we are here, my dear, is that since we are in no rush...'

'What do you mean *no rush*?' interrupted Trinity as she came to a complete stop. 'Daniel's missing! We *should* be rushing, especially if he's not in this realm anymore.'

'...I thought that it would be interesting for you to see the Faerie Transport Network,' Gydion concluded without missing a beat.

'The FTN? Really?' exclaimed Trinity as she jogged to catch up. 'Well, that *would* be interesting, as long as it doesn't delay us too long. I just hope he's okay, wherever he is.'

Gydion stopped, took his pocket watch out, and momentarily watched its hands rotate around its ornately designed Louis XIV face. 'Do not worry, my dear,' he said shortly. 'Daniel is fine. Time is still in our favour, so let us crack on.'

'And what's that supposed to mean?' she asked with a quizzical look on her face.

'All in good time,' came his reply. 'Now, do you know what this place is?' He gestured to the large grey building they stood beside.

'What?' Trinity was caught unawares by Gydion's question. She was still mulling things over about the missing Daniel as well as Gydion and his cryptic speeches. 'Oh, that's the postal sorting office.'

'Yes, the largest one in London, to be exact; the Mount Pleasant Sorting Office.' They began walking again as Gydion continued his tutorial. 'It was once a prison back in the nineteenth century but beneath it, things are more interesting. Not only does it have its own Underground train line, but below that is London's longest subterranean river which runs all the way from the Thames to Hampstead.'

'And that's what we'll be taking.'

'Exactly.'

A young man walked several metres behind them, totally oblivious to his surroundings, his attention completely focused on his mobile phone as he walked and texted. If he hadn't been so absorbed with his social networking, he might have noticed the aged man and young woman in front of him vanish. He momentarily stopped and shuddered when he passed the spot where they had been. Then he shrugged his shoulders and continued on his way.

On the other side of the invisible magical barrier, Gydion and Trinity found themselves in a seemingly unchanged environment; they were on the same stretch of road and the postal sorting office was still on the right. At that moment, a pedestrian walked through the spot they were standing on without breaking his stride, as if they weren't there at all.

Trinity reached out her hand and touched the barrier. Iridescent colours swirled around her palm where there was contact made. Their movement reminded her of the way colours flowed around a soap bubble in sunlight.

'It's a Reality Shifter Bubble; only magic users and those of Faerie blood can see it, I assume. Old Fungal seems to have made some upgrades. It was not so long ago that we would have had to stand before a wall in that shabby alley we passed, and traced some runes on it to reveal that,' Gydion explained. Trinity turned away from the Shifter Bubble to follow her father's gaze and for the first time she saw the brass spiral escalator before them.

It was like none other she had seen in her life. On its insides were gilt bronze relief panels apparently depicting scenes from the life of Fungal, which brought snorts of derision from Gydion. As they rode down, at regular intervals, the escalator hissed and blew out plumes of steam, almost as if it were breathing.

When they reached the bottom, they found themselves, along with all manner of Faerie, in a large ticket hall with vaulted ceilings and several columned arches down either side. In the centre was a large brass statue of Fungal; cigar in mouth, chest puffed out, and hands on hip in a heroic pose.

'I never knew Hobthrusts were so self-publicising,' a bewildered Trinity said.

'Usually they are not. Fungal is quite unique in that respect,' Gydion replied as he looked around until he spotted the sign which pointed the way towards the riverboats.

They followed the direction indicated to get to their transport. Trinity's head swivelled this way and that as she took in the sights of all the different Fae: Leprechauns, Redcaps, Dwarfs, and Fauns, to name but a few. The majority of them she had never seen before and had only read about them in the Encyclopaedia Magica, but seeing them up close was a totally different experience.

It was at times like this that Trinity wondered why Gydion hadn't introduced her to places like this before. He had taught her many druidic and nature spells, but at times seemed almost reluctant to allow her to search out other Fey. There were times when she felt more human than Faerie, times when she felt more Faerie than human, but she never felt completely one or the other; she was always only left or right of the middle.

Before long the pair had reached the river. There, sitting cross-legged on its bank, with a staff beside him, was a small boy. To Trinity's eyes, he looked no more than twelve years old. His long silver hair ran down his back, but as she got closer she could see that it wasn't totally silver; it had the faintest hint of blue to it. That was when she noticed the blindfold of white cloth tied across his eyes.

'Welcome to the Faerie River Services,' the boy said as he held out his hand. 'May I have your tickets please?' His voice sounded like that of a child, but it also had an older voice echoing in a harmonious tone.

'I can see that your sense of hearing is still good, old man, but what of your other senses? Surely I do not need a ticket.'

The boy paused a moment before he spoke again. 'I admittedly do not have much need to scan people's magical Essence here but there is no mistaking that of my good friend, Gydion.'

'It is good to see you again, Elganor.'

'You also,' replied the boy as he stood and embraced the mage. 'Who is this with you? Her aura seems familiar, but...'

'She is my daughter, Trinity.'

'I see. Well I am honoured to be in your presence.'

'As I am to be in the presence of a Calatin.' She almost felt a need to courtesy but restricted herself to a small bow out of respect.

'I am of no importance; it is my sisters whom hold that distinction.'

'Do not try and sell yourself short. She knows of our deeds during the wars.'

'Inconsequential. I did what I had to to survive. The consequences of failure were too dire. Heroes are not made fighting in wars.'

'True,' Trinity agreed, 'but the actions to save others makes them so.'

A silence pervaded as the trio paused to reflect on the comrades lost. Although Trinity had not been alive at the time of the Great Wars, when Gydion had recounted his experiences to her, he pulled her astral form into his memories, allowing her to see what the residents of Ariest had to endure; the terror that swept through the villages when the Shades, strange intangible creatures that devoured the magic energy of children, were deployed; the anguish that the warriors fighting under the banner of the Lady Alina felt when they witnessed their friends and allies skinned alive by the Frell and their brutish Gnolls. These were dark days indeed.

'Is Sayyidah not with you?' Elganor asked, finally breaking the silence.

'Sayyidah is no longer with us.' A faraway look came over Gydion's face as he spoke, a look Trinity had not seen him portray often, but before she could ask about the identity of the person, he changed the subject. 'We need to see Fungal, Elganor. That is why we are here.'

'That will not be a problem, old friend.' Elganor turned and made the few steps back to the river's edge. He gripped his staff in both hands and held it out before him, then chanted some arcane words, at which point the end of the stave began to glow brightly.

'The Calatins all have the same ability in senses,' Gydion said in hushed tones to Trinity, 'but whereas his sisters also have the ability to read premonitions, Elganor developed the ability to control and mould water to his will.'

The luminous end of the staff was plunged into the river and moved this way and that in large strokes as if Elganor were writing runes. Then he stopped and stood back. The water before him began to churn and bubble violently, growing in height, then just as quickly began to calm and ease. When it ceased, it had formed into the shape of a skiff with a paddle wheel on either side.

'This boat will take you where you need to go.'

'Thank you, old man. Be sure to come back home some time; do not be a stranger.'

'Actually, I do miss my sisters; perhaps I have spent too long away from them,' mused Elganor before bidding farewell to his friends, old and new. 'Until next we meet, Gydion and you also, young Trinity, I know you shall reach your true potential with him to guide you.'

Gydion helped Trinity onto the water-created paddle skiff. Though it was made of water, it was solid under her feet. Elganor's control of water was indeed absolute, she thought to herself as she ran her hand along a seat. It was warm to touch and left no wetness on her palm. As Gydion joined her on board, she wondered if she might one day be able to conjure such things, then she recalled something her father would tell her whenever she would question her abilities with magic: 'All things are possible if you have the imagination, desire, and will to achieve them.' In that moment, she knew that she would, because she had those qualities in abundance.

14

Trinity was finding it hard to enjoy the journey as much as she would have liked. She still marvelled at the paddle skiff they were sailing in; the rhythmic splash from its blades provided an almost Zen-like peacefulness, and the floating flames that lit the tunnels gave the whole place an atmospheric mood which she wasn't completely in the right frame of mind to fully appreciate.

The wellbeing of Daniel was still in her thoughts, but the question at the forefront of her mind was, who is Sayyidah? Judging by the way her father reacted to hearing the name, Trinity could tell that it was someone of importance.

She watched him intently as he sat opposite her. His eyes were closed and he breathed the deep breaths of someone in meditation. She was loath to interrupt him but her curiosity got the better of her and she asked the question.

Gydion's regular breathing stopped and he let out a deep sigh. 'I was wondering how long it would take you. Sayyidah is – Sayyidah *was* my wife.'

'Your wife? Blood hell!' Trinity exclaimed. 'I never knew you...I mean, you never told me.'

'It was something I have wanted to leave in the past. Besides, it is not something that comes up in normal conversation like: "This is the incantation for the Mystic Jump spell, oh, and by the way I was married once and she tried to kill everyone" does not sound very natural, does it?'

'Perhaps not,' responded Trinity. She looked down at her hands as she idly twiddled her thumbs whilst she got her thoughts in order. 'How is this for natural: "I think I may be in love but, not having experienced it before, I'm not sure." Have you ever been in love before, Father?'

Gydion looked at his daughter and smiled. 'Ok, ok, point taken.'

'Tell me about her; what did she look like?'

'What did she look like? Well, she had long black hair,' as he spoke, Gydion, using magical energy, began to mould the space in front of him, like a sculptor would clay. 'Her face was olive-shaped, her eyes were like two sparkling black gems, her skin was a dusky colour; she was from the deserts of second century Egypt, you see, that is where Penwyll found her. I have told you of him, have I not?'

'Of course, he was your Master. He taught you all you know.'

'He taught us all *he* knew,' Gydion corrected. 'Knowledge is not finite, there is always more to learn, it is just that some knowledge can be harmful and detrimental but it is up to us to know the difference.' Gydion finished his arcane sculpture and let it float there, slowly rotating in the air.

'She was beautiful.'

'Yes, she was; but it was her fire and determination which attracted me most. She came from a poor background and when Penwyll plucked her up from her life and showed her the magic she could wield, even though she had some knowledge already, she vowed never to go back to what she left behind, no matter what.'

Once again Gydion began to sculpt the Essence in the air until he was left with an image of himself, as he was as a young man, floating next to that of Sayyidah.

'OMG! Is that supposed to be you?'

'Hmpf there's nothing *supposed* about it, Trinity, it *is* me. Anyway, it was not long before he came for me; apparently, he saw something in me. Sayyidah and myself were of a similar determined character and soon became Master Penwyll's brightest Adepts and as such also became bitter rivals, but it did not take long for that rivalry to turn to affection and we became lovers.

By this time, we had become Initiates and were afforded the luxury of more free time, which we used to travel through time and to other realms searching for mystical items and magic books and increasing our knowledge. It was during this period of our lives that we performed the matrimonial rites at Beltane.

It was a great time for us; we loved, learnt, and quested to our hearts' content. Then the Firbolgs and Gnolls encroached further south than they usually did on their yearly drive and the Lady Amina, who was queen then, sent her armies to push them back. This was the First Great War. We defeated them, eventually, but not without loss, Master Penwyll was mortally wounded.'

Gydion paused a moment while he silently reminisced about his old Master, the man that was like a father to him, before he continued with his narrative.

'My Master put me forward to take part in the Trial of Succession before he died.'

'Which you won.'

'Obviously.'

'And what of Sayyidah? Was she resentful of you being picked over her?'

'No, she was very supportive. I doubt she would want to have dealt with all the responsibility that came with the position anyway.'

'Then what happened to her?'

'Patience, little one. Once I became Archmage, I also gained access to the Sanctum.'

'The room where I was born?'

'It is vastly more than just a room; we had very little time back then, or else you would have more appreciation for it. It is an abode that exists outside of normal reality and it harbours many secrets and artefacts of mystic nature. One in particular interested Sayyidah, a dimensional map of all the realms – well, all the realms that had been discovered by then – but there were more than we could have imagined; in all our travels we had not even scratched the surface. Her eyes lit up when she gazed upon it, and I must admit I was more than a little intrigued by its ramifications myself. Having directions to new realms reignited the adventurer and explorer in me, but it was no longer just myself I had to worry about. As Archmage, I have a duty to every mage in Ariest.'

'And Sayyidah had no such worries.'

'No, so I gave her access to the map, of course; she was my love...my life.'

'I think I see where this is going now. She died whilst adventuring in another realm.'

'Not exactly. The map was enchanted; it could tell you information about the realms. There was one called Salamida that it gave strict warnings about, and only an Archmage was recommended to go there. It is where the beings called Shade lived. Those shadowy, creatures that fed on Essence.'

'Like a vampire.'

'Indeed.'

'But she went there anyway.'

'She did, but I did not discover that until after the Second Great War.'

'So they killed her.'

'No. She unleashed them upon Ariest.'

'She did what?' Trinity couldn't believe what she was hearing.

'Sayyidah was the architect of the Second Great War.'

'But why? To save herself from the Shade?'

'I do not know, maybe it was, but that place certainly changed her. She was no longer the woman I loved, but I still could not bring myself to execute her.'

'So what did you do?'

'I stripped her of her magic and used a spell to banish her.'

'That's deep. I'm sorry she hurt you, Father.'

'Do not be, my dear. I have had many years to come to terms with it.'

'And yet you never loved again. I can see that her memory still affects you, despite her betrayal. That's the strength of love, I guess.'

'Is that how you feel about Daniel? I charged you with finding the boy, but you do not need to be a mage to see that it has gone beyond this.'

'I wanted to talk to you about it, because I didn't know what it was I was feeling, but hearing you talk about Sayyidah made me think about how great it would be if Daniel and I could be like you two were when you were young; travelling the dimensions and adventuring. Does that mean I love him?'

'It definitely is on its way to being so, and that is a good thing because he is going to need you to help him.'

'And you too.'

'Perhaps.' Gydion could see the confusion on his daughter's face but before she had a chance to query his reply he turned away. 'Ah, it would seem that we have reached our destination.'

The water-formed paddle skiff slowly came to a halt at the dock of their destination. They stepped onto the pier and the boat quickly dispersed back into its original state with a simple splash. At the pier's end was a single tunnel which Gydion and Trinity silently headed for.

The only source of light illuminating the passageway came from the flickering fires of the riverside, and as the pair walked deeper into the tunnel the darker it became until it was near pitch black, at which point Trinity held out her hand and in a firm voice said, 'Lumin!' A globe of intense white light appeared in her palm. She gently threw it into the air and it floated above and ahead of them and remained so, lighting their way as they continued down the passageway.

It wasn't long before they came to the end of the tunnel. Two huge gates that were padlocked together at the centre blocked their way. Each gate was securely held to the passage wall by three bolted hinges.

'Now what?' asked Trinity with a shrug.

'You tell me.'

'Well,' she began as she paced back and forth, 'we can assume that the padlock is just there to deter mortals.'

'A fair assumption, as no ordinary lock could stop Fey.'

'So, there must be some other magical defences in place on the gates themselves.'

'Possible.'

'Now, I could use a magic detection spell to determine exactly what it is and possibly negate it, but I believe that to be unnecessary.' As she finished speaking, Trinity held her hands out in front, her fingers loosely bent. She placed her thumbs and little fingers together and then her wrists to create a shape that resembled a tree. 'Eldritch Barrage!' she shouted and six emerald green bolts of magical power shot out of the shimmering ball mystic energy she had created between her palms. Each spiralling bolt blew away the wall that the hinges were connected to and, with nothing to hold it, the gates toppled backwards and fell to the ground, wafting great plumes of dust into the air. 'Et viola!' Trinity said with a satisfied smile as she shook the dust out of her skirt.

Gydion gave a sniff of disdain. 'You could have saved some Essence and a cleaning bill if you had used the detection spell; the gate was not enchanted.'

'Ah,' she replied, scratching her head with embarrassment. 'I guess I gave Fungal a bit too much credit.' A loud roar suddenly rumbled through the tunnel. 'Or perhaps I didn't give him enough.'

15

A bright light shone through Daniel's closed eyelids and he wondered if it was the light that people who had had life and death experiences talked about. If it was and he truly was dead, as he suspected, then the sound he could hear must be that of angels, although truth be told to him it sounded like whale song interspersed with a clicking sound. One thing bothered him, however. If he were dead and this were the afterlife, why would he still feel pins and needles in his legs?

He forced his eyes open. They were matted together, which hinted to him that he had been unconscious for a while. It took a little time for his eyesight to clear and, when it did, he discovered that the light source that had been shining in his face seemed to be coming from something that looked like a jellyfish. Then he heard the whale song again but it was quickly followed by a female's voice, which drew Daniel's attention.

'He is stirring, Ch'tan; speak the common tongue.'

If this female had been the first creature he had encountered in this world, Daniel might have been taken aback. With her light green hair, which had small seashells in it, turquoise-coloured skin, four small slits where her nose should be, and piercing yellow eyes, her features were striking, but next to the Bellowers and the demon horse with the shark teeth, it was nothing.

'Why should we have to lower ourselves to accommodate this surface dweller?' The second being that stood over Daniel was a male and even from his prone position Daniel could tell that he was large, close to seven feet tall and just as broad.

'Because I wish it,' the female replied. 'I have never seen a mortal like him before.'

'And you have never seen a Black Dragon before; would you bring one of them here also?' countered the male.

'Do not be ridiculous! This mortal poses no threat.'

'How do you know? Was it not surface dwellers that polluted our waters?'

'That was Gnolls, not mortals.'

'Surface dwellers are surface dwellers, Nyriel.'

'And by that narrow-minded view it would make you comparable to a Boda Whale.'

'Hmph! Let's hope that your father is as understanding if he discovers your new pet project,' Ch'tan said as he stormed out of the room.

The female sighed, looked down, and smiled at Daniel. 'Do not take any notice of Ch'tan. He is my personal bodyguard and he takes his duties far too seriously at times. Oh, you do understand me, yes?'

'Yeah, sure I do.'

'Ah, good. My name is Princess Nyriel. You are lucky to be alive. If I had not been in the area, searching for artefacts with Ch'tan, I fear your life would have been extinguished. You were already unconscious when we saw you, but Ch'tan dealt with the Kelpie and we brought you back here.'

'And where exactly is here?' asked Daniel as he sat up and took in the pearlescent qualities of the walls and floors, straining his neck to try and see out of the windows on the far side.

'Here is Pichini Palace in Murias City. You are in the medical chamber. Apparently being this far underwater is detrimental to a mortal's health, something about pressure, or so Ch'tan tells me, so we had to bring you here to give you an elixir.'

'We're underwater?'

'Of course!'

'But there's air in here.'

'Of course! A barrier surrounds the city. It was put there to protect my people from the pollution.'

Daniel found it a little odd having the shoe on the other foot; for the first time in his life he had no issues with the sun. 'So, what are you? If you don't mind me asking. Some kind of mermaid?'

'No, do I look like I have a tail?' Nyriel replied as she did a pirouette. 'I am an Undine. You really do not know much, do you?'

'Well, I'm not from around here. In fact, I'm not from this world.'

'I knew it!' exclaimed the princess as she excitedly clapped her hands. 'Who are you? Where are you from? Does your realm have Undines too? No, of course it doesn't. If it did, you wouldn't have asked what I was. I knew you were different! I could tell by your attire.'

At the mention of his clothes, Daniel noticed for the first time that his usual outfit had been changed for something akin to the blue diaphanous garb that both Nyriel and Ch'tan wore. 'Wait a minute, what's happened to my clothes?'

'Oh, I had to get you out of those,' she answered with slight embarrassment. 'Your material is not water resistant like ours.'

It wasn't too long ago that the thought of someone, especially a woman, seeing his undressed body might have given him concern, but Daniel had to admit to himself that he was beginning to accept the hand he had been dealt in regard to his albinism thanks in no small part to the way inhabitants of this realm, and in particular Trinity, accepted him rather than ridiculed him.

'Well, since you've seen me without most of my clothes on, you should at least know my name; it's Daniel Welsh from Earth.'

'Daniel Welsh from Earth? I have heard of this realm! It is the birth realm of the great Gydion! I read about it in the royal library.'

'The great Gydion?' an incredulous Daniel exclaimed.

'You know of him?'

Daniel nodded with a strained smile and through greeted teeth said, 'I think he's the reason why I'm here.'

'That must be amazing! I have never met him but my father has. A lot of our books have been translated into common if you would like to see the library,' she enthused, eager to show off her prized collection.

'I would like that very much.' Daniel pushed himself off of the table. His feet instantly collapsed under him and he fell into Nyriel who, much to Daniel's surprise, caught him with ease.

'I should have warned you about that,' she said apologetically, her face merely inches from his.

'Wow, you're kind of hot – I mean hot as in temperature hot! Not that you're not *hot* hot of course.'

Nyriel looked at Daniel quizzically. 'Of course I know what you mean by hot. It is how we Undines combat the cold water; we can change our body temperatures.'

'That's amazing!'

'Thank you. You should know, however, that it is an offence to hold a member of the royal family like this, except by their consort of course,' Nyriel playfully said.

'No, no I didn't know that,' Daniel answered as he quickly threw his arms back onto the table for support.

Nyriel couldn't help but smile at Daniel's embarrassment. 'I don't think it would be wise for you to walk through the halls like this, a little too conspicuous,' she said, looking at him thoughtfully. 'Wait here while I go and get something to hide your hair and face.'

She bounded out of the room, leaving Daniel alone. He could feel the pins and needles sensation receding from his feet and he gingerly took a step forward and then another until he was striding around the medical room freely and without hindrance. He was tempted to go to the door and have a look around but thought against it – who knows what he would run into out there? – so instead Daniel went to the window. The sight that greeted him almost took his breath away.

He knew he was deep underwater but when he looked out, to his amazement, he could see a sunny blue sky, with wisps of clouds. The city below was vast and stretched out before him from his high vantage point in the palace. All the buildings, from what he could see, were constructed out of the pearl material and their roofs seemed to be made of multi-coloured shells. He could see Undines milling about in the streets below, traders selling goods, others heading towards a marvellous building not too far in the distance. This was a far cry from battling for his life on the back of a Kelpie.

'The view looks even better from one of the tall towers,' Nyriel said. Daniel hadn't realised he was so zoned out and didn't hear the princess' return. 'If we get a chance I'll take you up and you can experience it for yourself.'

'I've been wondering, how is it possible to see the sky from down here?'

'That is thanks to Gydion. Before we used these glow fish to light the city,' she said, gesturing to the lights above them, 'but their light is not strong enough for that kind of mileage. When the Second Great War was upon us, the Gnolls polluted our waters as recompense for our fighting with the mortals during the first war and allowing them to use our city, which is why we have that elixir here. Gydion created this barrier to protect Murias and enchanted it to imitate the sky above but without the harmful ultra rays.'

Daniel looked back up at the barrier in awe and wondered if his first impression of Gydion had been wrong. No, it hadn't been, he surmised. He was an arrogant man and carried himself with an air of 'better than thou,' but hearing Nyriel speak about him with nothing but reverence urged him to consider giving the man a chance to explain himself. That is, if Daniel could stay alive long enough in this world to get back to Earth. 'That's pretty impressive,' he admitted.

'Of course it is, he is the Archmage,' Nyriel saw the questioning look on Daniel's face and answered his unasked query. 'The Archmage is the supreme magician, a mage of the highest rank, who presides over all others. They are guardians and holders of many artefacts and there is but one to a realm. Here, take this. You can find out more in the library. I took this from my father's chest; I'm sure he will not miss it. He has many cloaks and I cannot actually remember him ever wearing this particular one.'

The cloak she handed Daniel was a carnelian red colour and had gold embroidery around the edge and hood. He thought he saw it shimmer briefly when he touched it but dismissed it as a trick of the light.

He threw the cloak over his shoulders, fastened it, and pulled the hood over his head. 'How do I look?'

'Like it was made for you. Come on, let's go.'

Nyriel led Daniel out of the medical chamber and walked purposefully down corridors. Other Undines they passed bowed respectfully at their future queen. It was the first time that he had gotten any real sense of regality from her. To his eyes, it seemed like it was something she didn't relish, almost as if it were a burden to her.

As they walked, Daniel wasn't able to absorb his surroundings as much as he would have liked for fear of drawing attention to himself. He had read enough books to know that the way to 'blend in' was to act like you belonged there. And gawping at every fascinating object wasn't the way.

They rounded another corner and Daniel was expecting it to be another corridor but in actual fact it was a large gallery with paintings of past and present members of the royal family. Daniel saw a particularly stunning portrait of the princess herself and his comments about 'the subject matter making the picture' caused Nyriel to flush a darker shade at his compliment.

Next to her painting was one of a sour, stoic-faced Undine with a thick, bushy white moustache that hung down either side of his mouth. If Daniel had known beforehand that this was what Nyriel's father looked like, then he might have thought twice about sneaking around his palace. She, however, tried to convince him that the king's bark was worse than his bite, but he wasn't having any of it, so she grabbed his arm and dragged him off towards the double doors at the end of the gallery.

When she pushed them open, Daniel's jaw almost hit the floor. He could feel his heart pound as his wide-open eyes looked around in wonderment. Before him was a huge circular room, which went up three levels, and each level was at least three metres in height. All around the circumference of the library were books, scrolls, and other manners of literature Daniel didn't recognize. The floor, walls, and pillars were made of marble veined with gold, as was the large circular table in the centre. Daniel looked up and saw that the roof was a crystal dome. He could see the reddening of the sky on Gydion's barrier and knew that the sun was setting on the world above.

'So where would you like to start?' asked Nyriel, waking Daniel from his reverie.

'Everywhere.' He smiled like a kid in a candy store.

16

'I don't suppose you know what's making that noise, by any chance?' Trinity asked as she peered into the shadows.

'I cannot say that I do, my dear, but rest assured, Fungal can be a little...twisted at times. I think you should take point from here on,' Gydion said in a matter-of-fact way.

'What?'

'Why not? I would use this opportunity to see how far you have come in your studies, daughter.'

'But must it be in a life and death situation?'

'Do not be so melodramatic, Trinity. Besides, your survival gives you something to fight for, incentive to put all your effort into it, so to speak.'

'Couldn't I just take a written exam?'

'I was always an advocate of practical exams, myself. Theory can only get you so far.'

'Do you have any tips for dealing with an unknown adversary?'

'Yes,' Gydion smiled as he slowly began to vanish. 'Do not die.'

'The thought *had* crossed my mind,' Trinity said under her breath.

To say that she was feeling apprehensive would be an understatement. She knew a vast number of spells, enough to make her a Disciple or even a Master, if she were put forward for the mystic examinations. What she was concerned about was that she had never used them in real combat before. Simulated combat in a controlled environment, yes, but as Gydion said, there's no better teacher than real-life situations.

Trinity quickly made two more light spheres and sent all three down the passageway. Since she had no choice but to battle whatever it was that was blocking their path, at least she was going to do it with as much light as she could. She slowly followed the light and, eventually, two or maybe three hundred metres ahead she saw a silhouette. It jumped up repeatedly and tried to swat Trinity's intangible light spheres away. Whatever was ahead, it was humanoid, but that's as far as Trinity's identification could go because this creature had four arms and the noises it made, the roars, snarls, and growls were definitely not human in nature.

In her mind, she went over the mage combat 101. Personal Essence spells for defence, Planetary for attack. Realmic is no go because of the cast time unless your opponent is stunned or snared. Have two or three spells recited in your mind so that you only have to do the hand and finger gestures to cast them. Concentration is key; tension is a major barrier between our magic and us. Finally, whenever possible, enter combat with a full amount of Essence. Trinity took a moment to meditate and clear her mind. Her Essence flared around her like a green flame as she replenished herself before she continued on.

The creature at the end of the passage now came into full view but she still couldn't identify what it was; nonetheless, it still sent shivers down her spine.

It had the head of a lion and what looked like the body of a large-muscled man, except that it had four arms and at the end of each it had three-inch claw-like nails.

Trinity's balls of light had distracted the creature but now that she was closer to it, it caught her scent and slowly turned its head to face her. It snarled and bared its yellow teeth, saliva dripped menacingly from them, then it let out a blood-curdling roar before it dropped to its hands and feet and charged at Trinity.

She was momentarily stunned, like a doe caught in headlights, but a second later her feet shuffled her backwards, as she desperately tried to keep the distance between herself and the bizarre man-beast. She kept moving back until she trod on a loose brick and lost her footing. Trinity fell back but was able to use her momentum to roll through and regain her balance in a crouch just in time to see the hybrid creature pounce at her.

The young mage had just enough time to hold out her left hand and cast her mystic shield, which the creature slammed head-long into. The protection held and she gained knowledge of her enemy's raw strength. She wasn't sure her shield would hold for long if it came at her with a full-frontal attack, which is exactly what it did do.

Standing to its full height again, the man-beast used its four arms to batter Trinity's shield over and over again. The mental strain to keep the protection up was becoming unbearable and the shield was showing signs of buckling and fazing out. She needed to go on the offensive and cast her mystic barrage spell with her right hand. Three bolts of magical energy flew from her palm, each of them finding their target, and blasted the creature in its chest. It stumbled back with each successful hit it received, but was otherwise unharmed by the attack.

Trinity used this moment to increase the distance once again between herself and her adversary, who was once again prowling around her, waiting for an opportunity to strike again. Before it could, however, Trinity quickly performed the hand gestures for another spell and a fireball was cast at the creature, which exploded when it struck him. Again, little damage was caused by Trinity's spell.

'It would seem that this lion-man has some sort of resistance to magical attacks,' Gydion's disembodied voice said.

'I was beginning to think the same thing,' Trinity replied whilst keeping a firm eye on the beast. 'Any suggestions?'

'Just one. Don't use magic.'

'Wow, you've really outdone yourself with that gem of wisdom.'

'I resent that remark. Magic is not the only thing I have instructed you in.'

It took a moment for Gydion's words to sink in, but it also only took a moment for the man-beast to seize its opportunity. It slashed at Trinity with its two right arms, gashing her arm and across her abdomen. She was able to avoid its follow-up attack, which surely would have killed her, with some lithe movements borne from her gymnastics classes.

She felt a little stupid for letting her guard down and it had almost cost her. Magic wasn't the only thing Gydion taught her and she told herself that she shouldn't have needed his prompt to remind her; she should have just called her sword.

It was during the Second Great War, the war of shadows, when the Essence vampires known as the Shade came to Ariest, that Gydion changed mages' training. An enemy they knew nothing about decimated the mage army. When they had their Essence drained, they had nothing to fall back on and were easy pickings. Gydion had seen this weakness for a long time and, now in a position to change it, he did so by adding swordsmanship to the studies of all mages. Some of the purists were against it.

Trinity, however, was not one of these. She held out her hand and a schiavona, a renaissance sword with its intricately crafted basket hilt, appeared in her palm. The small smile of someone being reunited with an old friend crept on her face.

She flashed the sword in a figure eight before her, its white aura leaving a faint trail in the air, then she settled down into her en garde position; side towards her adversary, her right foot pointed towards the creature, while her left faced forward, her sword arm pointed down to the ground and her left rested on her hip.

The man-beast looked on with caution. It seemed it wasn't a mindless animal after all, Trinity thought. It raised its four arms and came at its prey again. Trinity rotated her wrist and waited for her opening. A second later it appeared and she struck with lightning quickness.

She struck up and spun on her right foot and her sword created a circular gleam of steel. The attack would have killed a normal person immediately, but all it did to this abnormal creature was leave a gash from its right hip to its left shoulder.

'Hmmm, it seems that the man-beast has some other protections in place too. Nice strike all the same,' Gydion's disembodied voice spoke again.

'If it does, they're not as powerful. The strike may not have killed it but it did cut it, and if it bleeds it can be killed,' a determined Trinity stated.

The man-beast slowly closed the gap again; it didn't run headlong into Trinity this time. She had changed her method of attack and now the creature did the same; no longer did it try to just run over its quarry, now it tried to weaken her with slashes and swipes. Trinity, however, was equal to its attacks, repeatedly parrying and countering time and again.

In no time at all the man lion was covered in cuts, nicks, and slashes all over its body. It panted heavily as blood dripped from its numerous wounds and it roared with anger as it entered a Berserker state of mind. It returned to its original attack method by using brute strength to overpower its opponent.

Sweat rolled down Trinity's face and she wiped her brow as she took a deep breath before she rubbed her aching arm. She felt the strength of the man-lion with every block and parry she made and the vibrations shot up her blade and through her body.

Again, Trinity took up her stance and once again the creature charged at her. She performed her windmill attack once more but, with her fatigue coupled with the creature's increased Berserker strength and disregard for its own wellbeing, it crashed through the assault and slammed Trinity into the wall. Her sword flew from her grip and clanged further down the passage.

A winded Trinity coughed and spluttered on her hands and knees as she tried to regain her footing. Before she could do anything, the creature grabbed her around the neck, its long claws dug into her flesh, and it hoisted her into the air like a ragdoll. It shook her with contempt before it threw her into the opposite wall with a grunt before stalking her again.

Trinity was barely conscious as she was repeatedly slammed into the wall by the man-lion. More and more blood erupted from her mouth each time her back hit it. She knew she couldn't expect Gydion to step in. father or not, she knew what he expected of her; she had to do this herself. But she was fading, losing cognisance.

The sudden pain of sharp teeth biting into her shoulder brought her back and she screamed in agony. She found herself held up against the wall by the man-beast's four hands and she wriggled desperately to free herself, but to no avail. The animal's strength was something she couldn't compete with. Not normally anyway.

That's when an idea hit her. The creature may have been protected from magic but she could still use magic on herself; she just needed to free herself from the man-beast's grasp.

It had left a horrific bite wound in her shoulder and now it snarled inches from her face, her blood smeared around its mouth. The repulsive stench of its breath forced her to turn her head or risk retching into its face. That's when Trinity saw her light spheres and remembered how troubled the creature was by them.

In an instant she had willed all three of them to fly down and strike the animal in its face. It howled in agony and slapped its hands over its eyes. Trinity fell to the ground, rolled away, and in the now pitch-black passageway, cast the spell of shapeshifting.

Trinity dropped down to all fours and her body began to convulse and grow until she was the equivalent size and weight of a large polar bear. Her head took on the shape of a large feline with two huge lower canine teeth and one large canine in the front row of her upper jaw; all three were at least twenty inches in length. A dense fur grew rapidly over her body, it was tri-coloured, black all the way down to the metre-long tail, bordered by a small band of white fur with the powerful legs and underbelly a dark orange colour except for its large white paws. Trinity's transformation was complete. Now she stood before the man-beast as a White-Toed Murato Puama.

Trinity had chosen this form for two reasons. Firstly, for its power and feline agility and secondly, and more importantly, for its ability to see in the dark; like most big cats, the Murato Puama could see in the dark as well as it could see in the day. The playing field had been levelled.

The lion-man had regained its vision, though she suspected that it might still be seeing spots after being hit in the face with her balls of light. The adversaries circled each other, posing and posturing, waiting for the ideal time to strike, and when the moment came they both took it.

Standing on her hind legs, Trinity stood taller than her adversary and she bore down on him, forcing him to take a few backward steps as they grappled each other in a clinch. Her claws ripped his back to shreds whilst he tried to squeeze her between his powerful arms but couldn't because her ribcage was too large for him to link his hands together. All he could do was throw her to the ground to get some respite from her incessant clawing. She rolled onto all fours and lunged at him again.

The lion-man attempted to fend Trinity off with one of his left forearms, but he was not to know that, to accommodate its three large canines, the Murato Puama could dislocate its jaw at will, much like a snake, which is what Trinity did now. She opened her mouth to grotesque proportions and clamped her jaws on its arm. The man-beast howled in agony as it repeatedly thumped her in her exposed sides with its free hands until she released him.

Trinity was relishing the experience of being a predator. Though she retained her normal thought processes, she also felt the primal instincts of the big cat. The thrill of the battle made her heart pump, and with her heightened senses she could smell the blood and fear seeping from her prey.

For a third time, Trinity pounced on the man-lion but this time it was ready for her attack and caught her by the forelegs so that she couldn't slash him with her claws. He held her at arm's length to prevent her from biting him and began to strangle her with his other two hands. He roared with satisfaction, thinking that he had her neutralised, that he had the upper hand; unfortunately for him, that wasn't the case. Her hind legs were just as lethal as the legs he held and she proved this by using them to push off the ground and slash the man-lion's unprotected abdomen, leaving several deep lacerations.

He released her and fell to his knees, clutching his stomach, trying to stem the flow of blood that seeped between his fingers. She circled leisurely, knowing the battle was ended, before she sauntered towards him to apply the coup de grace by crushing his windpipe between her jaws like other big cat predators.

'Stop, Trinity! Do not kill him!' Gydion suddenly appeared between his daughter and the man-lion. He projected a single light sphere that lit up the passage like it was daytime. 'You have done well, daughter, and I am most impressed, but this poor man does not deserve to die,' Gydion said, pointing at the hybrid creature.

Trinity had used her father's appearance to revert back to her true form. The injuries she sustained to her body from her ferocious fight were already beginning to heal, even the vicious bite she had sustained to her shoulder. Within time, the only evidence that would remain to suggest that she had ever been in a hard-fought battle would be her torn clothes and the blood stains.

'What do you mean, 'poor man?'' she quizzed.

'I have seen many creatures in my time, Trinity, hybrid creatures too, but I have never seen one such as this. So, whilst you battled it, I used spells to divine its origins. I had to cast Realmic spells to break through the magic protection that someone had placed upon it. This creature is a man, a normal mortal that someone has been casting spells upon.'

'Fungal?'

'Most definitely,' replied Gydion as he took a small vial from his inside pocket. He shook it and a purple glittery liquid swirled about inside; he then uncorked it and poured its contents into the creature's mouth.

'Was that –?'

'Yes, Dream Potion. He'll sleep peacefully for twelve hours and when he awakes he'll be fully healed and Fungal's spells will have been dispelled.'

'But he'll still be *here*.'

'No matter, once we have found out what we need from that troublesome Hobthrust I'll have him send the mortal home.'

Trinity looked down at her feet. She was almost embarrassed to ask because she didn't want to appear to be craving praise, but she did so anyway. 'Were you really impressed with what I did?' The fact that her father was an Archmage sometimes made Trinity feel pressured to succeed as a mage, and as such she pushed herself hard in her training, hoping to get some accolades one day.

Gydion turned from the deeply snoring man-lion and took the few steps to stand face to face with his daughter, then he lovingly put his hands on her shoulders, which made her wince slightly. 'You were marvellous, my dear. Even when things were looking dire, you were still thinking; you did not lose your focus. Ability to work under pressure is a key trait for a Master to have.'

'A Master?'

'Of course; that is what you are to become on our return, but you will go on to be so much more, Trinity, you *and* Daniel.' He pushed a few blood-matted strands of hair away from her face and kissed her forehead. 'Though I may not say it often enough, Trinity, you make me proud to be your father every day. Now let's go deal with this bloody Hobthrust.'

As Trinity watched Gydion walk off, she smiled broadly and wiped away the tears that were welling up in her eyes, before following her father.

17

A silence reigned supreme in the vast Royal Library of Pichini Palace. It was momentarily disrupted, at regular intervals, by the sound of pages from a book being turned.

Another book was slammed shut and pushed aside by Daniel and he began to read yet another. Nyriel looked on in wonder; she had never seen anyone read so quickly nor so relentlessly. She found the whole experience enlightening, as was the tome she was reading herself; it was a book about Earth realm by a Faerie explorer.

'Do the women in your realm still dress like this?' the princess asked as she held up the book to show Daniel the picture.

Daniel finished reading his sentence before he looked up and what greeted him was a picture of a woman with a 'bob' haircut under a cloche hat and wearing a knee-length dress with a dropped waist.

'I think your book needs a little updating, Nyriel,' Daniel smiled, shaking his head. 'From the look of it, I'd say that woman's from the 1920s, about ninety years ago. Things have changed a lot since then.'

'Maybe one day I will be able to go to your realm and complete our record.'

'It would be an honour for me to be your guide, princess.' Daniel looked up at her beaming face as she once again looked through her book. He could see that she had a desire and deep fondness for knowledge similar to his own and wondered if he had the same look on his face when he read.

Going through some of the old books salvaged from Earth, Daniel came across many disturbing entries regarding albinism. He himself had more than enough experience with tackling the social challenges of being an albino – experienced the alienation, the lack of social interactions, but he was thankful that he had never had to deal with the challenges that many cultures around the world had regarding albinos. 'You must think that all surface dwellers are monsters.'

Nyriel had been reading another one of her favorite books about the "roaring twenties" when Daniel made his despondent accusation. She looked over his shoulder to see what he was reading; it was an article about witch-doctors using albino body parts for witchcraft purposes. 'No. I wouldn't condemn the majority for the actions of the minority. There are monsters in the pasts of many civilizations. The Undany are no different, we just have to be mindful that we do not repeat the mistakes of our ancestors.'

Daniel turned his attention to a new book and continued his studies. He had already learnt about The Shade, a race of Essence vampires from another realm that came to conquer Ariest in the second war, the war of shadows. No doubt named after their ability to travel through shadows, Daniel assumed. He had also learnt that the Undines were one of four elementals that were created by the deities of the four winds; Boreas, Lord of the North and Gnomes, earth elementals; Eurius, Lord of the East and Sylphs, air; Notus, Lord of the South and Salamanders, were fire; Zephyrus, Lord of the West and Undines of water. As interesting as that had been, reading about the exploits of Gydion and his father Eric Mondragon along with the warrior dwarf, Grimgaard Thunderbeard and the elf, Archdruid Tavisum, proved to be more enlightening to Daniel.

The foursome were held in high regard in the chronicles due to their deeds and prowess. The more Daniel read, the more his respect for them grew; that didn't mean that he would just let Gydion off the hook for sending him to Ariest, Daniel thought, but he would let the man explain himself. After all, he was the Archmage and Daniel had secretly already made the decision to accept his offer of tutelage, but that didn't give him the right to just whisk him off without even giving him the chance to say goodbye to his parents, he counterpointed.

Mum must be worried, he supposed. It usually only took him being a couple of hours late from sixth form college for her to get into a panic. Sometimes he couldn't stand her molly coddling him all the time, but right now, he had to admit, that he missed it at that moment. And he missed his dad.

Reading about the heroic champion, Eric Mondragon, made him wonder why he hadn't noticed anything earlier. He loved combat sports, he was at the gym regularly, lifting weights and sparring, and he looked about thirty years younger than the birthdate in his passport. But who in their right mind would look at a construction worker and assume that he was a great Faerie warrior, who was apparently sired by dragons, just because he loved mixed martial arts?

Just as Daniel was about to start on yet another book, he heard a gasp from Nyriel. He looked up and saw a deeply worried look on her face. 'Nyriel, what's wrong?' he asked before he turned his head and followed her gaze. 'Okay, this doesn't look good.' At the entrance to the library were four figures in heavy dark purple hooded cloaks, their faces completely covered by highly reflective golden featureless masks.

'They are my father's royal guard, the Wraiths,' Nyriel said, anticipating Daniel's question. 'I am sure you must have read what happens to Fae when we die.'

'You return to your elemental state, water to water, fire to fire –'

'Yes, but the Wraiths were warriors who were granted this position for dying with valour. This is their afterlife.'

'So these are dead soldiers? Creepy!'

'I have never much liked it myself. They have no memory of who they were, of wives and children they may have left behind, and their masks shield their identities. To the populace, they are just honour guard who can strike fear in them.'

The four honour guards moved silently towards them, as if they were floating across the floor. They came to a stop around the table and all four spoke in unison. 'The Princess Nyriel and the mortal trespasser are summoned to stand before the king.'

Nyriel stood up in a fury and stomped around the table to stand before the guards. 'Daniel is *not* a trespasser! He is *my* guest!'

'Mortals are forbidden to enter Murias City.' Again the guards spoke as one.

'Come on, Daniel. I'm just wasting my breath trying to reason with these empty shells. The person I need to be convincing is my father.'

Nyriel and Daniel were led out of the library by the silent guards. Out of the corner of his eye he could see the seething rage on Nyriel's face. She muttered to herself as she power stomped her way to the throne room. Daniel was sure that if anyone were to confront the princess's anger now, they would instantly be cowed, but then he remembered the painting of her father. He gulped and a dread anticipation came over him.

It wasn't long before they were rounding another corridor and approaching another large set of doors; these, however, were flanked by two Wraith honour guards, who opened them as the contingent got closer.

The throne room was an impressive sight for Daniel to behold. The gold-veined pillars were as evident here as in the library. They were lined in four rows with the columns running the length of the chamber. The walls had several brightly coloured tapestries, the floor was a huge mosaic of Zephyrus, the Undines deity, and at the far end, dominating the room, was a high golden dais with a large marble throne standing strong upon it; on either side of it were smaller golden thrones. Daniel remembered reading, in the palace library, that four such marble thrones were carved from a single giant marble rock by the four wind deities and one was placed at each of their elemental palaces. He thought that it must weigh a vast amount judging by the size of it, and as he got closer he could see detailed carving all over the royal seat and couldn't help but appreciate the artistry of the work, if it be by deity or not.

So absorbed by the opulence of the throne room was Daniel that he failed to notice, at first, that the chamber wasn't empty. Down either side of the hall were Undines who were bowing with respect as Nyriel passed and standing by the dais itself was Ch'tan.

The procession came to a halt at the foot of the steps that led up to the throne and it was here that Nyriel had an epiphany. 'You told my father about Daniel, Ch'tan! How could you?'

'How could I not? I may be your protector, but I cannot go against the king or his laws, and as the princess you should be upholding them also.'

'How can I uphold something I do not believe in?'

'Silence for the arrival of King Noi D'Laani!' the Wraiths suddenly said, and in the quiet a hidden door on the back wall abruptly opened.

The king, a crown of spiral shells atop his head, strode out with purpose and with his golden staff stomped his way up the dais to his throne. His physique was a match for that of Ch'tan, if not more imposing, and even though his shoulder-length turquoise hair was fading to grey, Daniel could hardly tell that he was hundreds of years old.

King Noi sat there in an imperious posture much like The Statue of Zeus from antiquity, Daniel thought, only with added rage. He stroked his long beard several times before he spoke.

'You have disappointed me this day, daughter. Though I do not like you leaving the protection of Murias City in pursuit of your artefact hunting, I allow it because it is something you have a passion for. I understand this, even if it does make you neglect your duties as a member of the royal household. But bringing a surface dweller here is a flagrant disregard to my laws and a slap in the face as your father!'

'I did not seek to bring anyone here; it just happened.'

'It just happened, hmmm? He just found his way here of his own accord? I think not.'

'Yes, I brought him here but only to heal him. The Kelpie almost killed him. What would you have me do? Leave him to die?'

'If he was foolish enough to tackle a Kelpie, then yes.'

'Well actually,' Daniel interjected, 'I didn't know what a Kelpie was until Nyriel –'

'Silence, mortal! How dare you speak when the king does not address you and how dare you speak to the princess in such familiar tones?' King Noi D'Laani's booming voice made Daniel shudder.

'Forgive him, Father, he does not know our ways because he is not of this realm. He travels from Earth realm.'

'Then he has travelled a long way to die.'

'Die?' Daniel blurted out.

'That's the punishment for trespassers from the surface,' Nyriel whispered from the side of her mouth.

'And you were going to tell me this *when* exactly?' he whispered back.

'I was not going to. I was hoping not to be discovered.'

'Great!'

'Do not worry, I have an idea,' then she turned back to address the king. 'I protest, Father!'

'You protest?'

'You cannot execute this man.'

'Really? Why ever not?'

'Because I have chosen this man to be my consort!'

'What?' a panicked Daniel exclaimed.

'What?' the king shouted as he slammed the point of his staff down with a thunderous boom.

'Yes, I intend to marry Daniel.' She grabbed hold of him and kissed him full on the lips. Audible gasps rang out amongst the dignitaries. When Nyriel released him from their lip lock, Daniel staggered back a few steps with a smug smile on his face.

The king seethed as he watched his only daughter with her chosen mate. 'Why do you persist in trying to bring dishonour to my name, Nyriel?'

'I do not, but I cannot let you kill this mortal; there is something different about him.'

'If it is your intention to bond with this surface dweller then you have given me double the reason to have him executed.'

'You cannot do this, Father!

'It is law! Now, surface dweller, what is your name so that we may enter it into the chronicle?'

'My name? My name is Daniel...' And then it came to him, a last chance to save himself. 'My name is Daniel Mondragon, son of Eric Mondragon.'

The king scrutinized Daniel a moment before he spoke, 'Eric Mondragon has no offspring.'

'And he hasn't been seen here for years. That is because he went to Earth realm, married a mortal woman, and had a son called Daniel.'

'This is all very convenient,' Ch'tan suddenly said. 'He lies, Sire, to save his own neck.'

'Is this supposed to stay my hand, surface dweller? I suppose you think that Eric Mondragon would not take kindly to his son being executed?'

'I'm not even sure he knows I'm here, but Gydion does and I'm sure he wouldn't be happy if his student were harmed, especially in a misunderstanding.'

'See, I told you he was a special mortal, Father,' Nyriel said before she whispered to Daniel, 'You could have told me you were Gydion's student. This could have been dealt with a lot sooner if you had.'

'Well, technically I'm not,' he whispered back.

'What?' It was Nyriel's turn to panic.

'But I will be, as soon as I find him,' he said reassuringly.

The king spoke, interrupting their conspiratorial discussion. 'So now you claim to be a mage, under the tutelage of the Great Gydion, no less, as well as the son of Eric Mondragon? Is that correct?'

'Yes, your majesty, that is correct.'

'Then prove it.'

'Prove it?'

'Yes, show me what the Great Gydion has taught you.'

'Well, he hasn't – ow!' Daniel's yelp was a result of Nyriel treading on his foot to gain his attention. She gave an almost inconspicuous shake of her head when he turned to her.

'He has not what?' queried King Noi.

'He hasn't taught me much, but I can show you what he *has* taught me.'

'Might I make a suggestion, Sire?'

'Go ahead, Ch'tan.'

'Since Gydion is Archmage and has not taken an Adept since taking up the post, if he has indeed selected this Daniel to be his student, it would make sense that he would only take someone that is gifted.'

'A fair assumption.'

'So perhaps the Book of Azul...'

King Noi D'Laani stroked his beard and thought a moment before he nodded his assent. He then stood and, whilst holding his staff before him, he spoke in hushed tones. The king then banged his staff on the dais, and each slam created a cluster of sparks. Striking the staff three times ended the ritual and caused a thick blue-covered book with a golden clasp to emerge out of the dais and float up into the king's waiting hand.

'This is the Book of Azul. It was written by Zephyrus himself and presented to our ancestors as a gift and can only be opened and read by a mage of specific ability. If you are, as you claim to be, under the wing of Gydion, then you must surely meet these requirements. Ch'tan, give him the book.'

'This is a pretty flimsy test,' Daniel quietly said into Nyriel's ear.

'Then you will have no trouble passing it,' Nyriel replied in a matter-of-fact way, 'especially if you wish to keep your head.'

Daniel smiled thinly at the princess before he received the Book of Azul from Ch'tan. It was a lot lighter than he had expected; it was roughly A4 sized with upwards of three thousand pages, yet weighed no more than a book a fraction of the size. On the cover was an embossed image of Zephyrus, identical to the one Daniel now stood on, and surrounding it was Undany text.

He could sense the apprehension coming from Nyriel, as he looked the book over. Though she wouldn't be the one to lose her head, Daniel could imagine that she would face some sort of repercussions if he were unsuccessful and, the way things were going, it was beginning to look more and more likely.

The golden clasp had no keyhole but when he tried to force it open it didn't move an inch. Daniel didn't know where to begin and he could feel his face getting hot from the stress, like his face was about to break out in a sweat. He could hear one or two whisperings coming from the onlookers and with a quick glance up he could see the stern but hopeful look from the king.

The pressure was building; he had to do something. Anything was better than just standing there turning a book over in his hands. He tried to calm himself, take deep breaths, and think about the problem to hand. Thought back to the time when he evaded Bobby Brinkmeyer. Then, he had used Trinity's short lesson on relaxation to connect with his Essence to good effect. His only real option was to try it again or run away. He had a quick look around and saw the two Wraith guards standing by the throne room door. His only real option was to try it again.

He breathed deeply and felt the Essence rushing through his body. It was happening much easier than it had done before; he was becoming more proficient at the exercise.

Loud gasps from the spectators brought Daniel from his quiet state, and for the first time he saw the purple haze of his Essence flickering around him. His look of astonishment was mirrored by the look on Nyriel's face as she took a step back, and even King Noi D'Laani had sat up to attention as the Book of Azul responded to the touch of a mage and came to life.

It floated out of Daniel's hands and levitated before him. The gold buckle dissolved into a metallic liquid and traced around the image of the Undine's deity. When it had completed outlining the picture, there was a brief flash of gold before the book opened.

Although Daniel couldn't read what was written, his love of books and thirst for knowledge enticed him to flip a few pages of the spell book. Then a strange thing happened: the more pages he turned, the more Daniel was able to read and understand the lines and symbols that made up the Undany alphabet. To the astonishment of everyone in attendance of the throne room, Daniel began to recite word perfect what was written.

'I didn't know you could speak our language,' a surprised Nyriel said.

'Neither did I. It just seemed to rearrange itself in my head as I looked at it,' Daniel replied.

'It is the magic,' the king informed them as he strode down the dais steps, a broad smile on his face. 'There is no doubt in my mind that you are worthy to be chosen by Gydion! You should have said something earlier.'

'That's what I said.' Nyriel's attitude had been fortified now that she had been proved right in supporting Daniel, though she had to admit to herself that she thought he might have been doomed at one point.

King Noi gently held the head of his daughter and kissed her forehead. 'I am sorry I could not take your word on the matter, Nyriel. I hope you can forgive an old Undine.' She smiled and nodded in reply. 'And as for you, Daniel Mondragon, we have things to discuss.'

He placed one heavy hand around Daniel's shoulders, which nearly buckled the mortal's knees, and put his other hand around the shoulders of the princess, then he began to lead them away to his private chambers. Ch'tan dismissed the assembly before following his king for the clandestine gathering.

The door to the king's study was situated behind the dais and the décor of the throne room was continued here, but there was no grand marble chair. Instead, large mounds of plush cushions that the royal family sat upon took its place. After a gesture of invitation from the king, Daniel took a seat on the offered stack of pillows.

'I am sure you must be wondering why you are here. One minute you are moments away from execution and the next you are sitting in my private chambers. The reason is simple, I need your help, or, more specifically, the help of your master.'

'My *master*?' Daniel questioned before he realised, 'Oh, you mean Gydion.'

'Indeed. I have sent requests to have an audience with him but to no avail; he has not been seen...but perhaps his own student will fare better and succeed where my messengers have failed.'

'What is it you need from him?'

'There is a Shade loose in Ariest. It has already killed several of my subjects.'

'Its victims have been our priests and children; all have been discovered in their beds with the tell-tale marks on their bodies where it draws the Essence from them.'

'But how is it possible? Didn't the combined armies eventually turn them back?'

'Apparently not all. When we finally identified the perpetrator of these killings, I personally went to the Faerie Queen herself to ask for aid and she refused! After all we have suffered through allying ourselves with them during their war, the surface dwellers refused to assist us! The alliance we held meant nothing to them. And that is why I have closed Murias to them all.'

'I still think it is too harsh, Father.'

'I disagree, Nyriel,' Ch'tan responded. 'It is what they deserve. We welcomed them with open arms; Gydion had the elixir produced so they could survive under the waves. We allowed them to use parts of the city as a medical centre. And when we are the ones that need help, where are they? Nowhere!'

'That is why we need Gydion. Unlike other surfacers, he has honour; he has helped us in the past and I am sure he will do so now.'

Daniel had sat on his cushions listening to the three Undines, and the fact that the surface Fae had declined to help didn't add up to him. They knew how dangerous the Shade were, even if it was only one of the Essence vampires, but who was to say the one couldn't become two or even two dozen. No, it didn't make sense; it took the combined forces of those that fought under the banner of the Faerie Queen, both surface dwellers and those beneath the oceans, the Mortal Conclave and the Mage Armies to put a stop to the Shade's last invasion. Why wouldn't they do the same now to stop things from escalating? Could the surface Fae really think that they would be safe from harm? That would be a stupid assumption on their part, and also a selfish one too.

'Did the Queen Rhiannon give any reasons for not assisting you?' Daniel asked.

'That was the most vexing part. She said that she could not be bothered and that her people would share her decision,' growled the King.

'What? She said that?'

'I do not dwell upon it, Daniel Mondragon. The wellbeing of my subjects is my pressing concern, but rest assured I decreed that any surface dweller caught in my domain would be executed, and then I stormed out of her palace.'

'I understand that Gydion is your last hope,' Daniel cautiously said, 'however, you should know that he is not here; I left him in Earth realm.'

The silence that descended was palpable. It lasted a few moments before the king broke it.

'It is a little strange that he would leave you to your own devices,' mused the king. 'How are you to advance in your training without his guidance?'

'I guess his methods can...seem a little...unorthodox,' fibbed Daniel.

King Noi looked at the young man sceptically. 'I see. Then you will just have to wait for him to return to his Sanctum. Gydion must learn of our plight as soon as he returns.'

Daniel nodded his agreement as he began to nervously play with the material of his Undany clothing.

'Is something wrong?'

'Wrong? No, no, nothing's wrong.'

'I think he just wants his own clothes back before he begins his journey,' Nyriel suggested. Daniel at this point tried to use subtle facial movements to convey to her that that wasn't his meaning at all and soon decided that they didn't translate into Undany when he saw the blank and confused expression on her face.

'Are you sure you're all right?' the king persisted. He was beginning to think that his guest's peculiar mannerisms might be an Earth realm trait that they all had.

'Yes, I'm fine,' Daniel maintained. 'Well actually...I'm not entirely sure where – '

'Where Murias City is in relation to Gydion's Sanctum?' Nyriel had interrupted Daniel's confession just in time, as she finally realised that he didn't know where the home of Gydion was. 'If you would allow, Father, I would be more than happy to accompany Daniel to the surface to make sure that he takes the correct route.'

'And if I refuse, you would no doubt sneak out and go anyway,' the king surmised.

'True, but at least this way you can have a say,' the princess smiled back.

'Fine, you can go. It is understandable that you would want to spend time with your future consort but Ch'tan goes with you, to protect you as well as be your chaperone.'

'Chaperone?' exclaimed Nyriel. 'Father, there is going to be no wedding. I only said that to spare Daniel from his fate.'

'Oh, thank the waves!' the king sighed with relief as he sank into his cushions, before remembering that his guest was sitting right next to him. 'No offence, Mondragon.'

'None taken,' reassured Daniel.

'Even though kissing him was very intriguing and informative, I find surface dwellers to be a bit...ugly. No offence, Daniel.'

'None taken,' Daniel reassured the princess again.

'You are a cut above the rest, mind you,' she continued as she studied him from head to toe, 'and if I were to bond with a surface dweller you would be my ideal consort, Daniel Mondragon. I'm quite interested to know how the procreation process with an Undany and a surface dweller would work.'

'Well, I think I should be on my way now!' an embarrassed Daniel suddenly said as he shot out of his pile of cushions. 'The quicker we get to Gydion the quicker he can come and deal with your problem. Time is of the utmost importance.'

'Indeed it is, Daniel Mondragon. I want you to take the Book of Azul to your master and present it to him on my behalf. I saw him take an interest in it many moons ago. If I gift it to him now, he will know how desperate I am for his help.'

'Then let us be off,' Nyriel clapped excitedly.

18

The Boswick gate scraped open at an effortless gesture from Gydion as he stood at the entrance to the abandoned British Museum station. The gate clanged into the wall, causing plumes of dust to take to the air. The smell of dampness and rust invaded Trinity's nostrils as she and her father walked into the ticket hall.

'I take it Fungal doesn't get any of his Hobthrusts to do any cleaning down here,' Trinity said as she fought the urge to sneeze.

'It is all part of his illusion, no doubt, just in case there are any human trespassers.'

'A human getting past that creature? Are you sure?' mocked Trinity. The fact that she had the wounds, which still pained her, to testify how vicious the lion-man hybrid was, supported her belief that any human that managed to venture this far would surely have met a swift end.

'Why not?' Gydion replied as he looked around the station with interest. 'Stranger things have happened.' As he spoke, Gydion remembered the last time he had been at the station before its permanent closure in 1933. It was during the Roaring Twenties; Howard Carter had made his discovery of Tutankhamen's tomb and the second revival of Egypt mania had begun. The populace became so enraptured with the fad that they began to feed off all aspects of Egyptology, including its superstitions about mummies and the walking dead, to the point that a rumour began to circulate about a ghost of an ancient Egyptian haunting the station.

The story went that the ghost would emerge late at night and walk along the platforms wailing and moaning. It was enough to pique Gydion's interest and he decided to investigate things for himself. This was when he met

Fungal for the first time, since it was the Boggart that had been the so-called ghost.

The father and daughter duo continued to walk through the ticket hall area, with Trinity having to brush cobwebs out of her hair on several occasions. She was, however, enjoying the whole experience; it was like she was stepping back in time to the Twenties. Several posters of the day were still up on the walls. Some advertised the extension of the Northern Line, then called the City Railway and the Hampstead line, from Kennington to Morden, others gave passengers step-by-step instructions on how to conduct themselves when using the Underground. Trinity found, however, that due to the expansion of the Network, the majority were promoting the idea of living in the suburbs, places such as Edgware, Hendon, and Welwyn and commuting to work.

The faint scratching sound from the mice and the rhythmic footfalls from Gydion and Trinity were the only things audible in the abandoned booking hall, as they made their way to a door signed Station Foreman. It was just as dusty and web covered as the rest of the station was, as if no one had passed it in decades, but it was a completely different story when Gydion opened the door and their eyes saw what lay beyond the doorway.

To all intents and purposes, it looked exactly like a fourteenth century Scottish castle, but Trinity soon found out that it did not just look like a Scottish castle, as ludicrous as it seemed to her, it *was* a Scottish castle. She touched the wall and felt the cold, textured stone under her fingers. She had to take a quick look back through the door and into the station just to make sure her eyes were not seeing things.

They were in the banquet hall of the castle but there were several archways that led further into the out-of-place fortress. Torches in their sconces surrounded the room and a long, thickly cut but rather low oak table dominated the hall. Its twenty matching chairs were likewise built to a heavy-duty fashion with tall backrests and short legs.

More paintings and tapestries adorned the walls and all were of Fungal. Trinity was quite frankly beginning to get sick of the sight of him and his squat head, crooked yellow teeth, and giant sideburns.

She could smell a roast being cooked behind one of the doors that led off the hall. Her belly growled to remind her that she had not eaten since breakfast.

'This is some kind of reality-warping spell, right?'

'I believe so.'

'But how? Boggarts shouldn't be able to do things like that.'

'Quite right, they should not. They usually specialize in illusion generation, but this most definitely is no illusion,' Gydion said with some finality as he wiped his finger against the wall before speculatively tasting it. 'I think we should find Fungal and discover what he is up to.'

'Who's Fungal?' Trinity suddenly asked sincerely. 'Is he a friend of yours?'

'This is no time to play games, Trinity, you know full well who he is.'

'I do? I don't remember.'

'What do you mean 'you do not...'' Gydion spun around and saw that the door which they had walked through moments before had vanished, then the penny dropped. 'It seems that we may be in a spot of trouble, unfortunately more so you, than me.'

'What's that supposed to mean?'

'Well,' Gydion began as he frantically searched the walls, 'if I am correct, this warped reality of Fungal's is collapsing. The longer you stay here the more you will cease to exist. It has already begun to affect your memories; soon you will forget me and then you will lose your magic, and finally you will not remember anything about yourself, and then you will be no more.'

'Rubbish! There's nothing wrong with my memory!'

'Oh really? Then tell me about Daniel.'

'Who's Daniel? That's not fair! How can you test me on someone I don't even know!'

'Ah ha, here it is!' Gydion stood in the corner of the banquet hall where a sliver of luminescent light was fractionally growing. 'This place is quite literally coming apart at the seams.'

'Can't you do something about it?'

'This is Fungal's reality; I dare not use magic in these unpredictable conditions. Come on, we need to find him quickly.'

Gydion took Trinity by the hand and quickly led her through the nearest archway. They immediately came upon a staircase and they followed it up to the next floor.

Trinity had never seen so much concern on her father's face before, but it was understandable when she thought about it; the idea that she could forget who he was seemed a daunting prospect for them both. She squeezed his hand slightly tighter for reassurance.

The floor they arrived on did not fit in with the castle plan of the lower level. It was a long, corkscrewed corridor, which had large wooden doors lining either side, and it disappeared far into the distance.

'Whoa, that's a bit weird.'

'Indeed. That is the trouble with reality spells that are not of your creation; they twist your perception of what is real and unreal. A person with a low mental capacity would be lost here. Let's hope that our friend is behind one of these doors.'

'So where do we begin?'

'Your guess is as good as mine, so you pick a door.'

Trinity looked at the doors in her immediate vicinity; they all looked identical, no one door stood out, so it was going to come down to a combination of trial and error and sheer blind luck to get to their goal. They just had to hope they got there before this warped world collapsed around them.

She counted five doors down the right-hand wall. At the sixth door she grasped its ring handle, twisted it, and pulled the door open. The aroma of dew-covered grass hit the father and daughter duo as they surveyed the dark green forest that lay beyond the door.

'Okay, surely this can't be right. I don't remember a massive forest being in Holborn.'

'That is because there has not been for centuries. To be honest, I am not entirely convinced that this is Earth, much less London.'

'What makes you say that?'

'Those trees over there...I know for a fact that they are not indigenous to Earth realm.'

'An effect of the reality warping?'

'Quite possibly.' Gydion looked over his shoulder and saw that the sliver of light from the banquet hall had grown to become a luminescent void and was beginning to engulf the stairs. 'How are you feeling, Trinity?' Gydion anxiously asked his daughter.

'I feel fine,' she replied.

'Are you sure? You have not lost any more memories? What of your spells?'

'Spells?' she repeated, as she looked at him sideways as if he were insane. 'What spells?'

'Ah, I see. Keep checking that side whilst I check these doors.' An earnestness had become evident in Gydion's actions as he urged Trinity along. 'Just give a shout if you find a troublesome runt with sideburns.'

They began opening and closing doors in rapid succession. With every one he opened, Gydion became more and more worried. The reason for his concern came when he had discovered that the doorways were not caused by the reality-warping spell at all, they were actually portals to other realms. Several of the doors led to places he had already visited and others to realms he still planned to. He looked down the corridor, still not able see the end of it as it vanished into the distance, and wondered if there were doorways to every realm in existence. Then he wondered why Fungal would want something like this.

Gydion's reasons for apprehension were given gravitas when he heard Trinity's piercing scream from behind. Just as he opened another door, he turned his head to see what distressed her and saw several three-foot-tall featureless creatures grappling Trinity with their four-fingered hands. He knew them as the Waviast from Liera realm. Singularly they were rather pathetic creatures of limited strength and intelligence, but to get them on their own was the trick because they existed as a collective of ten, twenty, or more Waviast. They could work as a team as if they had one mind or they could form a gamut; both ways multiplied the individual Waviast by the amount in the collective. They had one ruler, a queen, who fed on females captured from other realms. Once she had fed, she could produce more Waviast.

Gydion was about to rescue his daughter, but since his attention was taken by her plight, he had completely forgotten about the door he had just opened, until it was too late.

Suddenly he felt the pull from the vortex world, O'sho, the realm that sat precariously on the precipice of survival and certain destruction on the edge of the great void. It was on Gydion's list of places to visit, but now was not the time.

He latched onto the doorframe to anchor himself from being dragged into the vortex, just as its power lifted him off of his feet. Gydion's lower body resembled the melting clocks in Dali's Persistence of Memory as his legs were wrenched into the maw of the swirling void.

Although Gydion was not a young man by any stretch of the imagination, his grip was strong; the doorframe, however, was not and it swiftly began to splinter under the extreme pressure exerted by the vortex.

Gydion knew he did not have much time to get himself out of his predicament. He tried to pull himself back through, and the muscles in his arms ached as he began to make headway. Inch by agonizing inch, the Archmage slowly pulled himself back into the corridor, but then the doorway came away in his hands and he tumbled into the waiting void.

'Noooo,' Trinity screamed as she caught a glimpse of the middle-aged stranger she had hoped would rescue her from her plight suddenly get sucked through a door.

With her hopes of rescue dashed, she renewed her efforts to escape from her assailants, knowing she could only rely on herself now. She wriggled, threshed about, and kicked two of her attackers off, but before she could do anything else, two more had come to replace them.

Demoralised and exasperated by her failed efforts, Trinity slumped in defeat. She did not know what her faceless aggressors wanted with her, and finding out was not high on her list. Trinity felt physically drained from fighting them but she had no intention of giving up; she just needed time to rest and formulate a plan before she made another attempt when, or rather if, the opportunity arose.

With their quarry now limp in their arms, the Waviast began to make their way back to the door that hid the portal to their world. One of the creatures grabbed the handle and pulled it to reveal their realm, but their way was unexpectedly blocked by a figure.

'I cannot allow you to leave with that young lady,' Gydion said tersely.

Trinity heard the voice and from her restrained prone position she could see the stranger, albeit from an upside-down view, standing in the doorway. With renewed hope, she once more fought for freedom.

'Calm yourself, Trinity, I shall have you free in a moment.'

She did as the man asked and relaxed her body the best she could, given her situation. She wondered why he had called her Trinity though.

'Firstly,' Gydion continued as he started to weave a spell, 'we free you by changing your molecular density to the point where the Waviast can no longer lift you.' Within seconds, Trinity had been dropped to the ground with a thump and, try as they might, the Waviast could not move her. 'Secondly, now that their prey is seemingly beyond them, they quickly turn their attention to the only other collection of matter in the vicinity...namely me, and in their angered state they rashly charge towards me, at which point I turn myself invisible and create an exact replica...'

At that moment Gydion vanished, only to appear some twenty metres within the Waviast realm of Liera. The aggressors immediately changed direction and continued their stampede towards Gydion's new position. As the last Waviast passed the doorway, however, it was slammed shut behind them.

'...Which draws the rampaging Waviast back into their own realm, where they will no doubt concoct another scheme to kidnap women from another realm,' Gydion summed up, as he slowly reappeared. Without delay, he went to Trinity and, whilst dispelling his own conjuration, helped her to her feet.

'Thanks for the help...but how did...I saw you...I mean, I thought you were...dead.'

'No, it's not quite my time yet, my dear. What happened was that I plunged through the centre of the vortex and discovered O'sho's twin planet within the maelstrom itself. O'nio, as it is called, is inhabited by beings known as Kinooksi. Tall and graceful, they are a race whose magic is nature based. For the year I was there I learnt a lot from them.'

'Did you say 'year'? But you were barely gone for a minute!'

'Time does not flow with the same regularity in all realms, Trinity.'

'Why do you call me that, sir? My name is Saxa.'

'Saxa?' Gydion asked; she nodded. 'A Boggart name?' Again she nodded. 'Then it would seem time is running short, but no problem. Whilst I was on O'nio I had time to construct this.'

Gydion pulled a small origami bird out of his pocket. He straightened its wings and stood it on his open palm. 'And now for the final piece.' Gydion blew on the paper sculpture. The bird absorbed the sparkling Essence-enriched breath that left his mouth and it immediately came to life.

First it tested one paper wing and then the other. Once the enchanted origami bird was satisfied, it flapped both wings and took to the air. With its newfound freedom of flight, the bird performed loops and circled Gydion's head. Eventually the Archmage held out his hand and his enchanted bird perched upon it.

'Now, little bird, it is time to do your duty.'

'And what is that?' Trinity asked

'Well, Trinity – '

'Saxa.'

'Quite. Well...Saxa you probably do not remember, but I told you earlier that I did not want to try to cast any spells in this collapsing warped reality because I could not be sure of getting the desired effect. When I was sucked to O'nio realm I made this enchantment to locate Fungal quickly and easily; I only wish I had come up with the idea earlier.' Gydion helped the little origami bird up into the air and it fluttered off down the corridor. The father and daughter quickly chased after it.

As they ran further and further down the corridor, Gydion could not help but notice that some of the doors they passed had rudimentary barricades across them, but before he could give anymore thought as to why, the little paper bird suddenly flew headlong into a door on the right, burst into flames, and was totally consumed.

'This is it, we have found him,' said Gydion as he took hold of the handle and opened the door.

'Och, it's about time yous two got here. What took yous so long?' the gruff Scottish voice said from beyond the doorway.

19

This was the room Trinity had expected to see when she and her father first opened the Station Foreman's door: dusty filing cabinets, a couple of desks, old wooden chairs, but the wall of monitors showing security feeds was an out-of-place addition.

Now that she was out of the warped reality, Trinity was slowly getting her memory about her very existence back. She no longer thought she was a Boggart named Saxa; she knew that Gydion was her father and she also knew that they were here to question Fungal and find out why he had sent Daniel to Ariest.

The Boggart himself stood in the centre of the room, in what seemed to be his favoured pose, hands on hips, chest out as if he were some superhero. Another Boggart was in the process of painting yet another portrait of the self-proclaimed Laird. As much as Trinity was getting fed up of seeing the subject of the portrait everywhere she turned, she had to admit that the artist was a talented imp.

'That'll do for now, Lowack, I got guests ta' tend to,' Fungal said as he stepped down from his podium. The Boggart named Lowack packed up his brushes and silently left the room.

A hush descended on the three Fae left in the office, although the reason for its appearance was beyond Trinity. She looked quizzically from Gydion to Fungal and could almost feel the tension between them. She wondered if there had been some episode connecting them in the past, when Gydion suddenly sat down, uninvited, in the most prominent and clean chair, no doubt reserved for Fungal himself, and it became clear to Trinity that the bad atmosphere was caused by nothing but a power struggle.

Fungal had positioned himself as a spokesperson for Boggarts, Hobthrusts, and all similar Fae and as such believed he deserved a seat at the table of The Assembly, the institution that guided and governed magic users. It consisted of six master-level mages, with the current Archmage at its head taking the gathering to seven members, all seven positions filled by the top seven finishers of the Test of Apollonius. The establishment acted much like a democratic senate; any new ruling had to be voted upon and would only be acted on with a majority backing.

The Assembly had been put in place to prevent any one mage having ultimate power over the rest, something which had happened frequently in the distant past for, as they say, if all power corrupts, absolute power corrupts absolutely.

'I suppose yer 'ere ta question me about the old crone,' Fungal stated in thick Scottish accent. Gydion did not reply. 'Ya *are* 'ere about the warping spell, aren't ya?'

'No, we are here about Daniel Welsh.'

'Daniel who?'

'The boy you sent to Ariest,' interjected Trinity.

'What? It cannae be me, lass. Ah've no sent no one ta Ariest...well no one 'cept that annoying Jim Rustin. Och, he's so sweet and nice he rots yer teeth,' Fungal growled as he shook with anger.

Trinity fought to stifle a laugh but could do nothing to hold back the snigger at his comical tantrum as she asked, 'Who's Jim Rustin?'

'He is the bane of my existence! He is the last descendant of the MacLeod clan.'

'By the Goddess, Fungal! You are not *still* hounding that family?' exclaimed Gydion.

'Why not? Fungal questioned. 'When we lose something that we love we fill the void with determination. Determination not to feel that loss again, determination to find something better, determination to make those responsible pay...'

No one spoke for a moment as they let the words sink in and they all reflected on past losses. Trinity saw the forlorn look come over Gydion's face again and she wondered what his 'determination' had been; to try and forget the woman he loved by becoming the greatest ever mage? She was not prepared to forget Daniel yet, especially since she had still to tell him how she felt.

'I'm determined to find Daniel,' Trinity said, 'so tell me about this Jim guy. How did you send him away?'

'What's the point? He's gone, not of this realm, ceased to be...hopefully.'

'Well, think of this as your last chance to reminisce.'

'Okay, okay. It was quite simple really. Yer see, I knew Rustin loved those old historic trains, so I sent him an FTN ticket to his place of work disguised as an employee of the month award.'

'And where does he work?'

'Belsize Park Station.'

'That's where Daniel lives,' Trinity said to Gydion before continuing to question the Boggart. 'Tell me, Fungal, exactly how friendly is this Jim Rustin? Let's say, for instance, that someone who had the same passion for history as him came through the station and let's say, for instance, that that person was upset and depressed...would this Jim Rustin give that person something to cheer them up? Let's say, I don't know, a ticket to ride a historical train.'

'Oh yeah, sure, without a doubt...oops!' The penny dropped.

Now that the evidence seemed to favour Daniel's unscheduled trip out of this realm, Gydion closed his eyes, hoping to hear an uplifting answer, as he gently asked his question. 'Fungal, what was the final destination of that train? Almedia? Elkim? Oceanside?'

'Well, no, ah didnae want him ta 'ave ah goodtime, it *is* Beltane ye know...so ah sent him ta Kincasel,' he mumbled.

'The western kingdoms?'

'Ah was hoping that he would run into a Puama.'

Trinity pictured the wildcat she had transformed into and shivered at the thought of Daniel running into an untamed version of the creature.

'So help me, Fungal,' Gydion said as he stood up, his voice amplified with magical fury. 'If anything has happened to the boy – '

'Och, d'nae worry. Ah'm sure the boy is fine.'

All Gydion did in reply was to give the Boggart a stern glare before beginning to cast a portal spell. When Fungal realised what the mage was doing, he quickly jumped out of his seat and began shouting and waving his hands about.

'Hey, ye cannae go yet! What about the reality spell?'

'What about it? The consequences you face are of your own design.' Gydion did not like when people failed to fully comprehend the delicate workings of magic. Any Adept could set a room on fire by magic, but only a Master-level mage could light a candle in that room using the same spells. He was about to begin casting again and leave Fungal to his fate when he relented. 'As long as you are not in the conjured castle when the spell collapses, you will be fine.'

'That's good to know. I assume that you'll be off to find the boy now then? There is a wee little something else you should know before ye go,' a suddenly bleak Fungal began. 'I d'nae know how informed ye are, but ah've heard from me sources, usually reliable sources, I might add – '

'Spit it out, Fungal,' an impatient Gydion interrupted.

'Well, ah've been told that the...that the Shade are back.'

'What?'

'That's not possible,' Trinity said.

'That's what ah said, but all the signs point ta them; Essence-enriched people, mostly youngsters, apparently dying in their sleep or just disappearing.'

'But how? Gydion and the other mages closed the portal to their world and they don't have the ability to create portals themselves.'

Trinity and Fungal watched the man in question, who had been pacing up and down but who suddenly stood stock still as if he had been struck in the face. 'Why did you add that corridor, Fungal?'

'It wasnae me,' he replied.

'Of *course* not. Why would you add a corridor such as that to your fourteenth century castle?' Gydion paced back and forth and continued to talk to himself in hushed tones as if he were thinking out loud. And it became evident that he was, as he suddenly stopped. 'Is it possible to open these doors from the other side?'

'Ah guess so, if ye know where they open in that realm.'

'Is that why you boarded up some of the doors, to stop things coming through?' asked Trinity.

'Some of the places ah took a wee peek at ye wouldnae want ta go back ta, lass.'

'How many doors have you opened?' the Archmage asked.

'Just a few.'

'Is there a door to Salamida?'

'Ah d'nae know.'

'Think, you odious imp!'

'Ah d'nae know!'

'Father, stay calm,' Trinity said in a soothing manner. 'Anger won't help us here.' It took the 'A' grade student only a few seconds to figure out why Gydion had been so harsh with his questioning of Fungal. 'Do you think that the Shade have used the corridor as a backdoor to Ariest?'

'I do indeed, Daughter, but who is to say that they have not gone through to any of the other realms...if not all of them?'

'Including Earth,' Trinity said uneasily as she turned to look at the door that led to the corridor.

Fungal followed her gaze and began to back away from the door. 'The Shade? Here?' he murmured. He swung around and shot a glare at the dark recesses to inspect them. He knew the Shade used the shadows to travel around, able to pop out and melt back into them with ease. On many occasions, a victim would be found dead behind closed and locked doors with no apparent access, but a sliver of shadow under a door, through and keyhole, would welcome the Shade and envelop them like a lover.

'If they *have* used this corridor system,' Trinity reasoned, 'then that would mean that they were being directed, coordinated by someone. You don't suppose –'

'There is only one way to find out,' interrupted Gydion as he deduced that his daughter had come up with the same prime suspect as himself. 'I need to go and see for myself.'

'Don't you mean *we*? I'm coming with you.'

'As much as I would like you to be with me, you, my dear, have other commitments. You must go to Ariest and begin the search for Daniel until I can re-join you.'

'Go to Ariest...on my own?' Trinity could not hide the apprehension in her voice.

'Not quite; Fungal has graciously offered to be your guide.'

'What?'

'After all, he does feel partially responsible for what has happened to the boy...is that not right, Fungal?'

The Boggart grumbled under his breath while Trinity looked into space and tried to ascertain if the fluttering she felt in her stomach was caused by a feeling of elation or trepidation. Before she could come to a conclusion, a thought came to her mind. 'What about Daniel's parents? We need to let them know what's happened to him.'

'Do not worry, I shall take care of that, since I will need Eric to watch for any suspicious activities that could be attributed to the Shade.'

Gydion did not need his magical abilities to sense that Trinity was worried when she did not respond. He could understand why; there was no telling how long he would be gone or what he would find when he arrived at Salamida.

He knew she was level-headed enough to eventually realise that he was only trying to protect her. Singularly, he believed that she would be able to cope with a Shade but on their home world it would be a different matter, and it would not be an ideal situation to be concerned with the distraction of having to look after her. No, this was the best plan for both of them, he decided, even if she did not like it.

Gydion took Trinity by the shoulders, gave them a reassuring squeeze, and kissed her forehead. 'Do not worry, Trinity, all will be fine,' he said as he took an old leather-bound book from his inside pocket, a book no bigger than a small notepad, and handed it to her.

'Your grimoire?'

'Yes, you will need it to begin Daniel's tutelage and also I will be able to easily find you when I return. I will see you soon, little one. Be safe, and remember all I have taught you.'

With the final goodbyes said, Gydion conjured a portal to Ariest. Trinity looked at her father as if it were the last time she would ever see him, like she was taking a mental picture so she would never forget his visage, then she quickly stepped through to hide the tears that were beginning to well up in her eyes.

'Be sure to safeguard my daughter, Fungal.'

'Aye, and ye be sure ta hurry up. Ah d'nae fancy hanging about Ariest if the Shade are there.'

As soon as Fungal had vanished into the portal, Gydion closed it behind them and created another one to Salamida. He quickly replenished his Essence, then stepped into the portal between realms and disappeared into the unknown.

There was no one left in the Station Foreman office. No one left to see the shadow in the corner, the corner Fungal had watched ripple unnaturally.

20

Ariest; known as Otherworld to some, Elseworld to others, was an idyllic place. It was rich in mineral deposits; food was in abundance and Essence flowed unheeded throughout the land. The Faerie Queen of the High Bourne, direct descendants of the Tuatha, the old gods that once called these lands home, was the ruler of Ariest. Cernunnos, the Green Man, the physical embodiment of nature and who ever held the position of Archmage, acted as her advisors. Throughout the realm, the different races of Ariest also had a ruler to keep order and their cultures alive.

This was nowhere more evident than in Almedia where the council of three reigned. Chief Seydou, Empress Xu Ping, and King Ewynn ruled equally in their city of diverse peoples with fair mindedness and impartiality and so it had been since the original settlers founded the city. But even in a seemingly perfect place you still had to be wary; brigands operated in Ariest, with none larger of more notorious than the mysterious faction known as the Shadow Dancers; assassinations, sabotage, and thievery were their forte.

Getting lost could also be detrimental to one's health since not all inhabitants of Ariest followed Queen Rhiannon. Finding yourself in a Frell, Firbolg, or Gnoll encampment could quickly turn your day sour.

That was what Nyriel and Ch'tan told Daniel at any rate. He had decided that it would be a good idea for him to learn a bit more about life in this strange new world, especially since he had no idea how long he would be here, and he had been more than willing to answer, to the best of his ability, all the myriad questions that Nyriel had about his own world.

'We are almost at Almedia,' Nyriel said. 'From there we will get transport to the imperial city where Gydion's sanctum is.'

Daniel was not certain how long they had been walking – he still felt energised and not fatigued at all – but he was sure it was longer than what he thought, because he could no longer see the beach that he and his two Undany companions had come to shore at and the first sun was also beginning to dip.

As soon as they had reached the coast after leaving Murias City, his escorts had taken on human guises. Relations were strained with the surface dwellers, due to the events King Noi described, and they did not want to reveal themselves to them; who knew what trouble it would cause? So Nyriel had taken the form of a pale-skinned beauty with the Twenties hairstyle Daniel recognised from the Pichini Palace library, a style she seemed to love, whilst Ch'tan disguised his large frame in dark skin and his hair became matted and locked.

Daniel turned his head this way and that, as any tourist would do. Eventually the party crested a hill and Ch'tan pointed to a large town, situated a few miles away, surrounded by a white wall that gleamed in the sunlight. 'That is Almedia,' he said.

'Impressive,' Daniel responded in wide-eyed admiration.

'For surface dwellers, perhaps.'

When they finally reached the city gates, the metropolis was even more imposing. The wall was a towering twelve metres in height and was clad in limestone. Daniel soon found out that the wall was even thicker than it was high as they walked through the ten-metre-tall bronze doors, which were flanked by two guards. They greeted the travellers and welcomed them to the city, first in something Daniel could only describe as gibberish, and then again in the common tongue. Nyriel greeted them in return, using the unknown language, and they were on their way.

'Isn't this a human city?' Daniel asked as they proceeded down the passage.

'It is,' Nyriel replied, 'for the most part.'

'Then what was that you spoke?'

'They call it Patgeon. The founders of the city devised it. I guess out of mistrust of the other inhabitants of Ariest.'

'And you know it?'

'Not really; hello, goodbye and a few simple questions, but I am learning.'

Now that Daniel thought about what he had heard and went over it in his mind, he could recognise that what the guard and Nyriel had spoken was a kind of mix using Asian languages and the clicking of certain African ones.

Approximately nine metres beyond the entrance was another set of bronze doors and two more guards. A further nine metres and the trio came to a third and final barrier with another pair of guards, and then they entered the city proper.

Almedia was a thriving, bustling city. Boys and girls with handcarts were going from house to house, collecting wood and straw and threatening anyone with bludgeons if they refused to contribute a toll. It was a strange thing for Daniel to see, but Nyriel explained that it was all part of the Beltane Fire Festival. A group of older teens, though supposedly part of the wood collection crew, considered themselves to have reached an age where they could dish out more of the bludgeoning and less of the handcart duty.

This was particularly the case for Finn Jesson. Her actual name was Finnuala, but nobody called her that, primarily because anybody that did happen to call her by her full name usually got a swift kick or punch from the feisty girl. Consequences like that tended to travel quickly around towns, but she rather enjoyed her reputation of being somewhat of a scrapper.

Finn was now of an age where she could add her name, along with other eligible bachelorettes, to the Beltane Games in the hope that, through providence and some luck, they could end up with a potential husband. Not that such things interested her as much as the two shiny new snub-nosed revolver guns she had on her hips, made especially for her by her Uncle Quinn.

The people of Almedia called him The Tinkerer but in actual fact Quinn Jesson was more of a master engineer, harnessing the power of steam to run many of his creations, such as the escalator in Fungal's beloved FTN. Such was Quinn's inventiveness that he had also experimented with combining his technology with Faerie magic...not always with successful outcomes. His Translocator, for instance, could be pinpoint accurate with its teleportation but then again, on some occasions, it could miss its mark by a couple hundred, sometimes thousand, miles.

Finn herself was quite a dab hand with an engineer's toolkit. Having spent most of her life with her uncle, she had learnt a thing or two about the profession. She always wore her blast goggles – you never knew when you

might need to do a spot of welding, she would say – although they were usually pushed up on her forehead as if they were a headband to keep her short
tousled violet hair in check.

As good as she was with a spanner and blowtorch in her hand, Finn was
even more impressive at gunmanship, since being a markswoman was her
true calling.

The custom-made bronze-coloured guns were small, a little over five
inches, yet were still beautifully crafted; each of its six barrels had a pattern
engraved on it, and the handle, which had crystal panels on either side, was
see-through and clearly showed the steam-driven gears which fired the revolver's hammer. A small gauge showed the psi of the steam. So efficient were
they designed that it only took a thimble full of water for the guns to func-
tion.

Quinn had constructed the weapons out of Tyrinnium ore, one of the
many minerals found on Ariest. It was strong but incredibly light, meaning
that each pistol weighed no more than a ripe apple.

'Come on, Finn,' Jimbo pleaded, 'put your name down for the Games. I
will if you will.'

'*You* will anyway,' Finn laughed as she continued to examine her pistols.

The two friends had pretty much grown up together and, as they did,
over the years, it became more and more apparent to Finn, judging by the
way Jimbo would always bring up the Games for no apparent reason and the
prospect of marriage and her views on the matter, that he was harbouring
feelings of a romantic inclination for her.

She liked being around him, but her views on the matter of matrimony
were that she could take it or leave it. She wasn't the kind of girl to go pining
after a boy, skipping about with flowers in her hair. It wasn't that she didn't
like boys – she had had partners in the past, even came close to marriage once
– but it had always been on her terms.

Most of the people of Almedia thought she was a bit of a tomboy; because she was one of the boys and she could scrap with the best of them, as
well as the fact that she was more likely to be found hunting than knitting.
The old women of the town put it down to the lack of a female influence
on her upbringing after the death of her parents. But as far as Finn was concerned, she was who she was and it suited her just fine.

'Jimbo, you deserve a good woman,' Finn said matter-of-factly as she slapped her hand down on his shoulder, 'but it ain't me. Not unless you're going to be happy staying at home looking after things while I go out and enjoy life.'

'Well, why don't we leave it up to fate to decide?'

'Because me and fate ain't friends,' Finn stated. 'She has been against me my whole life.' The young woman looked off into the distance, her thoughts drifting to the parents she could barely remember, but then her concentration was interrupted as three strangers caught her attention as they entered Almedia through the Western Gate.

She was interested to find out who they were, the one with white hair and matching skin more so than the others.

The whole spectacle of the town was an odd one for Daniel to witness. The cacophony of the city, the sounds of the many different accents and species, traders calling out to passers-by trying to peddle their goods, unknown aromas from unknown foods, music escaping from open windows. All the sights and sounds reminded Daniel of Oxford Street and he couldn't help but smile at the comparison.

'We should find a tavern or inn. Hopefully we will find someone there who will be able to give us transport,' Ch'tan suggested.

There was a definite buzz in the air, no doubt due to the imminent Beltane celebrations, thought Daniel, but there was also something else, an uneasy anxiety. The teens that had been collecting wood had stopped what they were doing and a girl with striking purple hair and funny goggles on her head watched him intently. He smiled back at her.

The anxiousness they felt was more evident when the trio asked a local for directions to the nearest alehouse. He looked them up and down with a suspicious eye before telling them where to go, and it was even more so when they reached that alehouse, called The Dirty Dog, and every patron seemed to stop what they were doing and cast a glare at the three strangers, some whispering in Patgeon, knowing that outsiders were unlikely to understand it.

Though Daniel didn't like it, he was used to being stared at, so he ignored it as he always did and led the way to the large rosy-cheeked woman behind the bar.

'Could you direct us to someone that might be able to give us transport to Imperial City?'

'Imperial City, you say,' the woman replied as she thoughtfully took a puff of the pipe in her mouth. She blew the smoke out of her nostrils and inspected them each, in turn, with a sceptical eye. 'You're not from around these parts, are you?'

'No, we're just visitors passing through in need of transport,' Ch'tan interjected. With his well-honed instincts, the royal bodyguard could see that she was one of those nosy bartenders and wanted to cut her off before she could pry any further into their business.

'Well, old Murphy runs the nearest coach station, but you got more chance of getting a pig to baste itself and jump in the oven than getting a ride during Beltane,' she stated matter-of-factly, 'so you might as well relax and enjoy the festivities when they kick off tomorrow. My name's Mavis and I just happen to be the proprietor of this establishment and I have one last room available if you're interested. It might be a bit of a squeeze,' she said, looking at Ch'tan, 'but I can put another bed in there for you.'

'I guess we'll just have to take it,' Nyriel said as she scanned the establishment. 'And bring us a round of your finest ale,' she concluded as she headed towards an empty table she had spotted at the rear of the tavern.

To get to the table, they passed the kitchen and the aroma that escaped invaded Daniel's nose and made his stomach growl. They didn't have to wait too long before a maid brought them their drinks. She asked if they wanted anything else and, after some financial reassurances from Nyriel, Daniel said he'd have a plate of whatever that great smell from the kitchen was.

'Sure thing,' the maid replied with a smile before leaving to get their orders. Before she could reach the kitchen, however, a man burst through the door of the tavern, swept her off her feet, and, whilst dipping her, gave her a long kiss which was met by the roars and cheers of most of the alehouse's patrons.

'Get off me, Tristan, I'm working,' the maid said after she caught her breath. She began to wriggle, desperately trying to break free of his strong grasp.

'Are you trying to say that you're not pleased to see me, Eveline?' Before she could reply to Tristan's question, he was struck over the head by a tray, which brought raucous laughter from the patrons.

'What have I told you about accosting my staff, you little ragamuffin?' Mavis said as she readied herself for another swing of her tray.

Tristan released Eveline, who hurried off to the kitchen with flushed cheeks, and held up his hands up in mock surrender with a smile on his face. 'Can a condemned man at least get a drink?'

'Can the condemned man pay for it?'

He jostled the moneybag at his waist and the sound of coin striking coin brought a big smile to the face of Mavis.

'Well,' she said in a long, drawn-out breath, 'since you put it like that, step right up to the bar!'

The clientele of The Dirty Dog tavern cheered in celebration and Tristan milked their applause as he walked past them. Whoever this Tristan was, it was obvious for Daniel and his friends to see that he was a popular man in these parts.

With a couple gulps from his flagon of mead to refresh his dry throat, Tristan turned on his stool and surveyed the patrons. He blew a kiss at Eveline as she came out of the kitchen, an action that prompted her cheeks to redden once more from the flirtatious behaviour of the swordsman.

His eyes followed her swaying hips as she carried a plate of food to the three strangers in the corner. Upon seeing them, he turned back to Mavis and asked, 'Who are the newbies?'

'They came in not long ago looking to get to Imperial City.'

'Is that a fact?' Tristan replied, his interest piqued. 'They don't look like the High Bourne type.'

'I didn't ask them their reasons for going. As long as they have good coin, their affairs are their own.'

Tristan took another gulp of his mead and looked again toward the strangers. 'Perhaps this is an opportunity to take some of that coin for my-self.'

Ch'tan, ever the bodyguard, had made it a point to be aware of his surroundings and knew that they were being watched. He leaned forward and spoke in a conspiratorial manner. 'It seems like we are attracting the attention of some of these surface dweller ruffians.'

'It might be a good idea if you went out and tried to buy some horses for us.'

'Are you sure? I do not agree with leaving you here.'

'Do not worry, we will be fine.'

Ch'tan was still in two minds about leaving as he rose from his chair. One final nod of ascent from Nyriel was enough to convince him and he turned and strode out of The Dirty Dog tavern.

Daniel ate the last spoonful of his Almedian hotpot with relish and rocked back in his chair with a full stomach and a content smile on his face. He was so content, in fact, that he forgot he didn't drink alcohol and almost choked on the ale in front of him when he took a mouthful.

'I thought all you surface dwellers drank this liquid,' giggled Nyriel.

'I'm not from around here, remember?' Daniel replied as he wiped his streaming eyes.

'Maybe the honey mead will be more to your liking. I'll order you some.'

'No, no that's alright,' he protested as Nyriel succeeded in getting Eveline's attention.

'How was the meal?' the waitress asked as she cleared up the table.

'The food was great!' enthused Daniel.

'Is there anything else I can get you?'

'He would like to try some of your honey mead.'

'Sure, coming right up.'

With his objections ignored, Daniel decided that he might as well let Nyriel order what she pleased; after all, she was the one paying for it. He leaned back in his chair again and soaked up the atmosphere. He didn't know how many taverns there were in Almedia, but surely they couldn't all be as packed as The Dirty Dog was.

The clientele were definitely a lively and rowdy bunch. There was a table across the room that seemed to have its own pipe-produced smoky atmosphere surrounding it. The people at the table, men and women, were playing a gambling game involving dice and every so often Daniel would hear the words 'advance,' 'retreat,' 'counter,' or 'conquer.' The cheers that accompanied this last word signalled to Daniel that this was the winning predicament and he could just about see the winner through the crowd, the purple-haired girl, as she smiled broadly and drew her spoils towards her.

Daniel was half tempted to get a closer look at the game play but wasn't totally convinced that these were the kind of people that tolerated strangers peering over their shoulder and thought better of it.

His mind soon turned to other things, in particular the Book of Azul, given to him by Nyriel's father, King Noi. Now that he was seated at a table, he decided that this would be an ideal time to take a closer look at the contents of the tome. He took the book out of the satchel and placed it gently on the table. He traced his fingers around the cover with reverence as if it were a delicate object of historical importance, which in effect it was. The book had been passed down through the Undines from monarch to monarch, having been apparently penned by the hand of Zephyrus, the deity of the Undines.

At this moment, however, Daniel wasn't convinced. Each page was blank, and as he flipped through the book he became more and more confused.

The sound of the pages being hurriedly turned attracted Nyriel's attention. She had been watching the entrance waiting for Ch'tan's return, hopefully bearing good news, but now she eagerly watched Daniel as he handled the sacred book.

In her heart, Nyriel was a historic diviner, what the Undines called an archaeologist. She had a passion for it, so much so in fact that frequently her royal duties suffered because of it. Nyriel had travelled all over Ariest, below and above its waters. She had made many significant finds and to have an artefact as ancient as the Book of Azul in your own home and then be told that you cannot see it until you have ascended the throne was a bitter pill for someone of her nature to take. She had read all about the book and now she had the chance to finally study it up close.

'You need water,' she stated.

'What?'

'If the book is used outside its water temple, Murias City, then you will need its element to reveal its secrets. In this case, water, or Essence-infused water, to be exact.'

'And where do I get that from?'

'You make it, of course. Your Essence should be strong enough to perform the task, we just need some water.' Nyriel's gaze rested on her half-finished flagon of ale and then she shrugged her shoulders. 'I guess it's water...of a fashion.'

Nyriel explained what she had seen the priests of Murias do when they performed service. How they had purified water and bestowed healing properties upon it by imbuing it with their Essence. Although there were subtle differences between what priests and mages could do with their Essence, Nyriel suggested that it was worth a try.

She made Daniel cup his hands before she poured the liquid into them. 'Now, surround your hands with your Essence and let it infuse the ale.'

Nyriel's plan was a good one; however, it had one flaw: she believed Daniel had more control of his Essence than he actually did, and as he tried to focus his Essence into his hands, his purple haze flared around his body. Unfortunately, this occurred just as Eveline was returning with Daniel's drink and the sudden appearance of his Essence startled her so much that she dropped the tray.

'You're a mage!' she exclaimed.

The sound of the tray hitting the floor didn't break Daniel's concentration but it did attract onlookers, in particular Tristan and Finn, as whispers that echoed Eveline's went around the tavern.

The ale slowly began to seep through Daniel's cupped hands. Each droplet that escaped had a purple hue and as they fell upon the blank pages of the open book, ever-increasing ripples extended from the point of impact. As each ripple reached the page edge, more and more of the book's text was revealed until at last it was complete and Daniel could once more read the foreign language.

A small smile crept onto Daniel's face as he read the unusual pictograms. He was still amazed that he was able to fully understand what was written, and he hurriedly began reading the page before him.

It turned out to be a spell of freezing rain, and it described the hand gestures that needed to be performed whilst casting the spell, as well as where in your body you should draw your Essence from to obtain optimal results.

This was fascinating to Daniel, as he avidly continued to read with wide-eyed wonder, but it was just as fascinating to Nyriel.

'This is fascinating,' she enthused. 'Apparently the spells in the book are different depending on the school of magic used upon it; druidic Essence would bring forth a whole different list of spells than what you are seeing now.'

Nyriel was giddy with excitement at finally getting up close with the ancient book. She took a mouthful of the fresh mug of mead that she noticed for the first time had been replaced, and that's when she became aware of the whispers milling through the gathered crowd.

'Is he here to banish the Shade?'

'He's too young to battle a Shade.'

'Why would the Council send a boy for something so dire?'

'It just proves that they have just as little regard for us as they do in Imperial City.'

The crowd was making the princess anxious as she and her companion fast became the centre of attention. She thought that it might be a good idea if they removed themselves from the prying eyes and went up to their room.

'Come on, Daniel, we should go,' Nyriel said as she shook her new friend's arm and tried to wake him from his trance-like reading state. She hadn't realised until now that his eyes had turned completely white whilst he had been reading and as he blinked a few times they returned to their normal yellow colour.

It took a few minutes for Daniel to regain his senses, for his heart rate to slow down to normal, for his awareness to be confined once more, for the 'rush' of magic to subside.

That was awesome! Is this what it was like to be a mage? The thoughts ran rampant through his mind as he stared down at the book and tried to comprehend what had just happened to him. *It was mad – like I had left my body and I was being enveloped by the writing – like I was absorbing the knowledge – like the spells, the magic itself, was becoming a part of me. The feeling was enlivening and it is something I want to experience again.*

'What's wrong? What's going on?' Daniel asked, as he was shaken out of his reverie.

'We need to go,' Nyriel replied as she leant closer to Daniel so no one else could hear. 'We were supposed to remain inconspicuous, but I fear we have failed that task judging by the throng around us.'

'Yeah, maybe you're…'

Suddenly there was a loud commotion of a fight brewing, cutting Daniel off mid-sentence. Angry raised voices could be heard to one side of The Dirty Dog.

Although fights breaking out were a regular occurrence amongst the rough and ready clientele of the tavern, the patrons still enjoyed watching a good dust-up; the more entrepreneurial among them would even take bets on the outcome if it wasn't a one-hit knockout.

Heads turned and people jostled for positions as they tried to see the skirmish, and even Daniel and Nyriel took an interest as they stood and craned their necks to see what was happening, but they couldn't tell where the trouble was.

Nyriel, slightly disappointed at not being able to see the fight, suggested that they use this opportunity to make their way upstairs. Daniel nodded in assent and turned back to their table to collect the ancient Book of Azul, only to discover, to his chagrin, that the book was gone.

21

The Dirty Dog had a renowned reputation of being the best tavern for food and drink in all Almedia. Eveline was an exceptional cook and as such Mavis paid her an exceptional wage so as not to lose her to a rival inn. Unfortunately, the tavern was just as infamous for being a hangout for the worst kind of rogues, scoundrels, and thieves in the city, a fact that Daniel and Nyriel were just finding out.

Daniel leapt up onto the table to see who had stolen the Book of Azul. Everyone was watching the scuffle...everyone except one girl, the girl with the violet hair and goggles on her head. She was looking in the opposite direction. Daniel followed her gaze and saw the slight hooded figure of someone quickly making their way towards the tavern door. The person moved with extreme agility, slipping in-between the revellers unheeded, as they made their escape.

'There!' Daniel shouted as he pointed at the entrance, before he jumped down and gave chase.

Nyriel swung her head around in the direction indicated and saw Daniel pushing his way through the crowd, following the unknown person. Catching up wouldn't be a problem for her, given her Undine strength; the difficulty would be not using too much of it since she didn't want to accidently injure any of these people.

As cautious as she was, one attentive pair of eyes could tell that she was stronger than the average woman of her build as she moved through the crowd. Seeing this further piqued Tristan's interest in the visitors and, after downing the rest of his drink, he jumped off of his stool and went after them.

'Stop the thief!' Daniel was buffeted this way and that as he fought his way through the crowd, and his shout carried no impetus as a result. Within a few moments the thief had burst through the tavern door and into the streets of Almedia, and straight into Ch'tan.

The huge frame of Ch'tan barely moved as the small, slight thief bounced off his barrel chest and landed on the ground.

'Oh, sorry about that,' Ch'tan said with genuine concern as he bent down to help the unfortunate person to their feet.

'Grab him, Ch'tan!' Daniel yelled as he burst out of the tavern.

Ch'tan and the thief both looked at Daniel and then at each other. Before the Undany guard could make his move, the thief pre-empted the attack and performed a back flip, kicking Ch'tan in the face with each foot before regaining a standing position.

The difference in size and strength of the two combatants was as disproportionate as the difference in speed and agility. Time and again Ch'tan missed with his lunges, only to be hit with a counter. The hits were not particularly strong but they were very accurate and it wasn't long before the cumulative effect of the blows began to take their toll, as his left leg became too numb to stand on and he dropped to one knee.

With his assailant incapacitated, the thief turned and gave a mocking bow, fleeing once more. As Nyriel came to the aid of her long-time friend and confidant, Daniel took up the chase.

Tristan, who had been standing with some other onlookers, smiled as the little pickpocket quickly despatched the giant. *This crook has skills*, he thought. His blood rushed at the idea of facing a new combatant and he also joined the pursuit.

Since he knew Almedia like the back of his hand, it soon became apparent to Tristan that if the thief continued in his current direction there could be only one place he could be heading, and Tristan knew a short cut.

He rounded a fish market and took a detour into a backstreet. As he passed the stall, Tristan knocked over a box, much to the chagrin of the owner who yelled and threw a fish at the adventurer, before realising that he was throwing his livelihood about and picked up the four-gilled trout and put it back on display, after dusting it off.

This was a new situation for Daniel to be in, being the chaser rather than the chasee. Instead of having to do whatever he could to lose his pursuers, usually Bobby Brinkmeyer and his cronies, in this role all he had to do was make sure he didn't lose his quarry and be ready to replicate any sudden moves they made.

It was all going well. Years of being bullied and pursued had given Daniel the stamina of a long-distance runner, but that couldn't help him when the thief found their way blocked by market shoppers.

'Stop that thief!' shouted Daniel. Two burly men turned to respond to the call for assistance, and within seconds they wished that they hadn't.

With two swift kicks, one to the knee of one and another to the abdomen of the other, both men were incapacitated and left in the perfect position to act as stepping-stones, providing the thief with a boost to a balcony overhead. They saw the level above was damaged and that they would need another way to the roof.

The thief brought his feet up beneath him and pushed off the balcony. He spread his arms wide and arched his back as he performed a perfect reverse swan dive. At the last minute he flipped over, landed on the springy canopy of a market stall, and was propelled even higher than before.

Twisting in the air, he latched onto another balcony on the opposite building. From here he was able to swing up another floor and then up onto the roof. With a bit of a run up, he was able to jump from roof terrace to roof terrace and back on to his escape route.

Daniel had watched it all with begrudged awe. He knew he couldn't get up there as easily as the thief had but he had to try; he couldn't risk losing him, and he couldn't risk losing the Book of Azul.

Okay, first things first, get up to the balcony. Daniel took a few steps back before sprinting at the still-winded market shoppers, vaulting off their backs, and jumping up to the ledge. He overshot it. By a long way. But instead of falling back down to earth, he continued going up, and up, and up. His arms and legs flailed about as he desperately tried to grab hold of something to stop his unexpected climb.

Nyriel and Ch'tan, who had been trying to get back into the chase, all of a sudden came upon a large crowd of Almedian citizens all, strangely, looking up into the sky.

'What are these surface dwellers do...' Ch'tan trailed off as he followed the line of sight of the masses.

'Zephyrus' beard!' Nyriel exclaimed as she saw Daniel drifting high above. She wondered what he was doing up there, then she saw her father's cloak, the one gifted to him by Gydion, glowing and leaving a multi-coloured trace behind the frightened mortal.

The stories surrounding the cape suggested that it could bestow the ability of flight to its wearer, but being a race that predominately lived beneath the oceans, she had never seen if that was fact or fiction; the princess wasn't even sure if her father knew for certain, since it was always locked away and she had never seen him wear it.

'Daniel,' shouted Nyriel, 'you're going to have to unfasten the cloak!' She made a gesture of removing the item, hoping that he might be able to see her, as she wasn't sure he could still hear her from his current height. Then she was suddenly startled, along with everyone else, by a loud bellowing voice of a young girl.

'Poppa, isn't that the traveller we passed the other day?' Nisset Mudd shouted.

'Hard to tell from this distance, dear, but you could be right!' Dilbert Mudd replied.

Nyriel, hands over ears, looked down and saw a family of Bellowers on the back of a Kitsune. She crouched and spoke to them. 'You sound like you know my friend.'

'We're acquainted!'

'Well, I need your help to get him down. He needs to take off the cloak but I don't think he can hear me.'

'I can do it, Poppa!' said Kanda and, before any of his family could say a word, he had taken a deep breath and bellowed with all his might. **'OI! TAKE THE BLOODY CLOAK OFF! YOUR FRIEND SAYS SHE'LL CATCH YOU.'** Several windows were shattered and the young bellower boy instantly got a clip round the ear from his mother.

Most of the crowd had dispersed when the Bellowers had first made their appearance, a usual occurrence, now the rest quickly ran off, fearing another assault to their eardrums.

The thief was close to making his escape through the Eastern Gate of Almedia. It was just as thickly built and sturdy as the other three and was likewise manned by the town guard, but the thief had nothing to hide from them. His pursuers were gone, no doubt trying to rescue the one that went floating off into the sky. The thief wondered how that had happened, but it was really none of his concern. The objective was nearing its completion; steal the book and meet the benefactor at the rendezvous.

To be sure that they wouldn't be followed, the thief, upon leaving the homestead blocks, had liberated a few pieces of clothing and was now using them to disguise himself. A change in stature and the addition of a slow, shuffling amble completed the masquerade.

Tristan suddenly came storming out of a side street and into the disguised thief.

'Sorry, are you alright? Let me help you up.'

'You youngsters,' the old voice croaked in reply, 'you should take your time. You're only rushing yourself to an early grave. But I'll be alright, nothing broken.'

'Glad to hear it, old timer,' Tristan said as he helped the elderly person to their feet. That's when the adventurer saw the footwear. If he had not seen the thief humiliate Ch'tan with a series of well-aimed kicks, he probably would not have noticed them. 'Nice shoes,' he said.

The thief stopped in his tracks, but before he could do anything, a crushing blow to the back of the head knocked him out cold.

'Sorry about the underhand tactics,' Tristan smiled, 'but the way you move about, this was the only way I could stop you to challenge you to one-on-one combat. It's been a while since I was truly tested but I think you have some ability, my friend. Now,' he said, crouching down beside the incapacitated thief, 'let's see who we have here.'

He pulled away each layer of the thief's disguise, pushed back the hood, and unwrapped the scarf from the face. When the reveal was complete, Tristan was surprised to see that the person who had stolen the book, who had defeated Ch'tan so easily, who had eluded them through the crowd with such skill, was a young girl.

Daniel had finally stopped his arm and leg movements. Partly because his limbs were aching and partly because there was nothing for him to grab hold of anymore since he had drifted higher than the rooftops of Almedia.

He could see for miles around; the western coast where he had come ashore with Nyriel and Ch'tan, the south where the hazy horizon indicated a hot climate, to the north, vast mountain ranges and the distant east, which seemed to be suffering from huge perpetual tornadoes.

If he could control his flight, if he wasn't floating up to his imminent death, Daniel knew he would have enjoyed this experience, but as it was, he just hoped it would be over soon.

His mind was swimming with melancholy thoughts, thoughts of coming to a foreign world and dying a slow, agonizing death...then he heard a voice.

It was so clear that at first Daniel thought that it was someone talking next to him, then he thought he recognised the accent. Was it the Bellowers?

Take the cloak off and she'll catch me? Really? That's the best they could come up with? Taking off the only thing that's keeping me in the air sounds kind of suicidal to me. I may have considered ending it all once upon a time, but I lived through it and I've got even more to live for now. But do I want to face the uncertainty of what's waiting for me above? It could be an airless solar system, like back home, but this place isn't like home at all, so who knows what's out there? It could actually be where the old gods of Ariest, the Tuatha, reside.

Daniel mulled things over in his mind for a few more moments before he closed his eyes and unfastened the cloak.

22

Some people claim that skydiving can be an intense and liberating experience, the solitude of the free-fall, the only sound being the wind rushing past your ears.

Intense? Liberating? What about the part when you're worrying if your chute is going to open or not, wondered Daniel, as he tried to come to grips with the solitude of free-fall, the only sound being the wind whistling in his ears, that and the flapping of the cloak given to him by King Noi. A chute malfunction, not being able to stop his plummet to Earth, would be at the top of his worrying agenda, as it was now; he just hoped Nyriel's plan to catch him, whatever that was, worked.

On the ground Nyriel was about to put it into action. She had been looking up into the sky, along with everyone else, waiting to see what Daniel would do.

'Do you think he will do it?' Dilbert Mudd yelled his question.

'He has to.'

'It just comes down to if he trusts you or not,' Ch'tan reasoned.

'What's not to trust?' So as not to be overheard, she spoke in a conspiratorial manner. 'I am a princess, after all; our word is our bond.'

'Do not forget that this boy is from another realm. I do not know what kind of courage or convictions his people have; do you?' Nyriel didn't reply. 'But it would seem that he is a courageous one nevertheless.'

'He did it?' There was a moment of astonishment in her voice, which changed to enthusiasm as she looked up once more. 'He did it!'

'Yes, he did. Now, should you not be doing your part now?'

'Yes...yes, I should,' Nyriel flustered as she suddenly realised that her plan was in motion. 'Water! I need water!'

Ch'tan had a quick look around and saw a man taking a gulp from his flagon of mead. The trusted bodyguard ripped it out of his hands.

'Hey, are you crazy?! That's mine!' A quick glare from the giant Ch'tan was enough to crush the man's boldness and he shrank back into the crowd.

'Here, will this do?'

Nyriel looked at the flagon, then at Ch'tan several times. 'I think I'll just use the river, but this will do for a start.'

Ch'tan placed the mug on the ground before Nyriel and, knowing that time was short, she had already begun to weave her hands in large fluid motions.

Members of the Undany royal family had been bestowed with the ability to control water and shape it to their wills, by their deity, Zephyrus. They weren't born with this talent, but when they came of age, they partook in a ceremony where they were bathed in a well of water blessed by their god.

Nyriel was drawing water from all around her, filtered from people's drinks, soups, even from a woman's cake batter. Little streams of liquid flew through the air; past an amazed Finn, as if attracted by the huge globe of water that was being formed by the princess.

'This will have to do,' she said as she looked up to see the plummeting figure of Daniel.

'What are you going to do? Catch him in that bubble?' Dilbert yelled.

'Of course not. Hitting the water at the speed he is travelling would be no different to him hitting the ground. So I need to be creative.' Nyriel suddenly threw her open hands into the air and the water globe shot straight up into the sky at a ferocious speed.

Daniel wondered what the hell was happening when the liquid orb flew past him. Was this Nyriel's plan? To shoot him down? Because if it was, he wasn't a big fan of it!

He was beginning to wonder if he had made the right choice, as the ground continued to rush up toward him, when out of the corner of his eye he saw the orb beside him, matching his speed. It began to move towards him, slowly enveloping him in its watery depths and, just before he was totally immersed, he took a deep breath.

The world around him became a rippling blur as he peered through the watery globe that surrounded him. He could no longer hear the whistling wind. The only sound he now heard was his racing heartbeat, which was amplified by being underwater.

The strain of controlling the water at such high velocities and then putting on the brakes was taking its toll on Nyriel; sweat was breaking out on her forehead and her human guise was faltering.

'Nyriel, you cannot keep this up,' Ch'tan whispered to her, his concerns growing as she began to shake from her exertions.

'I have him...must hold out...not much longer...he is almost down...'

Fifty feet...forty feet...thirty...twenty...ten, then the exhausted Nyriel could hold on no longer and collapsed into the arms of her bodyguard. The water orb fell the rest of the way and splashed down. Daniel was sprawled on the ground, spluttering and gasping for breath, a bit bruised but more than a little grateful to still be alive. As the crowd of onlookers cheered and whistled at the conclusion of the spectacle, he staggered over to his saviour, dripping wet, and hugged her enthusiastically.

DANIEL, NYRIEL AND Ch'tan were recuperating in their room at The Dirty Dog tavern. They had invited the Mudds to join them but Mavis had a strict rule concerning Bellowers ever since a group of them got drunk celebrating and started singing at the top of their voices.

'I can't believe I lost the book,' Daniel said morosely. He absentmindedly played with one of the fresh bowls of soup that Eveline had just brought up for them. She said that they were on the house; apparently, there had been an influx of customers hoping to see the three strangers get up to more craziness.

'You should not blame yourself. None of us were able to stop the thief,' Ch'tan said as he tried to console the boy.

'Maybe, but I was the one that had it, and he took it from right in front of me, right under my nose. I'm sorry, Nyriel.'

Daniel's apology fell on deaf ears as she sat in a corner totally engrossed with the king's cloak.

'I cannot believe I never knew what this thing could do,' she said to no one in particular as she eyed the material closely. 'I wonder if my father knew, or if Gydion even told him.'

Just then there was a knock at the door.

'I hope this is the waitress with more free food,' Ch'tan said as he finished the last of his soup and opened the door. He was shocked to see that it wasn't the maid at all but Tristan standing there with the unconscious thief slung over his shoulder.

'I think this belongs to you,' the swordsman said.

'The Book of Azul!' Daniel leapt out of his seat and grabbed the book as if he were reunited with an old friend.

Tristan walked past the surprised Ch'tan and unceremoniously dumped the thief on the ground.

'How did you catch her?' Ch'tan asked.

'Her?' The response came from Daniel and Nyriel together. They looked up from their items and saw the girl sprawled out on the floor. Her cowl had fallen.

She had a dark-red, coloured line, tattooed down the left side of her small heart shaped face, over almond-shaped eyes and high cheekbones, ending just past her well-defined lips. Her pointed ears, which had several earrings, the right one more than the left, poked through her long tresses, which shone golden, like a dawn sun. He estimated her to be of the same age as he was, perhaps even younger, but that theory was thrown out when Nyriel explained that the girl was elven and as such was a lot older than she looked.

'It wasn't hard to stop her when you know the city. I anticipated where she was going and caught her by surprise.'

'And why would you do that?' asked Ch'tan with a suspicious glare.

'After the way I saw her take care of you, I was hoping to fight her myself; well, that was before I found out she was a *she*, that is.'

'I suppose you do not fight women?' an offended Nyriel asked.

'Well, fighting women isn't the first thing that comes to mind in regard to the fairer sex,' Tristan laughed heartily.

'Just who are you?' an incredulous Nyriel asked.

'Who am *I*? I am Tristan Sturm, of course! Some people call me a hero around these parts, but I think of myself more as an adventurer. But I guess you wouldn't know that, being strangers to this fair city. So, what are your names and what brings you to Almedia?' Tristan asked as he casually leant against the wall.

Nyriel and Ch'tan were a bit reluctant to share their names with the stranger. Daniel, however, had no such compunctions.

'My name is Daniel and this is Nyriel and Ch'tan,' he said readily. 'We're in search of Gydion the Archmage.'

'Is that a fact? You know of his whereabouts?' Tristan asked anxiously. 'Because I have heard that he has not been seen in many years.'

A glare from Nyriel was enough to halt Daniel's loose tongue and none of the trio said a word in regard to Tristan's query.

'I see,' the swordsman stated. It didn't take much for him to know that they were hiding the information from him. 'Well, you should know that whoever is after you has deep pockets.'

'What do you mean 'after us'?' asked Nyriel.

'We're just delivering this spell book to Gydion,' blurted out Daniel.

'And what's the one thing this Shadow Dancer took?' questioned Tristan.

'Shadow Dancer?' Daniel looked down at the young girl, still unconscious on the floor, and wondered exactly how hard Tristan had hit her.

'Yes,' the swordsman replied. 'I didn't know they had elves amongst their ranks, but I saw the insignia on the hilt of her daggers. They are a sect of thieves, assassins, saboteurs and things in that line. They are the best at what they do, and hence do not come cheap.'

'But why would someone want the book?'

'I don't know, you're the mage, you tell me.' Tristan stopped and thought a moment. 'Or maybe you're not. Surely if you were, you could have stopped the thief with a spell or two. So I'm guessing you're one of those mage-in-training fellows.'

'You're very perceptive,' Nyriel grudgingly admitted.

'Nosey, if you ask me,' Ch'tan added.

'I get around, I see a lot of things. And I perceive that you need my help.'

'We do not need your help,' Ch'tan stated.

'I beg to differ. You are strangers here, and I know these lands like the back of my hand; where to go and the places to avoid.'

'And who is to say that you will not lead us into more of these brigands and hand us over to them?' asked Ch'tan.

'Not my style,' came the simple reply.

'And we should just trust that, should we?' Nyriel enquired.

'Sure.'

'We *could* use his help, Nyriel, as a translator at least,' Daniel reasoned.

'Maybe, but we do not have much money and cannot pay you.'

'Not a problem. I need to see Gydion also, so it will just be a case of helping each other out.'

'What do you want with the Archmage?' the princess suddenly became intrigued by the swordsman's motives.

'My business is my own, as your true origins are yours.'

Suddenly, the thief sprang up onto her feet, a dagger held ready in either hand. She quickly studied her surroundings with her pale blue, almost grey eyes, planned out potential escape routes, then she regarded her four opponents, paying particular attention to their stance to judge their combat prowess. Seeing that there was only one that could pose a threat, she smiled before leaping into a balletic spin, pirouetting, and letting fly stiletto blades in a continuous stream with unerring accuracy.

Ch'tan jumped to protect Nyriel and two blades sunk into his shoulder for his gallantry, while Tristan threw Daniel to the ground and deflected several of the small blades.

The Shadow Dancer used the flying daggers to shield her next attack and she dived at the swordsman like an arrow, her two daggers forming the tip.

Tristan barely had enough time to defend himself and then a furious duel began. Thrust, parry, riposte. They were evenly matched; neither combatant relinquished or looked likely to falter.

The continual sequence of attack then defend was at such an intense pace that the thief wasn't aware of Ch'tan coming up behind until he had grabbed her and thrown her towards the wall. The agile girl, however, was able to shift her body in mid-air, hit the wall with both feet, and instantly push off again. She tucked in her knees and barrelled into Ch'tan like a cannonball.

Tristan came at the Shadow Dancer again. As he neared, she put a hand into a hidden pocket in her cloak and threw a small pellet at Tristan. He easily deflected it, but as the object hit his sword, it exploded and filled the room with a thick smoke.

Since he was the closest to the door, Daniel made scrabble for it. He eventually found the handle and fell through the exit, choking on the acrid smoke. Nyriel, Ch'tan, and Tristan followed shortly and as the smoke dispersed they could see that the Shadow Dancer had vanished.

'So, you still think you don't need my help?' said Tristan smugly to Nyriel.

'Maybe we can use your sword after all. When can we leave?'

'After the festival, of course.'

The pounding of heavy feet suddenly interrupted them as Mavis came storming up the stairs and down the passageway. She had a studded mace in one hand and a bucket of water sloshing everywhere in the other.

'Whoever set my tavern alight is in for a bludgeoning!' she yelled, swinging her mace. 'Now where's the fire?'

23

Twilight had descended on the city of Almedia. It was a very different place at night than it was during the day, especially at this time of year. No one was in the streets; even the night watchmen were reduced in number, as everyone made their last preparations for the Beltane Festival. Hearth fires were extinguished throughout the city, as was the custom, in readiness to be relit from the great bonfire the following night. There were still several fires needing to be put out, although not all of them were visible from street level.

Buxton Mews was a very exclusive district of Almedia, although it had not always been the case; once upon a time it had been nothing but a barely used corner of the city. It had been gifted to the late Thomas Jesson, the father of Quinn and Martin, for his deeds in defending Almedia during the First Great War. Like his youngest son, Quinn, Thomas had been an inventor and engineer.

At the time of the Firbolg and Gnoll encroachment south, Thomas had been building an automaton for the purpose of labour-induced work, but once the skirmishes began he quickly changed its purpose and put it to the defence of the city he loved.

After the war ended and the Council of Three honoured the inventor, he renamed the district after his ancestral home, the East Midland town of Buxton, and quickly went about transforming it into a steam-powered marvel.

In time, the wealthy and well-to-do citizens of Almedia were attracted to the district by the amazing creations of the Jessons, thus in turn making them one of the richest families and land owners.

The largest property in Buxton Mews was naturally the Jesson family home, and its size was not restricted to being above ground for, beneath the earth, Thomas had installed an extensive workshop where Finn continued the family tradition for invention.

He spent most of his time there and it was here that Finn found him tonight.

'What are you still doing up?' he asked without looking up from his workstation.

'I could ask you the same thing,' replied the troubled teen.

'I'm putting the finishing touches to your rifle, if you must know. What's your excuse?'

'It's almost finished?' she asked excitedly. When he nodded, her elation eventually subsided and once more she was in a thoughtful mood. After being silent for a moment, she responded to her uncle. 'I'm having trouble sleeping.'

'You don't usually have problems. Is something wrong?'

These were the times that Finn wished there was a female in the house that she could confide in. Perhaps she would have felt a little less awkward to discuss certain matters. Like the time she had had her first monthly visitation; that had been a catastrophe on a whole new scale. Although she had great affection for her uncle and they discussed a great many things, the subject of love never cropped up, until now.

'I met someone today,' Finn stated as Quinn continued to tinker away, waiting to discover what the melodrama was, 'and I think I...I think I have a crush on him. When I see him, I get a funny feeling inside, kind of giddy, kind of nauseous really. I don't know how to explain.'

'Wait a minute!' Quinn had dropped his tools at this revelation and spun around on his stool to face his niece. 'Are you trying to tell me that you're falling in love?'

'How should I know?' she shrugged. There had been only one other that she could think of that came close to igniting these feelings in her, and her cheeks reddened with embarrassment as she remembered the family of nomadic shamans and the young man named Crellis. 'What I do know,' she continued, 'is that I don't much care for it, whatever it is!'

'Why not?' asked Quinn as he beamed at her. 'What's not to love about love?'

'The feeling of not being in control, for a start. When I first saw Daniel and his friends enter the city gates, it was like everything else vanished and there was just him and me; even Jimbo thought I was acting strange.'

'Wow! You really *do* have it bad, don't you?'

'Stop teasing! You're supposed to be helping me!'

'Okay, okay, I'm sorry,' laughed her uncle. 'So, who is this Daniel?'

'I don't even know! I don't know anything about him...except...' Finn went on to tell her uncle all she knew about the object of her affection, described his snow-white skin and hair, described his eyes like two golden-coloured suns, described his friends, the water-manipulating girl and the huge, broad-shouldered man. She told him about seeing Daniel perform magic in The Dirty Dog Tavern and about the chase through the city after a thief stole his book, culminating with Daniel flying through the air.

'Okay,' Quinn began when his niece finally finished, 'so you know what he's done around the city since he arrived here, but what about the boy himself? What about his history? Where he's from? What motivates him? What are his interests and ambitions in life? And, most importantly, what are his feelings towards you?'

'Like I said, I don't know any of that, and to be honest, I'd be surprised if he even knew I existed.' She slapped her hands over her face and shook her head in frustration. 'Arrggh! This is hopeless! I might as well forget the whole thing and carry on like I've never heard the name Daniel.'

'That won't solve a thing. You'll just go through life with regret wondering 'what if?' The only way to learn more about him is to talk to him.'

'And how do I get him on his own to do that?'

'On his own? Are you trying to tell me that my sassy, headstrong, assertive, and self-assured niece is suddenly having a crisis of confidence?' He smiled at the irony.

'Noooo! I just don't fancy having an audience when he laughs in my face.'

'That's not going to happen, and if it does you have my permission to kick his butt all around the city.' Quinn's reassurance brought a smile to the stressed-out teen.

This wasn't his area of expertise, sorting out matters of the heart, but he wanted to help Finn. He knew that she couldn't stay with him forever. He loved having her around, loved teaching her engineering, loved her as a daughter, but the time would come when she would have to live her own life. And it wouldn't be too long, now that she'd reached the age of a maiden.

'That's it!' he yelled, almost causing Finn to jump out of her skin. 'The Beltane Festival! Enter your name as a single maiden and, with providence's guidance, one way or the other, you will find out about your Daniel!'

'Vekt! Are you serious?' The idea of leaving her potential love life in the hands of her sworn enemy filled her dread.

'Of course! If he wins you, then you will have an evening meal alone in the palace to learn all about him and see what's what. And if he doesn't, then it is a union that was fated never to come to pass.'

'There is, of course, one flaw with your plan.'

'There is? And what's that?'

'It's all dependent on Daniel actually entering the contest himself.'

'Yeah, well, I can't think of everything.'

Finn was about to call the whole thing off when she suddenly had her own eureka moment. *Perhaps there is a way to give fate a gentle kick up the backside and show me some favour*, she thought. With her idea formulated in her mind, she gave her uncle a big hug, kissed him goodnight, and happily smiled her way off to bed, but not before telling her uncle to hurry up and finish the rifle.

The subject of Finn and Quinn's conversation, Daniel himself, used another candle that was still lit at this late hour. He sat in the corridor outside of the room he shared with Nyriel and Ch'tan. He had wanted to read the Book of Azul properly ever since Tristan had recovered it. Though there was space enough for the three of them in the bedroom, he hadn't wanted to disturb his companions with the candlelight while they slept, and it was a good decision, as he had been able to read through it three times already and was about to complete it for a fourth.

He hadn't needed to read it so many times, since it was committed to the database he called his memory when he finished it the first time, but when he had gone through it, he was expecting to be able to recite the spells and instantly cast magic. That didn't seem to be the case, however, because after several attempts he had failed to perform a single conjuration.

Daniel finished the last page yet again and felt thoroughly deflated. He had hoped he would find something he had missed; a magically concealed passage or a few hidden lines around the edge, but he had found nothing he hadn't read the first three times.

One thing he *had* discovered was that the book seemed to contain only water-based spells such as the Spell of Ice Shards that, to Daniel's understanding, showered an enemy with ice spikes. Then there were the Spells of Healing Water and even the Water Control spell Nyriel had used to save him.

The excitement he had felt when the book had been returned to him drained from Daniel and, with a deep sigh, he pushed the great spell book aside. Perhaps Gydion had been wrong about him; perhaps he wasn't mage material after all. But he wanted to be, so badly.

He *was* different, and he had learnt to accept that; with white hair, white skin, and yellow eyes, how could he not be, but to be different and be able to do all the things Trinity said he could, would be something he would accept with open arms. He wouldn't just be different, he would be different and better, better than all those that had teased him.

Just as Daniel was beginning to remember how he had felt when she had first spoken to him outside of their lecture room, he was awoken from his reverie by the voice of Nyriel.

'How are you finding the book?' she asked.

'Frustrating,' he replied in a depressed tone.

'It will come to you eventually. Casting magic is more than just what you read.'

'I hope you're right.' There was a moment of silence before he continued. 'I thought you were asleep.'

'I was, for a little while anyway, but Ch'tan and I have been discussing some things.'

'Like what?'

'The fact we have to leave.'

'Really? I was hoping to see what all this fuss was about with this Beltane Festival thing.'

'I think you have misunderstood. When I said 'we' I meant Ch'tan and myself.'

'What?'

'It is against my better judgement to leave you with this Tristan and it is not something I want to do, but it is a necessity.'

'What do you mean 'necessity'? What's happened?' Then Daniel realised for the first time that Nyriel was in her true form. 'Wait a minute! Your human disguise!' Daniel quickly ushered the Undany princess back into their room, where Ch'tan was getting their things together.

'I cannot keep it up much longer,' she stated, 'just enough to get out of the city, hopefully. I had not planned on us having to stay in the city nor having to use my powers to rescue you, so my levels are depleted but, more importantly, we cannot be here when the fires are lit.'

'Why not?'

'We are creatures of the ocean and although we can breathe air as you do, we cannot survive indefinitely on the surface; we need to return to water from time to time. Being near those bonfires would dehydrate us and could potentially kill us.'

'Alright then, why don't you just take a quick dip in the river here?'

'It might help a little, but salt water or fresh water is what we need. Besides, who knows what they dump into this river and there would be a lot of explaining to do if we were spotted. No, this is for the best, Daniel, but it will just be for the few days that the festival is on, then we shall return and continue our journey.'

'And how will you know when it's safe to return?'

Ch'tan pulled a shell from one of the bags and handed it to Nyriel, who in turn gave it to Daniel. He inspected it and turned it over in his hands.

'O...kay...what am I supposed to do with this?'

'You talk into it, of course. My father insisted that Ch'tan and I take them in case we were separated. You speak into one and he hears you from the other.'

'Oh!' Daniel exclaimed as the revelation hit him. 'It's like an Undany mobile phone!' The princess and the bodyguard both looked at him with blank expressions. 'You really need to update your books about my realm, Nyriel,' he said, shaking his head.

'Anyway, all you do is speak my name into it and the two shells will be linked and we return.'

'So where will you go now?'

'Back to Shimmering Lake; we passed it on the way here. It is less than a day from here.'

Daniel nodded as he remembered the silvery lake. 'When will you leave?'

'Now,' she said regretfully, 'while we have the cover of darkness.'

'Look,' Daniel began as he realised Nyriel's conflict in leaving him behind, 'I'll be fine. Like you said, it *is* only for a few days and if anything happens, Tristan is here.'

She wasn't particularly comforted by that news. 'Do not put your complete faith into him, Daniel. We know so little about him, and we do not know if he is completely trustworthy.'

'Okay, I'll be on my guard,' Daniel said as he tried to allay her fears. 'But what should I tell him if he asks where you have gone?'

'You could tell him that we have gone to see an infirm aunt,' Ch'tan suggested.

'Here, take this,' Nyriel said as she handed Daniel her coin bag. 'Where we are going we will not need it.'

Then it was time for the friends to part. Daniel and Nyriel embraced before he shook hands with Ch'tan. The bodyguard then led the way out of the room and down the stairs to the tavern entrance. The Undanys reverted back to their human guises and gave Daniel one last salute before they disappeared into the night.

They kept to the shadows as they stealthily made their way to the western city wall. There was little light emanating from the homes and establishments of Almedia, which made their escape all the easier.

One house they passed that did still have its hearth lit was the homestead of the Sanderson family, Emily and her son.

'Timothy, come on, let's get you up to bed,' she said as she gently shook her son awake. 'You know I have to put out the fire.'

'But, mum,' the seven-year-old pleaded. 'I need to protect my wood for the pyre tomorrow. If I don't, the boogieman will get them. I got some real good wood too!'

'Don't worry, I'll protect your stash, and then in the morning you can throw them on the bonfire.'

'And then eat lots of Beltane cake – mmmmm! And I won't get the charcoal one either.' The cake in question was a small fruit cake with a rough surface. It was made with less eggs and less sugar but one out of the many cakes would have a small piece of coal. The person who found that cake would be deemed unlucky and would have to jump through the flames to 'burn away' any potential misfortune.

'Yes, honey, after we've given thanks to the great goddess for surviving the winter months and wishing for a bountiful summer harvest.' She paused a moment as if in reflection, before she solemnly continued, 'We'll also offer up a prayer for your father.' Gavin Sanderson, her late husband, had been a miner, a lucrative career in Ariest, due to its rich mineral deposits. This path had its downsides, however, paramount being that the ores were not necessarily located in friendly areas. She wiped a tear from her eye and sighed deeply. 'Now, the faster you get to sleep, Timothy, the faster Beltane will begin.'

'Alright then, Mum,' Timothy said as he stretched out his arms to his mother.

'What's wrong? Can't walk all of a sudden?'

'My legs are already asleep,' he giggled.

Emily carried her son upstairs and tucked him into his bed. After wishing his mother goodnight, as soon as Timothy's head hit his pillow, he fell asleep. She smiled as she kissed him on the forehead. The doting mother shook her head in disbelief at the innate ability children had to instantly fall into slumber. She wished she had that ability as she made her way back downstairs.

The young woman poured herself a small glass of mead and sat before the hearth. She looked deeply into its flames and her thoughts drifted to the loss of her husband. It happened almost fifty years ago, but due to the slowed aging that occurred in this realm, Emily still looked like a woman in her early thirties. She had had many suitors over the years, but as of yet had not chosen to re-marry; she still couldn't let go of Gavin. He had been her first love from as far back as school. When he died, she felt like her world had ended but she had to go on for Timothy. He had been her rock, just like his father had been.

As his mother relaxed downstairs, the young boy slept soundly. He was deep into the land of dreams, but they were soon to become a nightmare. Even if he had been wide-awake, he still would not have known what peril was about to befall him; he would not have heard a thing for the simple fact that a shadow does not make any noise.

The impenetrable darkness on the ceiling above the bed rippled like a pebble had been dropped into its dark depths. The undulation was gentle at first but grew more and more violent until a black snake-like protrusion extended from its recesses. It positioned itself inches above the boy's face, and though it had no features, it seemed to inspect him as if searching for something. When it sensed what it sought, it quickly retreated back into the shadows.

Nothing stirred for a few moments, just the rhythmic rise and fall of Timothy's chest as he slept.

Suddenly, small hands, five each side, emanated from underneath the child's bed. They paused just above his body, and as the protrusion descended from the ceiling once more, they grabbed hold of the boy!

Timothy woke up but it took several seconds for him to become aware of what was happening to him. He was terrified to see the projection hovering above his face, but even in his frightened state he could recall the stories of the Shade: how they would always strike at night, how they seemed to bring the shadows to life. He struggled to free himself – he didn't want to die – and tears began to roll down his cheeks, but the hands holding him down were far too strong for the seven-year-old. His only hope was to call for help and hope that his mother would hear. The boy opened his mouth to cry out to her but, before he could, two arms with long, skeletal-fingered hands extended from the impermeable black mass and wrapped around his throat. His shout was stifled and his eyes bulged as the breath was squeezed from his body. The Shade opened its whale-like maw, above Timothy's face, and began to draw the boy's pale-yellow Essence out of his mouth and into its own.

Emily, who had been dozing, was woken with a start; she thought that she had heard something come from upstairs, but now all was quiet. She yawned as she lit a candle and extinguished the last embers of the hearth before she made her way up to bed. Timothy had a habit of kicking the bed sheets off while he slept so, as usual, she decided to check in on him before she turned in for the night.

She opened the bedroom door and was devastated by what she saw. A Shade was sucking the Essence and life from her son.

'No!' The heartache at seeing her son helpless in the hands of the creature gave her the strength and courage to charge the vampire, but her attack was cut short. Shadow is the playground of the Shade and in a darkened room such as this they are God.

Emily barely took a step toward the fiend when restraints from the darkness behind her suddenly grabbed hold and threw her against the wall. Just before she lost consciousness, she saw the Shade release the pale, lifeless body of Timothy, his head lolled to one side with a look of extreme terror on his young face before it swallowed him whole. Then everything turned to black for Emily.

24

Tristan quietly closed the door to Eveline's accommodation at The Dirty Dog and silently made his way out of the tavern. He had left her sound asleep in bed and had no reason to wake her. After the night they had shared, he chuckled and suspected that Mavis herself would have difficulty raising her this fine morning.

It wasn't long before he neared his destination, a small, unassuming store with the sign, Hyasda's Herb and Alchemy, swinging in the gentle morning breeze. Just as he was about to open the door to the store, a militia commander on horseback and four guardsmen rounded the corner and marched past him. He wondered what they were up to – perhaps they would need the help of his sword – and he was just about to turn and follow them when he remembered that he had prior business to attend to and he opened the shop door.

'Hyasda!' Tristan called. 'I have returned with your herbs!' There was no answer.

He had always found the shop of curios to be exactly that, curious. Bottles of strangely coloured liquids and flasks filled with stranger smells all lined the walls and shelves of the store.

Tristan had learnt quickly, in the early days of his association with the alchemist, that tampering with the numerous vials and beakers could be detrimental to his wellbeing. On one occasion, he sniffed a bottle of a sweet-smelling concoction and was halfway into being transformed into a goonygor, a three-legged simian creature found in the region, before Hyasda brought the antidote.

At the back of the shop, beyond the alchemist's cauldron and brewing area, was Hyasda's sanctum, where she apparently created her most secret and potent of elixirs. It was a room Tristan had never entered, nor could he, since it had neither lock nor handle, but as he neared it he thought he could hear a voice coming from the other side.

'Hyasda? Is that you?'

The voice stopped, then the young adventurer heard the familiar sound of his godmother. 'So, you have finally decided to come and visit your poor old guardian, have you?'

The door opened and a wizened old woman carrying a staff stepped out. You could imagine, judging from the ends of her long hair that still had traces of colour, that it had once been jet black but was now faded to white. Her skin, aged and weathered, told the story of countless years, but no matter how old she was, age hadn't diminished the twinkling youth in her eyes.

'Come, come now, Hyasda, you know how special Eveline is to me.'

'She is no more special to you than any of the other women whose arms you have found comfort in,' she spat, but softened after a moment and continued, 'but I do not care what you do, as long as you do as I ask.'

'And I have yet to let you down. See, I come bearing the herbs you requested.'

Hyasda opened the satchel Tristan handed her and peered inside. 'Hmmm, very good specimens. I taught you well.' She closed the bag and put it aside. She leant heavily on her staff and eyed Tristan. 'And what of my other requests?'

'Whoever informed you about Imperial City was correct. It is as if a haze of indifference had descended upon the town; no one was bothered enough to do anything. Even Queen Rhiannon and the Sisters of Calatin seem affected.'

Hyasda looked thoughtfully into the distance as he spoke. 'And what of the Gnoll chieftains? Do they know about this?'

'I do not know; their distrust of other races still stands firm, and I could not get to see them. According to some of the locals from the surrounding villages, there are rumours going around that they wait the return of the banished betrayer, Sayyidah.'

'I see,' she carefully mulled over his words.

'And what of my request?' he pressed.

'Gydion has not returned to this realm as of yet. There are a multitude of possible realms where he could be, and it will take time to find him.'

'Perhaps not much longer. I will be accompanying a boy and his two companions to Gydion's sanctum.'

'Is that so?' Hyasda suddenly showed an increased interest. 'To what end?'

'Apparently to deliver a book. He is a mage; a mage in training, at any rate.'

'Hmmm, an Initiate? Going to the Archmage? That is not Circle procedure, unless Gydion has summoned him directly...'

'Possibly...the book he has is a spell book, the Book of Azul, I believe he called it.'

'The *boy* has the book? Are you sure?' She couldn't believe what she was hearing. 'They entrusted it to *him*?'

'You know of this book?'

Hyasda ignored her ward as she began to process the information she had received. 'Who *is* this boy that the great Archmage Gydion covets him so? And the Undines even trust him with their sacred tome; Gydion himself, yes, but who else...his student?' she mused. 'Perhaps. Gydion has had no student since his wife...could he really have chosen this boy?' She turned her attention back to her ward. 'What more do you know about him?'

'Nothing, except that his name is Daniel. I don't think he is from this realm either.'

'If you had continued to practice my magic teachings instead of over-relying on your sword, you would have known for sure. He is no doubt from Earth realm...which makes me wonder if...' Hyasda didn't share her suspicions with Tristan – she very rarely did – only choosing to tell him what she believed he needed to know, which in this case was, 'I need to know more about this Daniel! Why he is here and, more importantly, his provenance.'

'We will be travelling together shortly. You will have all you need to know soon enough.'

'This cannot wait!' she snapped back.

At that moment the bell above the shop's entrance tinkled. Hyasda slowly walked to the front area, leaving Tristan in the back to greet her prospective customer and found Finn snooping around the shelves.

'Ahhh, if it isn't young Finn come to visit. Are you on an errand for your uncle? Is he in need of more Faerie dust?'

'No, I am here for my own needs.'

'Oh? What needs do you have, youngling?'

'I have decided to take part in the Beltane Games.'

It wasn't long before Finn was exiting the curio shop with a huge smile on her face. Her mind was totally focused on the purchase she had just made, so much so, that she failed to notice Jimbo watching her from around a corner.

'This girl could turn out to be rather useful.' Hyasda rubbed her chin as she watched the excited girl walk down the street.

'It was a stroke of luck that she came in when she did,' Tristan said as he joined Hyasda.

'You could call it that, but when you are on first-name terms with deities long thought dead, and other deities yet to be written about, you tend to carry favour with them and they shower you in their glory. Now, I must return to my work.'

'And I must return to the comforting arms of my special one,' Tristan replied with a grin, which Hyasda greeted with a sneer before she turned and made her way slowly back to the handle-less door and her secret sanctum.

DEEP IN THE LAND OF nod, Daniel was having a most strange dream, strange but rather enjoyable. In it he was the Wizard of Oz and before him stood Trinity as Dorothy, Bobby Brinkmeyer as the Cowardly Lion, Jack Thompson as the Tinman, and Willis Jeffries as the Scarecrow. But whereas the Wizard of the book and films was nothing more than an elderly illusionist, in his dream he was a powerful and mighty mage, and now these four waited to receive their wishes.

'Who wishes to go first?' Daniel asked.

'I – I w – w - will,' stammered Bobby the Cowardly Lion. 'I – I don't want to be a coward anymore.'

'You don't want to be a coward anymore? Is that a fact? That's your excuse for bullying me all this time? Really? Well, unfortunately for you, I don't buy it, and as such I cannot grant you your wish…but I can grant mine.' As he finished, Daniel clicked his fingers and the cowardly Bobby transformed into a donkey. 'So, who's next for a wish?'

The Jack Thompson Tinman stepped forward. He opened up his tin body and showed Daniel the clockwork mechanism inside. 'This passes as my heart but what I really want is a real one.'

'You want a real heart? That's your wish? That's your excuse for teasing me? Not having a heart? Really? Well, unfortunately, I don't buy it. No, I don't think you are deserving of a real heart, so I cannot grant your wish…but I can grant mine.' Again, Daniel clicked his fingers and Jack Thompson the Tinman turned into Jack Thompson the can of baked beans. 'I've heard they're good for the heart!' Daniel smirked and then turned his attention to Willis Jeffries the Scarecrow. 'Now Willis, what is it that you wish for?'

'I want to have a brain,' Scarecrow Willis stated.

'A brain? Really? Hmmmm, a brain. You have enough brains to know that what you, Bobby, and Jack were doing to me was wrong and yet you continued. No, I don't think you deserve to have your wish granted…but I can grant mine. Once more Daniel clicked his fingers and Willis turned into a haystack.

The Dorothy Trinity was the last one left and now she stepped forward. 'Great and mighty Daniel, I wish only to go home.'

'But you are home, Trinity, here by my side.' He took her by the hands and moved closer to kiss her. He could feel her warm breath on his lips and smell her flowery fragrance and hear a heavy banging on a door. Banging on a door? *Why would that be in my dream?*, he wondered. He soon found out that it wasn't.

The door to his room splintered as it was kicked repeatedly and finally blasted open as one of its hinges gave. Four town militia charged in, shields up and swords at the ready. They surrounded the bed, as if they were expecting Daniel to stop them; some looked decidedly anxious, even more so than

Daniel did himself, and he was the one waking up with swords surrounding his head.

The commander then stepped in, ordered him out of bed, and made him get dressed at sword point. When he was ready, they led him downstairs and out into the streets. The looks of disdain and even hatred from some of the people left Daniel in confusion. He didn't even know what he was supposed to have done. Every time he tried to ask a guard, they wouldn't reply, and they didn't even look at him. They continued to march him through town to the jeers of the citizens until they reached the three-towered palace.

As Daniel approached the structure, he could see that two of the towers were each connected by a three-storied extension to a glass domed building, also three stories, at the centre of the trio.

They entered the central hub of the palace and in its centre was a huge statue of three men, each with their right arm extended and their hand resting on a large sphere. Daniel couldn't read the plaque in front of the sculpture properly as he was marched passed it, but he wondered if these were the three that originally founded the city.

Eventually Daniel was directed to a large room with tiers of seats on either side. To his horror, they were filled with people, and with the three high-backed chairs facing him he couldn't help but feel like he was being led into some sort of courtroom. His theory was proved right when he was made to stand in front of the chairs, a few paces away from them, on an insignia of a Manticore, at which point three people were led in to take the seats.

They were all of a venerable age, but they still had an air of authority and respect about them. An Asian-looking woman headed the way. She was lavishly dressed in red and gold silk. Her robes were intricately embroidered, and a jewelled golden crown rested upon her grey-haired head. The two men that followed her both had similar crowns. The dark-skinned African, though not a young man, was certainly as fit as one, Daniel surmised judging by the powerful arms he had, which were left uncovered by the bronze-coloured tunic he wore. The third man in the procession was no slouch either as he strode to his seat, his white fur-edged blue cloak flowing behind him. He adjusted the sword at his hip before sitting down and stroked his white beard as he regarded Daniel with a stern eye. Empress Xu Ping, Chief Seydou, and King Ewynn, the council of three were ready.

'Your name is Daniel, I believe?' King Ewynn questioned.

'Yes – yes, it is.'

The deep baritone of Chief Seydou rang out. 'And you are a stranger here?'

'That's right, I am.'

'From where do you hail?'

'I'm from Earth.'

There were a few mutterings amongst the crowd.

'Only here a few days and yet it has been rather eventful,' the empress stated. When she saw the confused look on Daniel's face, she continued, 'We have heard all about you running through the streets of Almedia and in particular about you flying through the air.'

'And also about your two friends who saved you,' Seydou added.

'Where are they now?'

'They had to go. They went to spend Beltane with a sick aunt.'

'Where is this aunt?'

'They didn't actually say.'

'And they left you behind?'

'I really wanted to be here to experience the festival.'

'When did your two friends leave?'

'Last night.'

King Ewynn nodded to one of the guards, who immediately bowed and left the room. 'On foot they could not have gone too far.'

'Can I ask what this is all about? Because it's sounding like a cross examination.'

'It is.'

'What? Are you serious?'

'The Council of Three are always serious.'

'Especially when a child named Timothy Sanderson is murdered.'

'Murder? You can't think it was me?'

'You or your absent friends.'

'The Shade has not been here in the city for many, many years and now one returns the same time three strangers arrive and then two decide to leave during the night.'

'It's nothing more than a tragic coincidence.'

'Coincidence or not, your friends are suspects and by association so are you. Bring forth the sphere.'

The sound of steam being expelled at regular intervals was suddenly heard. It was interspersed with the not-so-familiar rhythmic click on the marble floor as a brass quadrupedal contraption walked in. It housed a black sphere approximately twelve inches in diameter at its centre, which seemed to be suspended somehow.

'Now you will be judged and it will be determined if you will be held in perpetuity until your friends are found and brought back here.'

'This isn't right. I haven't done anything.'

'Do you have anyone that can vouch for your integrity?'

Daniel looked around, hoping to see Tristan stand up from the crowd, but there was no sign of him.

'Very well, since no one is willing to come forward, we will continue.'

'Being an outsider, you are probably unaware of what this is. This is the Gem of Truth. It has been used for generations, as far back as the founders, to ensure that our decisions are our own and not influenced by each other nor any other outside interference. Do you understand?' Daniel nodded. 'Then your fate shall now be determined.'

The Council of Three all stood and moved toward the sphere. As one, they each placed a hand on it, and almost at once the darkness within the crystal began to swirl and move as if it were alive.

Eventually it was still once more and suddenly Daniel heard a tinkling voice, almost crystalline in nature, which seemed to emanate from all around.

'The question has been asked,' the voice said, "should the accused be held in perpetuity?' And the question has been answered, with a vote of three to zero. Yes, is the verdict.'

'And so it shall be.'

'Guards, take him away.'

Daniel couldn't believe what was happening to him and he didn't know what he could do to stop it. Perhaps telling them that he was a student of Gydion might carry some weight here like it did in Murias City. But then again, perhaps not, especially if they asked for a demonstration too. He wasn't sure if he could concentrate enough to produce anything. He was speechless and he could feel his legs beginning to turn to jelly.

Two guards were about to take the confounded youngster by the arms and lead him away when, suddenly, the doors to the courtroom were blown open and the two guards that were posted there came sliding, unconscious, along the marble floor.

'Take your hands off of him!'

Daniel raised his eyebrows at the sound of the voice. He had wondered when or even if he would ever hear it again, as he swung his head around to be sure he wasn't dreaming, and he was elated to see that he wasn't. 'Trinity...and a little hairy dude in a hat!' he exclaimed.

Trinity strode past him, her auburn hair flowing, with a determined look on her face. She glared at one guard and then the other and they immediately backed away, then she faced the Council of Three.

'Whatever you are accusing Daniel of, you are mistaken in your judgement.'

'How dare you burst in here!' Seydou yelled as he got to his feet.

King Ewynn was likewise incredulously at the effrontery. 'Who do you think you are?'

'I am Trinity Evergreen, daughter of the Archmage Gydion.'

The gasps and hushed whispers that went around the courtroom suggested to Daniel that the 'student of Gydion' line might have worked after all.

'Gydion has no daughter,' stated Empress Xu Ping.

'And when exactly was the last time you saw him to know such a thing? Fifty years, perhaps? The same as my age.'

The Council of Three were unimpressed by the declaration.

'Och!' Fungal was exasperated. He had just wanted to do what Gydion told him to do and get back to his beloved FTN. The Boggart Laird had been standing behind Trinity but now he stepped out and puffed on a freshly lit cigar he had taken from underneath his top hat. 'She is who she says she is.'

'Fungal.' King Ewynn said the name with disdain.

'You expect us to believe you? By your very nature you are a liar,' the Empress said.

'That would hurt if it wasnae true. But you dinnae have to believe me, you can believe yer little gemstone there.'

'Even if she is the daughter of Gydion, it changes nothing. The boy is accused, along with his missing friends, of bringing a Shade to Almedia and using it to murder a child,' revealed Seydou.

'*That* is complete and utter rubbish! My father is already looking into how the Shade have returned and Daniel has nothing to do with it.'

'And what of his friends? Do you speak for them also?'

'I don't know them.'

'*I* do and they would never do any of the things you accuse them of,' Daniel insisted.

'If you believe in their innocence so much, you should have no objection to your judgement,' countered Seydou.

'I don't,' Daniel replied after a moment's thought. 'What I object to is having to languish in your prisons while we wait for them to return.'

'May I make a suggestion?' Fungal said, blowing the end of his cigar, agitating its burning embers. 'Why don't you release him to Trinity's charge? I'm sure she will promise to stay within the city until the boy's friends are found.' She nodded her agreement. 'So, the question now, lads and lass, is d'you do the right thing and hand him over, or does she take him?'

'What?' Trinity shot Fungal a glare of disbelief, but he just brushed her protestations away as if he had everything under control.

The regents of Almedia looked at each other before King Ewynn spoke and told the trio that a second vote would be cast. Once again, the council members each placed a hand on the black sphere. The mists inside swirled for much longer this time, reflecting the turmoil in the minds of the regents. Daniel could hear the murmurings from the crowd, and the tension of the situation was getting to him. Trinity could detect his anxiousness so she took his hand and squeezed it, just to let him know that he wasn't alone. That's when the sphere settled down to its dormant state. A decision had been made.

25

Empress Xu Ping raised her hand and a hush quickly fell across the crowd. Then the tinkling crystalline voice could be heard again.

'The question has been asked,' the voice said again, "should the accused be remanded into the custody of his protectorate?' And the question has been answered with a vote of two to one. Yes, is the verdict.'

When he heard the word 'yes,' Daniel punched the air in celebration and gave Trinity a big hug. He could have been mistaken, but he was sure she was squeezing him just as much, if not more so. He became self-conscious of his show of affection and released her with much umming ahhing.

They left the Palace and Daniel began to lead them back to The Dirty Dog tavern. As they walked, he couldn't help but steal occasional sideways glances at the girl who had been on his mind since the first time he had met her. He had missed her green eyes and her auburn hair. 'It's good to see you, Trinity,' Daniel admitted.

'You too, Daniel,' enthused Trinity, and her rosy cheeks blushed a deeper red. 'I'm so glad you're okay. Here, you left this.' She handed the peridot gem to Daniel and he was glad to have it back.

He could have sworn he had left it in his bedroom, but those thoughts left when he saw the way that her face practically beamed; he could tell she was genuinely happy to have found him. But if that was the case, why hadn't she stopped her father sending him here in the first place? Daniel was about to broach the subject but Trinity's little companion got in first.

'Right, lass. Now that you've got yer wee little lover boy back, we can get out of here.'

'He's not my *lover boy*, Fungal, he's...wait a minute! What did you say?'

'We can get out of here!' exclaimed the little Boggart. 'Yer didnae really think I was going to stay in this place, did yer?'

'Well, after *you* gave them *my* word, I kinda thought, yeah, you would.'

'Are yer out of yer wee little mind? I only told those eidiots what they wanted to hear.'

'Unfortunately, unlike you, I keep my word.'

'And Nyriel and Ch'tan will be back in a couple days, and I have to wait for them.'

'Who are these friends of yours, Daniel? Can you really trust them?' Putting her neck on the line for Daniel was not an issue for Trinity, but she was effectively putting her faith in these people she had never met and knew nothing about. What if they really did have something to do with this death? Then Daniel could be implicated by association alone.

'Considering they have saved my life twice already, I think that's a yes.'

'Nyriel?' Fungal mused. 'Now why does that name sound familiar?'

'Probably because,' Daniel had a quick look around to make sure there were no eavesdroppers, 'she's the Undany princess.'

'What? Are yer all mad?! If the regents discover who she is Unda –' Trinity slapped her hand over Fungal's mouth before he could shout out the name. There was no need to attract any more unwanted attention considering that people were already pointing at Daniel and whispering as they passed.

'He does have a point, Daniel, but if you believe and trust them, then that's enough for me and it's enough for him,' Trinity said as she hit Fungal on the head to emphasise the point. The little Boggart just grumbled about him being taken advantage of as he stomped off ahead of his unwanted companions.

'Put a sock in it, Fungal! I should tell you, Daniel, this little ball of trouble is the reason why you're here in the first place.'

'What do you mean?'

'I don't know. He said something about a train ticket meant for someone else.'

'Bloody hell! He must mean the ticket Jim gave me. And all this time I thought it was you and Gydion,' Daniel laughed.

Trinity, however, had stopped and did not see the funny side of his mistake at all. 'You thought what?!'

Daniel reacted like he had been hit in the face. He had so little experience with girls that he didn't realise that it was a bad idea to tell one that you thought they had been involved in anything underhanded.

'That was just one theory, but you have to admit that Gydion would be a number one suspect.'

Trinity did agree, but she didn't tell Daniel that. 'If that's the way you feel then you probably won't be interested to know that Father has told me to begin your training,' she said as she powerwalked her way past him.

'He really said that? I can begin my training?'

Daniel's reaction put a smile on Trinity's face but she didn't let him see. He was as excited as a kid, and to be honest so was she.

This was the biggest responsibility that her father had ever given her. Training an Initiate was not something to be sniffed at. It laid the foundation for all that the student could become. If the concepts of discipline and patience were not instilled in them, the consequences could be disastrous, for themselves and for all around them.

'He even gave me his grimoire, his personal spell book to help. He must think that you need a little help catching up with the other Initiates.'

'What other Initiates? Aren't I going to be Gydion's student?'

'Eventually, possibly. You see, all Initiates go to the Academy to begin their training and when they pass their trials, *if* they pass their trials, they become Adepts, then a Master will choose one to continue their tutelage.'

'Great, back to college huh?' he huffed. 'How long does it take to progress?'

'That depends on the student. A year, maybe two years, but father told me stories of some that did it in half the time. At the Academy, when you're ready, you're *ready* and with Father's spell book you will be ready in no time.'

'I'm not so sure. I mean, I read through the Book of Azul several times and I still couldn't cast anything. Maybe it's going to be harder for me to become a mage than we all think.'

'Don't be stupid, Daniel,' Trinity said as she hit him on the head with a knuckle. 'If you could cast a spell just by picking up a book and reading the incantations and following the gestures, then everyone would be doing it. It takes a little more than that. You need to tap into the correct energies for the spell, Personal, Planetary, or Realmic, and then you need to focus on the area within that energy that pertains to the element of the spell you are trying to cast; arcane, fire, earth, air, and water.'

'I did notice that all the spells in the book seemed to be water-based. So, I would need to concentrate on the water area of Personal energy whilst reciting the spell and repeating the gestures, right?'

'Exactly! There you go, you're learning already! But the more powerful spells will call upon Planetary or Realmic energies.'

'Seems like a lot of multitasking is involved; how do I access the energy, anyway?'

'By being calm and putting yourself in the trance like I taught you. Then you have to concentrate on the energy centre of the type of Essence you wish to use. Although our Personal Essence flows throughout our bodies, its reservoir is located here.' Trinity placed her hand on Daniel's lower abdomen, just below his belly button. The unexpected touch of her soft hand made him flinch and she smiled innocently at his awkwardness towards her contact. She smiled even more when she moved her hand up to his chest and felt his heart beating fast. 'This is where the Planetary Essence reservoir is and finally,' she placed her hand on his forehead and became aware of the cold nervous sweat forming there, 'this is where you access the Realmic Essence, right between your eyes.'

She looked deeply into Daniel's yellow eyes and he was lost in her own dark green ones. They were so close that he could feel her warm breath on his lips and he noticed the light dusting of freckles across her nose for the first time.

Neither spoke as the intimate moment overwhelmed them, before it was replaced by an awkwardness brought on by their inexperience at dealing with such familiarity. Trinity removed her hand and quickly continued walking down the street after Fungal, and she hoped Daniel had not seen her cheeks redden.

She was getting into the swing of being a tutor to Daniel; the fact that she enjoyed his company made the potentially daunting process more manageable and she was determined to put him on the right track to reaching the greatness her father believed he would scale.

'The reservoirs are like batteries,' Trinity resumed after clearing her throat and regaining her composure. 'They can be depleted, but they can be recharged using the technique I taught you the other day. They can also be temporarily boosted beyond their normal capacity, making your spells more powerful. More accomplished mages are even able to shift their Essence from one reservoir to another. That technique is particularly useful in combat, especially when you know that you will be using one type of energy more than another.'

Daniel had been listening intently to Trinity but he barely paid attention to what she had just said, due in part to the girl herself. You hear about instances when things click and serendipity shines on you, when the heavens align and you have a 'moment.'

Daniel believed he had just experienced his first.

'Och! We're going the wrong way!' Fungal suddenly said as he pushed past them and headed back the way they had just come from.

'What do you mean? The tavern's just over there.'

'And it'll be closed, like every other shop we've passed or have ye been too gooey eyed with ye lass there ta notice that?'

'What are you talking about? I'm not gooey anything!' Daniel was quick to protest the Boggart's comment but as he looked around he saw that Fungal was right; shops were closed or were in the process of closing. The streets of Almedia were a lot quieter than they were when he had first arrived in the city and what few people remained were all headed in the same direction. The trio soon followed, since there was nothing else they could do, for the Beltane Festival was about to begin.

As they headed out of the Eastern Gate and proceeded towards the near-by fields and eminences, Fungal took it upon himself to explain the meaning of the great festival to his two uninitiated companions.

Each of the four main events of the Faerie calendar, Imbolg, Beltane, Lammas, and Samhain, celebrated the life cycle of the Great Goddess and her consort from youngster, maid, mother, and finally her transformation to crone. Legend tells that together they had given birth to the Tuatha, who in turn created Ariest, amongst other realms.

Beltane, the time of union and pleasure, signified the first day of summer and was the time when the Goddess, as the maid, entered into marriage with her consort. Maypoles and garlands, music and dances were all part of the modern fair, as well as competitions and the great feast later in the evening.

When Daniel had first come to the city, he remembered seeing lots of children going about with handcarts from house to house collecting wood. Now he saw those carts again and the wood being thrown onto a giant pile in preparation for the lighting of the sacred fire and several smaller ones.

As the trio entered the field, a bunch of flowers were suddenly thrust into Daniel's face.

'Welcome to the greatest Beltane Festival in all of Ariest!'

Daniel took a deep breath of the intoxicating scent of the flowers before he lowered them and saw that they were being offered to him by a familiar person. 'Oh, it's you!'

'You remember me?' said a surprised Finn.

'Of course. I saw you when I first came to the city, although we didn't talk, and then again at the tavern. I didn't get to thank you before, but if it wasn't for you I would never have seen who had taken my book.'

'Did you get it back?'

'Yes, I did, with the help of Tristan.'

'He's always looking for adventure and enjoying himself, that one.'

'So I gather.'

'But I'm glad you got it back.'

'Thanks again and thanks for these,' he said acknowledging the flowers. 'What's your name, by the way?'

'My names Finnuala; people just call me Finn though.'

'And I'm –'

'Daniel, I know. Well, enjoy the festival, Daniel.' All of a sudden, Finn turned around and disappeared into the growing crowds.

Trinity had been watching the whole encounter with Fungal at her side and was about to question Daniel about his new friend when he was unexpectedly and rather immediately taken to one side and led into a gazebo; Trinity herself was taken to an identical one on the other side, their protests ignored. Fungal, left to his own devices, shrugged his shoulders, lit another cigar, and wandered off into the throng.

'Come along,' a motherly woman said as she fussed around Daniel. 'It's almost time for the Wheel Run.'

'The what run?' he questioned. She was in the process of tying on a sweet-smelling belt of herbs around his waist when he suddenly heard Tristan's voice behind him.

'The Wheel Run. It's a big part of the Beltane Festival. The single men partake in a few events to determine what single woman they will marry in the future.' He put his hand on Daniel's shoulder and led him to the opening of the tent. Tristan pointed across the field at a large tree with aerial prop roots that were thick and woody which were indistinguishable from the main trunk. The canopy of the tree had spread out laterally using the prop roots to cover a wide area. It looked like a group of trees but, in reality, it was only one very old tree. 'That is the second event, the Climb of Affiance,' Tristan stated. 'In that event you will need to climb one of those Fir trees that are standing in those brushwood-filled pits. Do you see at the tops, there? Before the event, the single women will send flower fairies to attach rose garlands to the tops of the Firs and that's what we, the single men, will retrieve.'

'Are you nuts? I'm not looking for a wife! No, no, no, no-way am I taking part!' Daniel began to struggle with the herb belt as he tried to take it off.

'It's too late, it's deemed bad luck to remove your belt now,' laughed Tristan. 'Are you sure you don't want to participate? After all, I saw that redhead you came here with; quite a beauty, I must say. She was taken to the single women tent, so no doubt one of those garlands up there belongs to her. Surely you wouldn't want her ending up with some village yokel? And it seems young Finn has taken quite a fancy to you too, for some reason.'

Daniel had a look around and saw a man with his finger so far up his nose he thought he must be scratching his frontal lobe!

'Don't look so worried,' Tristan continued. 'I got Eveline through these games a few years ago, and we're not married.'

'Then what are you doing here again? You looking to build up a harem?'

'No, I'm here for the competition,' he said, slapping Daniel on the back. 'Do not stress yourself, my friend, you have to pass the first event before you can start contemplating the marriage part.'

'And what is the first event?'

Tristan directed Daniel's gaze to the top of the steep hill on the other side of the nearby lake. At its summit stood a number of huge wheels. 'That is the first event, the Wheel Run. It's also the only event that you will be working together with another single man. Basically, the two of you will run the wheel down the hill and into the lake.'

'Well, that sounds simple enough,' Daniel said with some relief. Tristan was about to continue his explanation of the event, but at that moment he was interrupted.

'Okay, boys, come along, come along. It's time!' The woman that was in charge of getting the single males prepared for the day's events led the assembly of single men out into the grassland to the cheers of hundreds.

It was a beautiful May morning; barely a cloud in the pale pink sky and the light blue and lilac suns shone brightly. Daniel and the other contestants filed through the crowd that seemed to part before them. They were applauded as they passed and a feeling of elation came over the earth boy. *So this is what it felt like to be adored,* Daniel thought as he looked over at Tristan, who was playing up to the crowd, as usual, and enjoying every minute of their adulation. He spotted stalls selling drinks and snacks and then others with fairground games that looked similar to the ones back on Earth.

Then he saw that the single women were also being led out of their tent and when Daniel spotted Trinity he couldn't help but smile. Everywhere she went she made friends. She had a welcoming ease about her that people seemed to gravitate to, and the way she just seemed to 'fit in' like she had always been there intrigued him, especially since he himself usually found it so difficult looking so different to everyone else.

She was holding her sandals as she walked barefoot through the field, laughing and talking with the other girls; everything around her seemed to disappear and the world slowed down as he watched her.

Then Daniel caught sight of Finnuala; she was entered into the games also! She seemed to be rather popular with the other girls too, but for different reasons. And then he thought back to what Tristan had just said about her 'taking a fancy to him.' Surely, he was mistaken; they had only just met, after all. But as he looked on he would be lying if he said he wasn't intrigued by her; her short, tousled fuchsia-coloured hair with its violet highlights, her brass-rimmed goggles pushed up on her head, the interesting guns she had with her. To Daniel's eyes, she was definitely someone who valued her individuality and wasn't one to conform for the sake of conforming.

Just then, Trinity looked up as if she were suddenly aware that she was being watched. She caught sight of Daniel through the crowd and a big smile broke across her face as she waved at him. She attempted to make her way over to him but was shepherded along with the other single women by their doyenne, which prompted her to smile and shrug apologetically towards her friend.

As Daniel came back to reality, he could hear mutterings from amongst the single men concerning the red-haired one.

'Are you *sure* you still want to pull out?' Tristan pressured the still-reluctant Daniel. 'Because there seem to be quite a few fellers that might be willing to chance their luck at finding *her* garland, me included.'

Daniel looked at Tristan incredulously, stunned by the obvious challenge. Perhaps he had been wrong to trust Tristan so implicitly so quickly. His good experiences with Nyriel, Ch'tan, and the Mudds had possibly given him a slanted perspective of the inhabitants of Ariest; maybe they all weren't as helpful as *they* had been. But Tristan *had* caught the thief and recovered the Book of Azul; to his own gain, admittedly, and where was he when the Council of Three was accusing Daniel of murder?

He gazed down at his feet as he continued to follow the other singletons and pondered Tristan's actions. His mind drifted to the last person who threaten Trinity's virtue, Bobby Brinkmeyer.

Those days seemed such a long time ago, literally worlds apart. He was becoming a different person now though, more assured of himself, not so willing to cower away and accept things as they were. He didn't know if it was the fact that here on Ariest he *was* different not because of how he looked but because he could do magic, and it instilled in him a self-confidence that he had lacked most of his life. One thing was certain now, he wouldn't be bullied anymore.

'You won't get Trinity's garland; in fact, the only time you are going to see it is when I bring it down myself.'

Tristan turned to his young companion, smiled, and slapped him on the back with a hearty, booming, and ever so slightly mocking laugh.

The doyenne brought the gathering of unattached men to a halt in front of a raised platform on which stood three chairs, similar to the ones Daniel had seen at his trial. Behind the dais was a huge draped curtain that stretched right across the glade, obscuring everything behind it. When two men pushed through the curtain, Daniel, and almost everyone else, craned their necks and tried to get a glimpse of what was hidden behind it, but their attempts failed.

The two men carried a brass box that had several conical horns on either side, in ever-increasing dimensions. They placed it down a few steps in front of the three chairs and then left the platform.

Their departure was a cue for the curtain to be once again parted and the Council of Three filed out. They wore even more regal attire than they had before, especially for the celebration, Daniel assumed, as he watched Empress Xu and Chief Seydou take their seats whilst King Ewynn stood before the brass box.

Almost immediately, the top opened and what looked like a microphone head floated out of it and called to a stop level with the king's mouth. 'Welcome, one and all, to the best and greatest Beltane Festival in all of Ariest!' Cheers and applause rang out all around the field. 'And I do not make this claim because I am one of the regents of this city. No, I make this claim because of you, the beings of this world, who travel here from far and wide to sample the festivities for yourselves. So, once again I say, welcome one and all! Now, before we get the first event of the Beltane Games underway, I would like to extend a hearty gratitude to Eveline Durling for another magical spread,' he said and gestured toward the curtain behind him. 'I do not know how you manage to top yourself year after year, young lady, but you do it each time.' The young cook waved to acknowledge the applause. 'We would also like to thank all the taverns, alehouses, and bakeries of Almedia for allowing Eveline the use of your kitchens. Now, let us celebrate the union of the maid incarnation of the Goddess and her consort! Let us find the ones whose union is fated to be and shall be blessed! Let us find the ones who will bring favour from the Goddess and ensure a bountiful harvest! Let us begin the Beltane contest!'

26

The male entrants of the contest, to discover the representatives of the Goddess and the Consort for this year's festival, had been brought the short distance to the bank of the Didas Bay. It would have been an easy, short walk but they were transported in horse-drawn carriages all the same; Daniel was told that they would need their stamina for the event itself.

The procession of Beltane revellers that had been following the carriages was now lining the shore. They hadn't stopped singing and dancing the whole time and the atmosphere was so infectious that even Daniel was responding to the adulation that they were showering upon the contestants.

He felt like some sort of sporting hero as he waved and acknowledged the crowd, much like Tristan did. This was a whole new experience for Daniel, but it was something he thought he could learn to enjoy, as he and the other men stepped off the coaches and into several oar-less wherries.

The enchanted boats sailed themselves across the gentle waters of the Didas Bay, each one ferrying competitors to the start point of the Wheel Run, the first event of Ariest's annual celebration.

The Didas Bay was a major estuary in the south west of Ariest. It was fed by the Calloap Sea and many of the waterways of the region were linked to it; the Shimmering Lake and the mighty Akerhern River, which ran far to the north, were two such bodies of water.

A few miles out to sea, beyond the mouth of the bay, was a four-mountain range known as The Giant's Fist. This was the course heading of the enchanted boats. They resembled knuckles rising out of the water and Daniel was told the legend that claimed it was the hand of a giant that was encapsulated, in the core of Ariest, when it was formed. When the ground quaked, the olden folk would frighten the children and say that it was the giant trying to break free.

The boats came ashore and the doyenne disembarked, followed by the men. There was a mix of emotions amongst the group; some excited patting each other on the back and gearing themselves up for the event, others quiet with dread trepidation almost like they had been forced into the games by their parents.

Daniel couldn't understand what the fuss was all about; after all, how hard could it really be to push a wheel down a hill? Admittedly, the hill was a mountain and it was a bit bigger than he had first expected it to be, but the elevation wasn't anything drastic and at the end of the day it was just a matter of running downhill. No wonder Tristan was walking with such an air of confidence, Daniel thought, as he tried in vain to emulate his companion's stride.

The doyenne led them up the beach towards the foot of the mountains, and eventually came to a halt at a large gold glassless mirror-frame.

'Gather round, come closer, that's it. Now, I am Doyenne Swanston and, as you are all aware, this is the Wheel Run. The rules are unchanged but I will go over them anyway for the first timers. Anyone who does not remain in contact with the axle of his wheel will be eliminated, along with his partner. The winning pair will have uncontested choice of a garland in the next event. The Climb of Affiance has a staggered start so where you finish in the run will determine where you start in the climb, so my advice to you, don't dilly-dally. And finally, the Beltane Games may be a contact sport but let's try to keep the casualties down this year.'

'Casualties? What casualties?' Daniel exclaimed before being shushed by Tristan.

'Now,' the doyenne continued, 'if each pairing would like to walk through the portal, you will all be randomly assigned to a wheel.'

One by one each twosome went through the mirror frame and instantly vanished; Daniel, however was still too concerned with what he had just heard to fully appreciate the idea of instant teleportation.

'So,' he started nonchalantly to Tristan as they waited for their turn, 'these casualties...'

'Nothing to worry about really, one guy tried to use an enchantment to take over another runner's wheel, but not being a real magic user, he did not have the necessary ability to control it, ended up crashing it into his wheel and three others, killing five in total including himself.'

They stepped through the mirror frame and in the blink of an eye they had gone from the foot of the mountain to its flattened peak. Daniel and Tristan reappeared in a line with the other participants that had already been transported. In front of each pair of runners was a large wicker wheel, at least fifteen feet high. Daniel looked at it in a perplexed manner as the final few runners appeared.

He was in a quandary because he couldn't figure out how a wicker wheel could have killed five people. Sure, it was big, it might give you some cuts and bruises, maybe even break a bone or two, but kill, nah.

The doyenne was the last to appear and after a quick glance down the line of suitors, just to be sure everyone had been assigned a wheel, she proceeded with the final preparations. 'Now that the selection process is complete, we are about ready to begin; just one final thing to do.' She took a small box from her pocket, roughly the size of a box you would get a watch in, and flipped the lid open. 'Come on, my little fire sprite, it's time to wake up and do your stuff.'

A flame rested in the centre of the box and grew in size until it was a fiery cherub floating above the doyenne's hand.

'Can I at least get something to eat first?' yawned the fire sprite.

'Of course.' She gave the sprite some tinder from her pocket and the elemental greedily ate it down, each mouthful creating little puffs of smoke.

Once the fire sprite had finished its meal, it rubbed its belly and with a satisfied smile on its little cheeky face, leapt into the air. It left trails of fire as it spun through the sky performing loops and barrel rolls.

After a few moments, it came to a stop above the competitors, a perfect height to fulfil its role as the Beltane fire starter. It threw its arms open in a flamboyant manner and sent fireballs at the wicker wheels, igniting them in blazing infernos, all the while singing a merry tune.

Several of the competitors started at the sudden infernos, Daniel more than most. It now quickly became clear to him how it was possible to have casualties in a so-called simple downhill race.

He could feel the sweat getting ready to break out on his forehead, and it wasn't just from the heat; his nerves were skyrocketing. Daniel took a glance at his companion, perhaps hoping to get some strength from him, but he got even more nervous. Tristan had a determined glare on his face. He was a winner; he loved the competition, the battle, and he was getting in the zone for another bout. Daniel didn't want to let this man down, but, more importantly, he didn't want to let himself down.

'You ready for this?' Tristan asked, sensing Daniel's anxiousness.

'Nope.'

'It's simple; just hold on, don't get too close to the fire, and run as fast as you can.'

'That simple, huh?'

'The time has come, gentlemen,' the doyenne suddenly said. 'If you would all take hold of your axles now, we are about to begin the run.' She looked down the line, first one way then the other, to make sure everyone was ready and on their marks. After a few moments of jostling, when they had all settled down, she signalled the fire sprite. At her command, the elemental threw fireballs into the air that exploded into a fiery three-second countdown. When it reached zero, the men heaved on their axles and charged down the hill.

The Wheel Run contest had begun!

27

As the runners set off, Daniel discovered that the wheel was a lot heavier than he had thought it would be, as it immediately began to veer to the right, since Tristan was applying more force on his side of the wheel.

'Come on, Daniel!' Tristan urged. 'Pick up the pace! We need to straighten up!'

It was already too late, however. The wheel continued to travel off course. The runner next to Daniel screamed at his partner to speed up, but it still wasn't fast enough and he was forced to release his hold and dive out of the way as the wayward flaming giant wheel collided with their own.

Along the mainland coast, spectators clapped and cheered as they witnessed the first action of the annual race.

'Yer beau seems to be struggling a wee bit there, lassie.' Trying to get a rise out of people was Fungal's favorite pastime, after tormenting poor old Rustin, of course, and he seemed to have found the perfect mark in Trinity.

'Well, it's a new experience for him. He can do it, you just watch. He'll pull through, I believe in him' she said optimistically. 'And he's not my 'beau',' she finished firmly.

'Keep telling yerself that, lassie, maybe one day you'll believe it!' he laughed.

Back in the race, Tristan had slowed down his pace enough for his companion to straighten up the wheel. 'Are you still with me, Daniel?' he asked. 'Good,' he continued after hearing Daniel's response. 'Now, I am going to need to you to run as fast as you can and I will match. Let us see if we cannot catch these stragglers!'

The race was beginning to unfold. Of the nine remaining wheels in the run, Daniel and Tristan were in a distant last place. The three front-runners had broken away and the chasing pack jostled for position.

To get anywhere in the race it really was necessary to cooperate with your wheel partner; sync your steps for a smooth run, pull back when he pushed forward, and vice versa, when steering. It was something that a few of the runners were failing at and what Daniel was starting to get the hang of.

Daniel and Tristan were steadily closing in on the back-markers when the true competitive nature of the race was revealed. Ahead of them, in the middle pack, three explosions sounded, in quick succession, which rocked the ground.

'That was no doubt Charles Simmons. He always brings a bag of tricks with him! Be on your guard, Daniel!'

It was a timely warning. There was another series of explosions and since they were closer to the other runners now, Daniel could actually see the explosives. They reminded him of helicopter seeds from a maple tree. He was almost mesmerized by their floaty rotational flight, but that soon turned to horror as one of the tennis ball-sized objects hit one of the wheels in the chasing pack, blowing it apart and sending the runners flying through the air. Daniel and Tristan were once more last in the race.

'Isn't there something you can do with your magic?' Tristan yelled. 'You're supposed to be a mage, aren't you?'

'In training,' corrected Daniel. 'Anyway, it wouldn't help if I was because I can't take my hands off the axle, so how am I supposed to cast a spell?'

'That didn't stop you from making it snow in the tavern.'

'That was an accident.'

'Well, we could do with another one of those accidents if you want to progress to the next round, or have you decided to let someone else win your friend's hand?'

Not a chance! To Daniel this was his opportunity. He couldn't tell her about the feelings he got when he was near her but if he were to win her garland it would mean that fate was on his side and perhaps she would see it like that too. But coming last in this Wheel Run would put a swift end to his plans.

So, what can I do to make sure that we get through?, thought Daniel. *I'm already running as fast as I can, and I feel like I'm holding Tristan back, to be honest. I guess I'm more built for long distance than sprinting. So, I guess that leaves only one thing...magic. But how? Like I told him, I can't use my hands to cast, but I've made things happen before by thinking about it, like when I made myself invisible. Trinity said it was because I don't have control of it and it leaked out. I guess that's what happened at the tavern too. All I was doing was reading the grimoire then I was lost in the spell.*

A sudden jerk to the right brought Daniel back to his senses. Tristan was forcing them wide, but the size of the flaming wheel blocked his view of his partner. 'What's going on?' he yelled over the roar of the fire.

'These bastards are trying to crash us! It's us or them and they're looking to make sure it's us!'

'Then I guess we have no choice but to try and use some accidental magic then. But I hope you know that this might not go as planned.'

'Well,' laughed Tristan, 'it is better to fail trying than not to try at all!'

While Daniel and Tristan ran their hearts out, Trinity was having the time of her life, having fun and enjoying being swept up in the euphoria of the celebration. It was a whole new experience for her, like being at the Grand National, but with a little less formalwear. With all her years on Earth accompanying Gideon, she had never been to any occasion like this before. There was never any time for such things; it was either training or searching for the person in Queen Rhiannon's visions, moving from city to city, school to school. But now that they had found Daniel, maybe she could enjoy the things in life a bit more.

All around her, people were watching the event across the sea, cheering and shouting encouragement to the runners. Trinity followed suit by enthusiastically rooting for Daniel as if she were his own personal cheerleader. That was, until Fungal made an observation.

'Ye do realize that yer wee little beau isnae doing too good, right? Take a good look and ye can see him struggling...at the back,' he smirked. 'I guess he won't be bringing ye yer garland back huh? Oh well, I'm sure ye will find happiness with the man lucky enough to get it for ye,' laughed Fungal. 'And another thing, his Essence levels are rising; I think he might be trying to do something stupid.'

Trinity didn't reply; she just looked more carefully at the race, and sure enough, there were Daniel and Tristan being forced off of their race line. Surely, he couldn't be thinking about attempting to cast a spell.

With a few lightning quick hand signs, Trinity cast a spell and sent her astral form across the sea. Seconds later her ethereal form floated beside Daniel.

'Trinity!' Daniel was startled by the sudden appearance of his friend. 'What are you doing here? How did you get here? And why are you so...see through?'

'What? I can't hear you!' Tristan yelled

Trinity giggled at Daniel's naivety. Having the power that she knew he had within him and yet having next to no knowledge of the basic fundamental of being a mage amused her. *This is my astral form, I've made it so only you can see it at the moment. My body is still across on the other shore.*

'It's like I can hear you in my head.'

'Yes, so you have no need to speak; just think it and I will know it.'

'Man, do you know how distracting this is?'

'I came over because Fungal seems to think that you're going to use some magic. You surely couldn't be considering doing something as stupid as that, could you? Especially after what I told you about being a loaded gun and the dangers involved with untrained Initiates using magic.'

'I've done it before.'

'Really? Did you call upon the magic? Mold it to your will and release it?'

'No. It just kind of happened,' he admitted.

'And that's a big difference. If you don't know how to properly control the energies summoned, it's very easy to lose control. You could kill everybody here, maybe even yourself.'

'I have to do something. Tristan is counting on me. Maybe you haven't noticed, but I'm kind of at the back of the race.'

'Big deal! It's not worth playing with fire, Daniel.'

'It is to me! Some of these guys are hoping to pick up your garland, and - well, I don't think they would be a good enough suitor for you.'

If Daniel didn't have his eyes focused straight ahead he might have glimpsed Trinity's coquettish smile. *'And how do you know who is and isn't a good suitor for me?'*

'Well, something told me, and I don't know what it was, but I just got this feeling that you wouldn't be interested in a guy that would be speaking to you with his finger jammed up his nose.'

'Okay, you may have a point there,' she agreed. *'So, you want my garland for yourself then?'*

'No! I mean yes, but only to protect you from them!'

'Like you protected my virtue against Bobby Brinkmeyer?'

Just then the cheers reached a new level as the first runners crossed the finish line and their flaming wheels hissed as they submerged into the ocean, creating great plumes of steam.

Time was running out for Daniel and Tristan. There were two other teams of runners left in the race and they were both pulling away. They had used enchantments during the race but since none of the four was a mage or a master of enchantments, they had to rely on vendors. But, like so many things in life, you get what you pay for, and as they were not particularly flush with gold, they had to shop at the lower end of the magic establishments.

Using these kinds of places was a hit or miss affair; either your item worked perfectly or it didn't. The unevenness and roughness of the race-course revealed that what Tom had left in his bag were misses.

His satchel bounced up and down as he ran, an action that caused the poorly crafted enchanted bombs to become unstable and shoot sparks into the air. Tom ripped the smoking bag off of his shoulder and threw it into the air behind him. He sighed with relief, having narrowly avoided disaster. A few moments passed before it dawned on him exactly what he had done. In his panic to get rid of the bombs, Tom had used both of his hands, and in so doing, had eliminated himself and his partner from the Wheel Race.

The bag of explosives flew through the air, sporadically dropping its payload; impact craters began to pepper the racecourse, where the little items met the ground. One such indentation happened just in front of Volston Fontonby, causing him to almost lose his footing, but it was enough to slow him to a stop. His partner, Sam Nessby, unaware of what had befallen his comrade, had continued his run, forcing their wheel to eventually end up pointing to the left.

'Now is our chance,' Tristan yelled. 'Push on! We can still make it!'

'He's right, Daniel, you can do it! And without magic, you just have to believe in yourself.' With those final words of encouragement, Trinity's astral form vanished.

Believe in yourself. Believe in yourself. Since Volston and Sam had to straighten up and began running again, from a standing start, Daniel and Tristan gained on them so quickly that Daniel did start to believe. The course was no longer as smooth as when the race had begun but, with Tristan's competitive nature and Daniel's newfound determination, the potholes couldn't slow them.

They were edging past their opponents when, in desperation to cling onto his position, Volston swung a backhand at Tristan. The strike was evaded, barely, but what ensued was a ferocious one-handed battle between the two. It continued unabated until Tristan and Daniel's wheel hit a rut, which juddered both of them, forcing the former to lose his footing, momentarily giving Volston the slimmest of opportunities which he pounced on and pummeled Tristan with several heavy blows.

It looked like Tristan and Daniel were about to be eliminated when, in a moment of rashness and defiance, Tristan made one final attempt to secure their position with what could be an all-or-nothing move. 'Hold fast,' he shouted to his partner. Another strike was about to crash down on him, but before it could hit, Tristan moved into action.

He switched his right hand into a supinated grip and swung underneath his side of the wheel axle, until his body was parallel with it. His feet dragged along the ground before he brought them up and into a tuck position. He hung there for a second, taking aim, and then, with two rapid strikes, he fired out his feet and hammered the side of Volston's knee. In an instant, Tristan had swung back to an upright position, at the same moment his opponent's knee collapsed, his feet dragging behind him as he clung onto his axle, desperate to finish the race and progress to the next round.

To Volston's credit, he did just that but, unfortunately for him and his partner, it was behind a jubilant Daniel and Tristan. Although it wasn't as high a position as Tristan was used to being in, he was happy enough not to have come last. Looking over at Daniel, who was flushed, sweaty, and breathing heavily, but who still had energy enough to celebrate as if he had won the whole event, put a bigger smile on his face and he couldn't help breaking out into a hearty laugh.

And he wasn't the only one pleased. Trinity applauded happily, jumped up and down, and cheered Daniel's efforts.

'You do realize that he barely came in second to last?' Fungal pessimistically said.

Trinity stopped and, in a determined manner said, 'Maybe he did, but he just learnt an important lesson. He learnt that he doesn't have to rely on magic for everything.' She turned to face Fungal and said, 'Besides, a personal victory is still a big win no matter how small others perceive it to be.'

28

Now that the first event had ended, it was time to eat. It was a buffet banquet, but it was like no buffet Daniel had ever seen before.

The curtains and dais that had been there at the start of the Beltane Festival had been removed to reveal a large clearing, roughly the size of a football ground, surrounded by trees. There were long rows of tables covered with food, one with fish dishes, one with meats, another with vegetables and side dishes, and one with desserts.

Some of the foods on offer Daniel could hazard a guess at their earthly comparison; others would remain a mystery unless he were courageous enough to try them, but one thing was certain: there were endless combinations of meals available. Daniel's stomach suddenly growled as he realised he was very hungry after his efforts in the Wheel Run.

The bachelors and bachelorettes were given first access to the open-air dining area. Daniel looked around, hoping to see Trinity. To his dismay, each of the ladies had a chaperone, a stony-faced doyenne, but there was Trinity enjoying herself.

Daniel was about to try and get her attention when all of a sudden, he heard a familiar voice behind him.

'Congratulations on getting through, Daniel!'

'Thanks! Finn, wasn't it?'

She nodded and smiled inside. *He remembered my name.*

'To be honest,' Daniel continued, 'Tristan did most of the work.'

'It takes two to push one of those things, so as far as I'm concerned you did your fair share of the work.'

'Yeah, I guess you're right,' he smiled shyly. 'Aren't you supposed to be with a chaperone?'

'I've been dodging oldies for as long as I can remember. I'm a bit of a dab hand at going undetected.'

'That must come in handy.'

'It does!' Finn replied with excitement. 'Sneaking out of bedrooms, leaving without paying for stuff, even doing the odd bit of thieving...' She caught herself when she saw Daniel's raised eyebrows and realised she may have exposed a little too much of her nature. She was leader of a gang, after all, and, as such, she prided herself at being able to lead by example. Pilfering a berry pie was an easy way to keep the troops in line by showing that she was one of them; not everyone got that though. 'What I'm trying to say,' she continued defensively, trying to rescue the situation, 'is that it comes in pretty handy.'

Daniel couldn't hide his look of shock and awe as he studied Finn more closely; her purple-streaked, violet hair, the blast goggles on her head, the slightly broken nose and small scar on her top lip, and then there were those guns. She had a unique style; well, it would be back home, he thought, but here it seems to be the norm.

'Look, Daniel,' Finn suddenly said as she angrily pointed a finger at him, 'I may not be the perfect little princess like your friend Trinity, but that doesn't mean you have to stare at me!'

'Whoa!' said Daniel as he held up his hands in surrender. 'I'm sorry, I didn't mean to. I'm just a bit blown away, that's all.'

'Blown away?'

'Yeah, I've never met a bandit before.'

An incredulous look passed Finn's face. 'A bandit? I'm no bandit! A scallywag, a sassy scoundrel, maybe a rebel rouser,' she said as she counted off each of the names she had been called over the years. 'Delinquent, mischiefmaker, rapscallion, reprobate, ruffian, gamine, hoyden even whippersnapper, but never bandit. The women in town say I need to put down my guns and stop hanging out with the boys, else I'll never find a husband, but that's not causing me sleepless nights.'

'But I thought you were with someone. That guy I saw you with when I first got to the city?'

'Huh? You mean Jimbo? Vekt! Goddess no! He's a good friend, part of the gang. I know he wants more; we've been hanging out together for so long everyone expects it, but I can't give it to him. He's like a brother to me.'

'He's in the competition; he could end up with you.'

'I think fate has other plans for me,' she said with a twinkle in her eye. 'Are you ready for the next event?'

'No, I'm not much of a climber either...except for when I'm being chased.'

Daniel saw the confused look on Finn's face and he explained how things were for him back home, how he had been ostracised all his life, how he had been looked upon as a freak, an outsider, ridiculed, and bullied.

'But you're a mage! Why would you let them do that to you?'

'There are no magic users in my world, so I didn't know I was a mage until recently, when Gydion told me.'

'No magic?' She turned this concept over in her mind as she tried to imagine what a world without magic would be like. 'Well, you could use your hands, fight them.'

'Have you seen me?' he replied, opening his arms wide to emphasise the point that he wasn't a fighter. 'Besides, I promised my parents that I wouldn't, even though my dad is some Faerie warrior hero.'

'Well, if I was there with you, I'd kick their butts all over the...wait a minute! Your dad's a hero? Who is he?'

'Eric Mondragon.'

Finn's mouth dropped in astonishment. She had read about the heroic exploits of Mondragon since she was a child. He was more than a hero to her, he was a legend, and now she found out that the boy she was attracted to was the son of her idol. '*The* Eric Mondragon? You're jesting me, aren't you?'

Before Daniel could offer a reply, a hand clamped down on the shoulder of his companion. 'You thought you could escape me, Finnuala Jesson?' the doyenne challenged. 'You know you shouldn't be fraternizing with the young men! Now come along.'

Finn tried to free herself, but the elderly doyenne was surprisingly strong and she soon gave up the struggle as she was carted off. 'Good luck in the climb!' she called over her shoulder. 'And don't eat too much!'

The two suns of Ariest had begun to set, casting long shadows of the forest across the field. The revellers didn't seem to pay any attention to the passing of time; they had enjoyed a thrilling race, had eaten well, and now waited anxiously for the next event.

Of the ten wheels that had started the first Beltane event, only six had crossed the finish line; twenty runners had been whittled down to twelve and they now stood in the order that they completed the race and prepared themselves for the next event, the Climb of Affiance.

The crowds were a lot closer than they had been during the previous event, separated then by the lake, but now their cheering and hollering hit Daniel like a wall of sound. He glanced around and saw a look of genuine joy and happiness on every face, lit by the flickering flames from the torches placed everywhere, heard the crackling, and smelt the burning fires of the giant bonfire in the distance. How could someone not be taken by the infectious euphoria? It was the season of laughter, freedom, happiness, and music. He was feeling it, the Beltane Festival, and he smiled.

The lead doyenne once more stood before them and held up her hands as she shushed the audience to silence. 'We have witnessed the first event,' she began and cheers rang out in agreement, 'we have once more enjoyed Eveline's feast,' cheers again replied, 'and now it is time for the second event of the Beltane Festival, the Climb of Affiance!' The crowd roared its delight. Quiet eventually descended to allow the doyenne to continue. 'The climb will pit bachelor against bachelor as you each try to retrieve a garland and then at the end present it to the bachelorette you believe it belongs to. If you are correct, then as a couple you move on to the next round. If you are wrong, then fate has not shined upon you and you will be eliminated from the competition. One more thing: climbers are allowed to collect as many garlands as they wish, but any that fall and hit the ground become void, as does the bachelorette it belonged to. As always, the winners of the Wheel Run will each be allowed to choose a garland and ascend to it uncontested. At one-minute intervals, the rest of the competitors will be released in the order they completed the run; Tobias Goodwyn and Isaac Maynwaring will be next followed by James Wallace and Charles Simmons then Kwame Thorn and Huang Evyngal, Adacram Lee and Rodan Taylor, and finally Tristan Sturm and Daniel Welsh. Now, if Simon and Steven Waltonware would step up, and can I have the rest of you line up behind them in finishing order, we will get this event started.'

The spectators showed their appreciation as the competitors followed the instructions. There was a short countdown before, with the eruption of the crowd, the Waltonware twins set off, but rather than the expectant flying start of a sprinter, it was more akin to a leisurely stroll through a park.

The brothers collected their respective garlands, waved, and held their prizes aloft. The fans met their roars of elation; now they could relax and see who would be joining them in the next round.

5...4...3...2...1, go!

The next pair, Tobias Goodwynn and Isaac Maynwaring, were off. And this time there was no languid stroll; they sprinted off like their lives depended on it. Thirteen garlands left for the ten remaining hunters would usually be good odds but by the time it was Daniel's turn to ascend the tree, he had noticed that, whereas Charles, Kwame, and Huang had all beat a hasty retreat upon retrieving their prize, Jimbo had stayed to collect more, to increase his chances of finding Finn's own wreath.

'Excellent!' Tristan roared with jubilation. He was aware of his companion's confused look at his outburst. 'Whereas the physical contact in the run is mostly accidental,' Tristan explained rubbing his hands, 'physical contact is all but guaranteed in the climb, especially if you are one of the last hunters.'

On hearing this, Daniel glanced back up at the tree and saw Jimbo and Rodan grappling over a garland. The tussle went back and forth until Rodan lost the wreath, along with his footing. Daniel winced as he heard the loud crack of Rodan's arm breaking as he hit the ground.

Jimbo's gaze fell unerringly on Daniel as he pulled the third of his prizes up his arm. Three garlands equalled three chances to succeed in winning her hand. All he needed to do now was to block Daniel and make sure he didn't get any.

29

Time was running out for five of the remaining six competitors. They climbed, jumped and swung their way up higher and higher into the magnificent tree, hunting down a festoon of flowers.

Daniel had spotted one, simply made with six pink and yellow flowers together on a wreath of green leaves. It was a few branches above him and on the other side of the tree trunk, but it seemed no one else had seen it.

He wondered whose it could be as he made his way as quickly and safely as he could along the branch. When Daniel reached out his hand and grabbed the garland, the wind suddenly changed and he caught the scent of freshly baked cinnamon rolls, the scent of something irresistible, something that seemed to call to him, something that he unexpectedly desired, something he needed to have.

He turned on his heels, determined to find the source of the aroma. 'Come and find me,' beseeched a voice in his head. 'I am the one you need, the one you want, come to me.'

'You're not going anywhere with that!' snarled Jimbo. He had jumped down and landed on the branch behind Daniel, his gaze fixated on the garland the off-worlder held. 'I've waited too long for this day, too long for fate to favour me and Finn, and I'm not about to let that chance go now that it's here, no matter how she looked at you. She should be with me, everyone knows that! I'm not about to lose her to you!'

'I don't know what you're talking about,' Daniel replied, shaking his head, 'besides, look at how many garlands you have already; you could have hers among them.'

'And then again I might not, so hand it over.' He held out his hand as he walked toward Daniel. With each step he took, Daniel stepped back, keeping the distance between them, until his back hit against the tree trunk.

Jimbo thought that was it, that his prey had nowhere else to run. Daniel, however, had other ideas. He still held the scent and he quickly made his escape, scampering up the tree in pursuit of its source. The native of Ariest was not so easily eluded and he took off after Daniel.

Being a much stronger climber, Jimbo was soon on the heels of his quarry once more. Daniel knew he couldn't outpace him, and as they climbed higher and higher, he knew that there was only one option left to him if he was to get away.

He threw the garland.

It hit Jimbo in the face like a bunch of flowers, which in affect it was, and although it didn't hit with any real force, it was still enough to distract his pursuer, who flayed about trying to catch the garland, but to no avail.

Daniel looked over his shoulder as he saw the garland Jimbo so badly wanted drift away, only to be snatched out of the air lower down the tree. A smile broke across Daniel's face as he watched Tristan add his newly acquired wreath to his other one.

Well, if Jimbo wants it he can try and get it from *him*, Daniel thought, confident that he had finally gotten rid of his nemesis.

His elation was short-lived, however, as, after a short pause, Jimbo resumed his pursuit.

More fire torches had been put up as the suns of Ariest had almost completely set, which would signal the climax of the second round of the festival games, and as Daniel continued his climb into the upper branches of the trees canopy, he knew he was within reach of his goal...the sweet spiced scent was so strong now. One final drive up and there it was. Nestled in some foliage at the end of the branch, oblivious to the troubles it had caused.

Daniel gleefully retrieved the garland but before he could take a single step towards making his way down, he heard the tree branch creek and he spun around to see Jimbo once more.

'So, this is the wreath you were truly after, and now it is the wreath that I will be taking from you.'

'Why do you want it? You've got more than enough.'

'Do I?' Jimbo replied as he held out his arm and pushed off his prized collection of festoons. 'Oops! It seems I don't have any. Oh well, I'll just have to take yours then.'

'You can't have it! It called to me, not you! It's mine!'

'I knew it! I bloody knew it!' Jimbo cried as if he had just uncovered some great secret. 'Gimme that garland!' Jimbo moved menacingly toward Daniel. 'You saw what happened to Rodan? What do you think would happen to you way up here if you fell?'

Down on the ground, Trinity couldn't believe what she was seeing, and she shot a look of accusation at Finn; it was her friend threatening Daniel, after all. If she had started his training proper, he could have just 'ported himself down; she thought that maybe she should send her astral form to lend a helping hand.

Daniel didn't get a chance to answer Jimbo's question as, all of a sudden, terrible screams pierced the twilight sky. Everyone left in the tree looked down and saw the crowds of people running this way and that. It was a chaotic scene, and individuals were pushed over and trampled by the stampede as people tried to escape with their lives, but escape from what? Daniel could see nothing. What was it that instilled so much fear into the populace?

Daniel! The sound of Trinity's mental shout in his head made him flinch with pain.

'*Ow!*' he replied as he rubbed his sore head. '*What's happening down there? What's going on?*'

'*Get out of the shadows! The Shade is here!*'

'The Shade?' whispered Daniel. As the words left his lips, out of the corner of his eye, he saw the shadows behind Jimbo begin to shimmer and ripple just before an ebony tentacle shot out of the inky blackness. 'Duck!' Daniel screamed as he grabbed Jimbo's arm and dragged him down. The person who was moments ago threatening him was now staring in wide-eyed terror as an appendage of the Essence vampire snaked overhead.

Daniel looked around anxiously, trying to find a means of escape before the tentacle could take another swipe at them. 'We have to jump,' Daniel said with dread realisation.

'You what?' Jimbo shouted before he saw the uproot Daniel was pointing at, and slowly nodded in agreement.

'We have to jump,' Daniel repeated. 'We slide it down as far as it goes and climb the rest of the way down.' He had barely finished explaining his plan before Jimbo had jumped for the root and slid his way down to the lower branches.

Now it was his turn…but his turn for what? He suddenly couldn't remember what he was supposed to be doing. A malaise had descended upon him and he didn't feel like doing anything; all Daniel wanted to do was sit down against the tree trunk and let everything pass him by.

Daniel turned to do just that, but in doing so he came face to face, so to speak, with the hideously stretched maw of the Shade that had begun to feed on Daniel's purple-coloured Essence. The realisation of seeing the creature made Daniel lose his footing. He desperately tried to keep it but he failed and toppled over the side of the branch and headlong toward the ground.

As soon as the creature from the realm of shadow had made its startling appearance, Trinity had sprung into action and helped with the evacuation of the field. It was what Gydion would have done, had he been there, and she had decided to take up the mantle in his absence.

Tristan returned to the ground as quickly as he could and helped clear the area, directing the guards and procuring a weapon for himself. Finn helped also, as soon as she finished making sure her guns were ready for the battle ahead.

'Forget the guns! They're useless against this thing!' shouted Trinity.

Finn looked at her unperturbed. Her heart was pounding with nervous excitement; too much to worry about what the 'princess' had to say. She knew she was an adventurer at heart and battling beasts is what adventurers did. She had always wanted to get out of Almedia for good and see what the world had to offer, pursue her dreams. She had had a chance in the past to leave, but the consequences that chance came with would have stifled her more than staying with her Uncle Quinn.

Fungal, unlike the others, was nowhere to be seen. He was no doubt doing what Fungal did best, looking after Fungal, Trinity concluded. She was just about to call the bogart, but she was cut short by Finn screaming Daniel's name. Trinity looked up at the tree, just in time to see her friend plunging to the ground.

In the blink of an eye she had transformed into a cheetah and raced towards the tree; a few seconds later she leapt into the air and transformed again, this time into a giant Roc. She beat her powerful wings, intent on catching Daniel on her back.

As fast as Trinity's reactions had been, she could only watch on as the Shade swooped in beneath Daniel and he plummeted into the creature's inky black depths and promptly vanished.

Trinity had no time to grieve the loss of her friend though, as the Shade immediately turned its attention to her, almost as if it sensed another being of significant levels of Essence. She took evasive action, swooping under and over every attack the Shade made at her. Even though it had grown to almost fifty metres in height, it still could not lay a tentacle on her. Eventually, when she had opened up a big enough space, Trinity had the time to land and go on the offensive, by transforming back to her normal body and letting off a volley of magical blasts.

Her vision blurred as tears welled up in her eyes. The loss of Daniel was beginning to take effect on her, no matter how strong she tried to be. He was gone and she hadn't had the chance to share her feelings with him. Hadn't had the chance to tell him that she had always liked his quiet nature, how she had felt a connection with him from the first day she had seen him, how she had always hoped that he would overcome his shyness and self-doubt and approach her, even if she were the popular girl and he was the outsider, then she could have told him that she had never felt this way before. That's what gave her tears of sadness a tinge of anger, anger at the extra dimensional creature that had taken her friend before a relationship had a chance to blossom, and she fully intended on letting the Shade feel her rage.

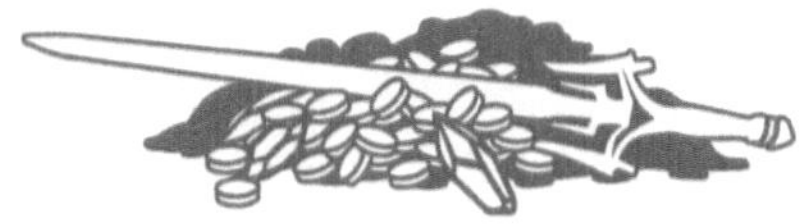

DANIEL OPENED HIS EYES and initially thought he was dead. All colour had been drained. Even the once brightly coloured garland Daniel still had on his arm was now different hues of black and white. Then he noticed that not all colour was gone; a deep purple corona surrounded his body.

He doubted that when Iris Apfel first came up with the phrase 'the world is not black and white, there are lots of shades of grey' was talking about this place even though that's exactly what this location was.

He scanned the monochrome landscape, not that there was much for Daniel to see; a desolate black vista, the meandering path he stood on disappeared into the panorama. In fact, the only thing that was interesting to see were the wispy wraiths that lined the path. His curiosity persuaded him to try touch one of them.

'They are the remnants of the beings this Shade has consumed,' a voice suddenly stated from behind Daniel, a fact which made him almost jump out of his skin and he quickly withdraw his hand. The voice belonged to a short, elderly, ruddy-complexioned woman who seemed to pop out of nowhere.

'Who are you?' Daniel asked after his heart had slowed a few beats.

'I am Aradia, matriarch of the Tolgarr people.'

'I am Daniel of...of Earth, I guess,' he replied awkwardly. 'So these floaty things are people?'

'What's left behind of them. The Shade feeds on Essence, that bright hue around your body, and it usually drains it away before it swallows its victims. But on occasion, it will consume them whole, like you and me, and slowly digest them here.'

'And where is here?'

'This? This is the belly of the beast. It is like a pocket dimension, a limbo,' she expounded. 'Anyway, I've been waiting for you...we need to go.'

'Waiting for me?'

'Well, not you specifically, just someone with enough Essence left to destroy this thing once and for all.'

'But Gydion already discovered that they have a weakness to cold, that's why...'

Aradia suddenly stopped mid-step and turned to Daniel with wide eyes. 'Gydion discovered? Did he now? Taking credit for my hard work, is he? I'll have words with him when I get out of here. How goes the war, anyway? Has it turned in our favour yet?'

'The war? Well, I read that the mages won it, but that was some fifty years ago.'

'Fifty years? Already? Goddess, my family! This limbo must exist beyond the bounds of time.' Then a thought suddenly struck Aradia. 'If what you say is true and we won the war, where did this Shade come from?'

'It attacked us at the Beltane Games in Almedia.'

'You don't understand,' she stated before running off down the path. 'Come on! We need to see if we can end this.'

Daniel watched the old woman for a few seconds, wondering what she was on about. 'What don't I understand?' he asked after catching up with Aradia.

'I was there, in that war, with my people, when this creature got me.' She waited for the significance of that fact to sink in; however, when Daniel made no comment she became exasperated. 'How can you be a mage and be so dim-witted?'

'About that –'

'If the Shade were all destroyed,' she continued, 'how did this one survive?'

Daniel thought for a moment and then it clicked. 'You've been here since the war...the Shade feed on Essence...so it was storing you...like a hibernating bear over winter...'

'And feeding on my Essence bit by bit to stay alive.'

'But that means –'

'Exactly! Cold attacks outside slow them but don't kill them, so there could well be more hidden in Ariest.'

'Then we need to get back and warn people!'

'And we will, as soon as *you* get us out of here.'

30

As a practitioner of druidic magick, Trinity was a savant at using nature and elven Faerie spells. It was Earth magick, so it drew strength from the powers of nature, meaning that in certain places her spells performed beyond normal level, places such as the fields they were in now.

She called upon the forest to aid her, and they answered her summons by sending their roots bursting forth from beneath the earth with unerring accuracy at the Shade, but what could such an attack do to a creature that could become intangible at will, allowing the roots to pass through its form?

Trinity cast several offensive spells at the Shade but all to little or no effect. If she hadn't let her rage cloud her judgement and entered the battle with a clear mind she would have realised sooner what a futile waste of Essence it was to attack in such a manner. Gydion would be most displeased.

As soon as she broke the enchantment over the forest, the Shade was on the attack once more. With its arms formed into solid darkness, it pockmarked the ground as it tried to impale Trinity, who gracefully evaded each attempt. She wasn't just avoiding the spear thrusts, however, she was also casting her magic.

Most magic users needed some sort of ritual when they called upon Realmic Powers; entreating beings from other realms is no easy task, but Trinity had what she called Spell Weaving, using dance as her ritualistic medium.

Finn, Tristan, and the guards that had remained looked on in awe as she began to glow bright green with arcane power. The balletic moves of her spell weaving started to work their magic; the earth goddess had answered.

In moments, the weather control spell was unleashed upon the Shade. Storms, rain, and wind were summoned and lightning bolts struck the Shade, but it wasn't until the temperature dropped and the wet storm turned into a blizzard, with its driving snow and strong freezing winds, that the Shade's attacks were halted.

The onlookers cheered and shouted encouragement; they had seen a Shade take a backward step. Could she actually defeat the Shade on her own? She is the daughter of the Archmage Gydion; if anyone could, it would be her.

It might well have been the case had it not been for her initial rashness, which came back to bite her now. Just as she was gaining the upper hand, her Realmic Essence pool emptied.

She had broken the cardinal rule of any war mage worth their sword; enter a battle half full and your opponent is already halfway to victory. Her father had told her that many times over, but at her first trial all his teachings left her. Theory means nothing without practical application. It was a lesson learnt all too late as her mistakes looked certain to condemn her to death at the hands of the Shade.

The creature used the shadow beneath Trinity to hold her fast, although in her weakened state she could barely stand, much less put up any fight, but this didn't deter the Shade, as it slowly advanced upon the young druid.

'We're running out of time, Daniel!'

They approached what Daniel perceived to be nothing more than a large tar pit. Whatever the ebony liquid in the lagoon was, it swirled and bubbled like it was alive or something in it was, at least.

Around the lakeside, Daniel could see a number of the wraiths; he was still finding it hard to believe that that was all that remained of these former beings. He was contemplating these formless objects, wondering who they had once been, what they did, what they once looked like, if they had families that missed them, when he noticed someone sitting, hunched over beside the undulating ebony lake. Daniel could see that whoever they were, their pale-yellow-coloured Essence was all but gone.

'Look, there's someone over there,' Daniel pointed out.

Aradia squinted with her old eyes to see what was there. 'Oh, that's little Timothy. He is a new addition here.'

'Timothy? Timothy Sanderson? The council thought I had sent the Shade to kill him.'

'Well, they were right about one thing. You can see that the Shade fed before he swallowed the boy. Come to think of it,' the old woman mused, 'his Essence seems lower than when I saw him last...which can only mean...' She turned as if she knew what was about to happen and saw the sky open and a beam of black light strike the ground, not far from where Daniel himself had appeared. When the dark light had receded a dazed and confused Almedian guard was left in its place, quickly followed by a second then a third.

'The Shade is under attack,' Aradia revealed.

This was music to Daniel's ears. 'It must be Trinity, Finn, and the others,' he enthused. 'They're my friends. Trinity is Gydion's daughter, actually. They probably think I'm dead after seeing me fall into the Shade.'

'Gydion's daughter, you say,' Aradia replied with a sceptical sidelong glance. 'Seems like I have missed quite a bit on the outside. This just means we must expedite things. If your friends are doing enough damage to force the Shade to feed then it won't be long before it finishes draining the Essence from Timothy and myself. You must destroy its heart with your frost magic.'

'About that,' Daniel started awkwardly. He was never any good at this kind of thing. He could see that Aradia was relying on him and he was about to disappoint her. He was just about to make his reveal about his lack of magic abilities when a thought popped into his head. 'I don't see a heart.'

'It is in that,' she replied, pointing at the ebony lake.

Daniel looked at the bubbling blackness. 'You want me to go wading in that?'

'Of course not. What *you* need to destroy only reveals itself when the Shade feeds, so no, you won't be going out there. I will be the bait.'

'But you'll become a wraith!'

'And it will be down to you to trap my form before that happens. All we need is something to contain it,' she said as she searched her pockets for something suitable.

Things were escalating far beyond Daniel's liking. Aradia's plan depended entirely on a wielder of magic. He had to tell her that he wasn't that person; he couldn't put it off any longer.

'I'm not a mage!' Daniel blurted out.

Aradia paused a moment as if processing what she had just heard. 'Not a mage,' she scoffed, 'who are you trying to fool? With Essence so strong and vibrant, how could you not be?'

'I didn't know magic was real until Gydion sought me out.'

'You are truly untrained? Can it be that you are the Mortokai?'

'The what?'

'Never mind that,' she dismissed Daniel's question. 'It is not my place to explain it to you, Daniel, but I'll tell you this; if my suspicions are correct, you are in grave danger. They will want to control you and if they cannot...they will kill you.'

Daniel was startled. 'Who will?'

'The Faeries.' The statement brought a sceptical look to Daniel's face. 'Do not be so foolish to think that all Faeries dance around maypoles scattering Faerie dust!' she said, imitating them by skipping and flapping her arms like wings. 'I am talking about the old Faeries, the dark fae, the ones parents tell their children about to scare them. My advice to you, train hard and learn fast or abandon your ideas of magic and lose yourself in your banal world.'

Daniel didn't know what to make of what Aradia was saying. Surely, she was being overdramatic; why would anyone want him dead?

'I suppose it is a moot point anyway,' Aradia admitted, 'since you are trapped in here, destined to be fodder for this Shade; we all are.'

'I won't have your deaths on my conscience. I'll do what I can help, but I've read a book, a spell book, the Book of Azul...' Daniel could almost see her ears prick up at this. 'The problem is, none of the spells worked for me.'

'How much do you remember of it?'

'All of it.'

'Show me.'

She kicked some of the black sand across the white path, creating a makeshift writing board. Daniel knelt down and wrote down the first pages of the grimoire.

'Extraordinary!' she gasped. 'I think I understand the problem. You have seen the words but you have not heard what they sound like. They may look like ordinary words but these are arcane letters, they are pronounced and sound completely differently, and these runic letters at the end, they are part of the spell too, denoting the hand gestures used.' She glanced again at the spell and then looked sternly at Daniel. 'This might just work, Daniel' Aradia said with a twinkle in her eye.

THE SHADE EXTENDED its solid black arm at the fatigued Trinity, but try as it might, its elongated fingers could not grab hold of her, as if an invisible barrier surrounded her.

A moan of frustration escaped the creature's distended maw, but it was soon replaced by the unfamiliar groan of pain as the Shade reeled from the sudden attack from Finn.

The young girl charged into the fray, firing shot after shot, each striking the Shade in its ebony mass. When it retaliated, she dived over its low attacks and slid beneath its high ones, all the while not missing a beat in keeping her guns firing. The gunfire assault was enough to force the shadow being to relinquish its hold on Trinity.

'Now's yer chance, lad!' Fungal shouted at Tristan. The bogart had cast an invisibility spell on himself as soon as the Shade had made its appearance. It had been his intention to wait out the whole confrontation, but when Trinity had gotten involved, he had no choice but to get off his arse, not to be the hero or out of any sort of loyalty to her, but just to avoid the wrath of Gydion.

'Don't worry, princess,' Finn yelled out, guns still blazing, giving Tristan covering fire as he ran in and collected Trinity. 'We got this!'

All of a sudden, the Shade used its morphing form and dove into the shadow of a nearby tree and then another and another. Before long, it had covered a significant distance, giving Almedian guards cause to cheer and declare victory over their retreating opponent.

'We haven't won anything,' Tristan revealed, 'it is not running away – it is heading to town!'

ARADIA WENT THROUGH the spell with Daniel, word by word, arcane letter by arcane letter, and then he recited it back to her verbatim. She was astonished by him but also fearful, not *of* him, but *for* him. Most mages needed to recommit spells to memory once they had cast it, but Daniel had the potential to become a living sanctum; who knew how much arcane knowledge he could retain?

She knew that if the wrong people became aware of his existence, he would find his life fraught with peril, and by teaching him the ways of magic it would be like putting up a hoarding announcing his arrival, especially if he were to use realmic spells to entreat extra-dimensional beings.

'Now you have the spell words and the hand gestures perfected, we need to go about powering the incantation. Unlike shamans, who only can use realmic energies, other magic schools have three pools; personal, planetary, and realmic.

'Isn't it a disadvantage only having one pool?'

'Realmic spells cost more Essence, but our pool is significantly larger than the realmic pools of the other schools, meaning that we can cast more powerful spells for longer. That's the trade-off, but ultimately it comes down to the skill and wits of the practitioner. Look, we have little time; these are questions for when your formal training begins. What we need to do is get you ready to destroy this thing when it comes to claim me.' Daniel nodded to acknowledge that he understood what was needed of him.

'Good. Offensive spells primarily use universal Essence so that is what we will be using. The universal pool is located in the chest cavity. Breathe deeply and visualise the pool.' She watched him close his eyes and perform the routine. 'Do you see it? Can you feel it?'

Daniel felt similar to how he felt when Trinity had first taught him the meditation exercise. It was similar but so different. With each breath he could feel Essence pulse from within his chest, around his body, down his legs, along his arms. His skin crackled with the new sensation of what resonated within him. The power built, expanded, and spread. Then something snapped in his mind.

He was suddenly aware, as if he had just woken up from a deep sleep, like a newborn taking its first unaided breaths. Momentarily, Daniel's senses expanded beyond his own body, extended around Aradia, around the limbo he was in and beyond. For a single moment in time his mind was everywhere at once and when that moment passed a tear rolled down his cheek.

'Your mind has been awakened,' Aradia said buoyantly. The moment of crossover had always been a joyous occasion to witness. 'It is a far cry from your previous banal existence, yes? You have started your magical journey along the mystic path.'

'It's like I've been reborn.'

'You have,' she stated. 'We are almost ready; all we need now is something to store my form before it is completely devoured.'

'I think I have just the thing.' He only hoped he hadn't lost it during the Beltane events. 'Will this do?' Daniel asked as he brought out the olive-green peridot crystal Trinity had given him.

'Perfectly!' Aradia explained to Daniel that what she was about to teach him was actually a spell of entrapment but that it would work perfectly for their needs. 'One final thing I must ask of you, my dear: if all goes well and we survive this, take the gem back to my people...they will know what to do.'

'Of course I will. It will be an experience to meet the Tolgarr.'

'You're suddenly so certain of getting out of here, hmmm?'

'I've taken the first step on the mystic path, as you've said, I've glimpsed what it is to be a mage, and I'm not about to let this obstacle stop me from fulfilling my potential.'

'Well said,' Aradia gushed as she patted Daniel's arm. 'If you're ready, I guess it is time for my swim.'

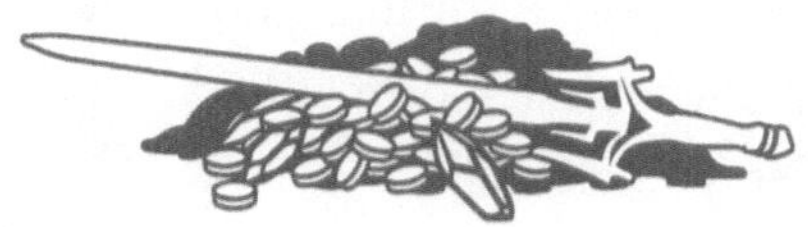

'COME ON,' FINN SHOUTED over her shoulder as she started to run back to Almedia. The city guard took off in hot pursuit. Tristan was about to follow them when he was called back by the weakened voice of Trinity.

'Those guns Finn uses,' she began from her crossed-legged position on the ground, 'where did they come from?'

'Those are from her uncle; he made them. They are mixed with Faerie dust, or something like that...that's what she says anyway.'

She fell silent for a moment, and seeing the warrior anxious to join the upcoming battle, Trinity knew she couldn't hold him any longer. She clapped her hands together and as she drew them apart her shimmering white schiavona appeared before her. 'You'd better take this,' she said. 'It will do well against the Shade.'

Tristan took the gleaming weapon, tested its balance with a few practise swings, and smiled about the damage he was about to inflict onto the creature before setting off after the others.

'How could I have been so stupid?' She pounded her fist into the ground as she admonished herself. 'I know ordinary magic attacks do nothing against the Shade. I know they are susceptible to frost attacks and enchanted weapons. I know this! And what did I do? I run headlong into battle, unprepared, waste my Essence, and almost get myself killed. I've wanted to test myself in real combat, without my father over my shoulder for so long, wanted a chance to prove myself, and when I finally get an opportunity I screw it up. I'm just glad he wasn't here to see it.'

'Dinnae be so hard on yerself, lass. We all go a wee bit loopy when we lose our loved one.'

'Loved one? What do you know about –?' Her sentence was cut short as Trinity suddenly gasped as an unseen force touched her consciousness. 'Did you feel that?' she asked Fungal.

'Yes, what was...'

'It was Daniel!' she enthused. 'He's alive! I don't know how or where he is, but that was him.' With renewed hope, and a smile, Trinity began her replenishment spell anew. 'Go on ahead, help the others and I'll catch up.'

31

Finn couldn't believe the chaos that was ravaging the city. Buildings were smashed and the people, who had left the forest seeking sanctuary in the city, were now in the front line. They ran every which way in a vain attempt to evade the rampaging creature. Almedia's massive protective wall proved useless, for what good is a wall against a creature that can use shadows to travel?

And that fact grabbed Finn's interest. She knew the stories of the third war, how the Shade used stealth to attack, launching strikes from the darkness. This one was now running amok, completely out of character, as if it were desperate.

She checked the steam levels of her guns and, seeing that they were still good to go, she walked out into the main avenue. People ran on either side of her, trying to get away from the Shade, whilst she walked straight towards it. The danger and excitement fuelled her adrenaline.

Once Finn was in range, she raised her brass guns and repeatedly fired them. Just as before, the creature let out a haunting moan of pain, but this time instead of running, its huge form split and divided itself into hundreds of human-sized Shade. At least two dozen continued the Shades battle with Finn while the rest terrorized the citizens of Almedia, swallowing any that were caught in its darkness.

Duplicating itself had made the creature from the shadows able to attack multiple targets at once, but also even more vulnerable to Finn's highly accurate gunfire. She took out one...two...three Shade, and each one evaporated into the ether as it ceased to be. Eventually, however, the numbers began to tell as, all of a sudden, she was dealt a heavy blow from behind.

Dizzy, Finn dropped to one knee, valiantly firing off shots, in a vain attempt to fight off her attackers in what was fast becoming a desperate situation for her. More blows rained down on her, and it was all she could do to cover up as she suddenly heard the sound of rushing wind past her ears and the desire to fight left her.

She was losing consciousness fast when, through her blurred vision, she saw swords flash by, slicing this way and that, the wielder of the blades, vaulted, and somersaulted like an acrobat, the swords, an extension of their body.

Finn reached out her hand to the hooded figure, just as they vanished, and Tristan came into her vision, then she succumbed to her wounds and blacked out.

She didn't know how long she had been out for, but when Finn came to, she had been moved into the doorway of a nearby homestead and Tristan was battling the Shade with a gleaming white sword. She struggled to her feet, leaning heavily against the wall as he despatched the last one.

'Ah, you are awake,' Tristan smiled broadly. 'You had a good sleep?'

'If you can call it that,' replied Finn as she rubbed her aching body. 'Who was that person that saved me?'

Tristan shook his head. 'There was nobody here when I got to you, just two Shade.'

'There were at least twenty! Whoever they were, they went through the Shade like they were nothing.'

'You must have been hit pretty hard, but I hope this person is not just a figment of your imagination, because I would like to cross swords with them and see how good they truly are.' He smiled at the prospect of finding a potentially worthy combatant. That grin disappeared, however, when Finn drew her guns and pointed them at him.

'It's not a figment of anything!' She squeezed the triggers, sending bullets flying either side of Tristan's head, and into the two Shade that had been coming up behind him.

He turned just in time to see the creatures dissolve. 'Okay, Finn, you have convinced me,' he admitted.

Having a moment of respite, with no Shade duplicates to deal with, gave both Tristan and Finn time for their minds to fall upon loved ones. Hyasda never bothered with the Beltane Festival. In all the years they had been together, Tristan had never seen her attend the festival. Quinn Jesson, however, had promised Finn to be there, because of her participation, but she hadn't expected to see him there until the round after the Climb of Affiance, where any courter with a garland would present it to the lady of his choice. If it was the garland which she had made, then they would both move on to the next round, the Test of Fire, so she was expecting to see him still at the house, if the Shade hadn't reached there yet.

The Council of Three, instead of taking the opportunity to head for safety, were showing why they were so loved and respected among their people by leading the defence of the city themselves. They charged down the streets on chariots, rallying the troops and rescuing citizens of Almedia.

But not all of its citizens needed rescuing. As in any large city, there are those that have and those that have not; Almedia was no different. The people that were affluent enough to be able to reside in Buxton Mews were happy to pay the premium for two reasons: the technological advances Quinn and his father had made to the properties set them far and above anything else in Ariest, and the second reason were its defences.

Apart from the enchantments that were in place around the Mews, six steam automatons, each eight feet tall and just as broad, were situated in the grounds of the complex. They had their roots based on the one Thomas Jesson had built and used during the War, only Quinn had incorporated some upgrades of his own.

They were the perfect foil against the Shade. Not only did they have no Essence to feed the shadow vampires, but their many weapons, rocket-propelled fists, surface-to-air missiles, solar beam, and turbine-propelled boots, which allowed them to leap huge distances, were all powered by Faerie dust.

When Finn and Tristan arrived at Buxton Mews, it was completely untouched by Shade activity; in fact, the immediate area was devoid of Shade presence. Apart from scorch marks, presumably from the automatons' attacks, you would be hard pushed to see evidence of the city's apparent peril.

There was but one of Quinn's fantastical creations left guarding the mews, but this one was a particularly special one, as the pair discovered when it suddenly spoke.

'Finn! I've been worried sick! I should have known you'd be able to take care of yourself,' the steam automaton exclaimed.

'Uncle Quinn, is that you?' she asked as she tentatively approached the mechanoid.

A sudden burst of steam escaping from a vent stopped her dead in her tracks. There was the sound of whirring gears as the chest cavity slowly and smoothly moved forward and upward to reveal Quinn Jesson strapped inside.

He unbuckled himself and jumped down, a huge grin on his face. 'Well, what do you think?'

'Vekt!' she cried enthusiastically. Finn's love for gadgets and inventions was matched by only one other person, her uncle.

'What have I told you about your language?'

'And what have I told you about keeping secrets?' came her retort as she inspected the interior of the automaton. She had seen them for years, but she had never known them to speak, but then again, she had never seen them in action before. 'This is amazing, uncle! No wonder it's taken so long to finish my rifle.'

Quinn scratched his head and smiled with embarrassment.

'That's okay, I forgive ya,' Finn said as she climbed into the automaton, 'This'll more than make up for keeping me waiting for the gun.'

'What do you think you're doing? This is far too advanced for...'

Finn had already strapped herself in and found the switch to close the hatch.

'Sometimes I wish I hadn't been such a good teacher and you hadn't been such a precocious child!' Quinn yelled through the gap just before the chest cavity sealed shut.

'I love you too, Uncle,' Finn replied in a mechanised voice. Having looked around her cockpit more thoroughly, she noticed something interesting. 'Am I right in thinking I can command the other automatons and coordinate our actions from here?'

'Yes, but they're not just mindless hunks of metal. They can operate individually but I've also made this one a command module. Haven't I, Vincent?'

'That is affirmative, designate Quinn Jesson,' Vincent replied.

Finn stared at the automaton with wide eyes. 'I think you've outdone yourself, Uncle,' she gushed.

'I know!' her uncle replied excitedly. 'So please be careful with him.'

'Well, I'll do my best, but I am going to test the vekt out of him!'

Tristan didn't really have an interest in any of these inventions. He had been standing aside yawning and testing his sword arm whilst Finn had been fawning over Quinn's tin man. That was, until something the tinkerer said lit a flame in his mind. 'Did you say you can control your other creations with this one?' When Quinn nodded, Tristan thought for a moment. 'This could work. Having the Shade duplicates all over the city is stretching our resources and making it difficult to tackle them and protect the people. If we could force them into the city centre it would be easier for us to finish them off once and for all.'

'It's worth a try,' admitted Finn before she let out a battle cry as she activated the propulsion boots and leapt off down the road and over buildings. Tristan patted Quinn on the back with a heavy hand before he headed off to find Hyasda.

Although Aradia knew what she had to do, it did not necessarily mean that she was overjoyed with the fact that it relied so heavily on Daniel, someone whom she had just met but, more importantly, someone who wasn't an accomplished practitioner of the arcane arts. 'Are you sure you are ready for this?' asked the shaman.

'As ready as I'll ever be,' Daniel murmured, as he traced his thumb around the cut edges of the peridot gem. He played through the sequence of his role in the coming events through his mind, just to be sure of how it was supposed to go.

Aradia let out a deep breath before she took her first tentative step into the viscous lake. It was warmer than she had expected, not that she had known what to expect. She knew very little about this area of the Shade's limbo, only that beings with dangerously low Essence were somehow drawn to it, as if summoned, and that when they made their way out to the centre of the ebony lake they were dragged beneath its depths only to re-emerge moments later as a wraith. Every time it had happened, the rhythmic thumping sound of a heart had accompanied the occasion, so Aradia had naturally thought that there was something there that played a pivotal role in the survival of the Shade, something that could be eliminated.

Her plan was based entirely on speculation since she had never seen anything actually in the blackness, but every great discovery was preluded by a leap into the unknown. She hadn't told Daniel any of this. And the only reason she could think of for not doing so was because of her own selfish needs. Firstly, she needed to be free of this place; she had been here too long, missed so much of her family and her people. What if by telling the youngster that nothing in the plan was guaranteed to work...would he have still gone through with it? It was a risk she wasn't willing to take. And secondly, she knew that if they were successful it would bring great glory to her and her clan, a risk she was willing to take even if it meant someone else unknowingly taking that risk also. After warning Daniel about the dark fae potentially using him, she was now doing the same, and it didn't sit right with her. She prayed she would get the chance to explain one day.

As Aradia moved further and further away, Daniel began to wonder if there was any range factor to deal with when the time came for him to capture Aradia in the gemstone. She must have been having the same thoughts, as she suddenly shouted to Daniel that he might have to get into the ebony lake after all, if she had to keep wading out there.

That wasn't necessary, however, as all of a sudden, the bubbling lake became more violent at its centre and the sound, not unlike a heartbeat, rang out.

'This is it, Daniel!' Aradia called out, 'Be on the ready!'

He was as ready as he was ever going to be, Daniel admitted to himself. As he looked on, the bubbling epicentre had begun to swirl, eventually becoming a waterspout. The current of its rotation was pulling Aradia into it, and as it did so, she could feel her Essence being syphoned away.

'Do it now, Daniel! The plan isn't going to work! Whatever is draining me is beneath the...'

Aradia's sentence was cut short, as she became stock still, frozen like a statue, as whatever was within the inky depths of the water funnel began to feed on the last of her Essence. The plan was unravelling fast.

Within seconds of the Tolgarr's pleas, Daniel had reacted by casting the spell she had taught him. He held the peridot gem out at arm's length, towards Aradia, as he recited her words. The moment he finished them, the green stone began to glow before a bright green light spiralled out and engulfed the shaman. Moments later her astral form was pulled free from her body and along the light, shortly followed by her physical body.

He was alone. The realization dawned on Daniel that the destruction of what was in that liquid fell solely upon his shoulders now. He held up the gem and peered into it, hoping that he would see Aradia and be able to commune with her. She was there but, unfortunately, seemed to be in some sort of stasis and unable to talk to anyone.

Daniel let out a deep sigh, which was immediately overtaken in volume by a blood-curdling screech emanating from the ebony lake. Whatever was in there wasn't happy that he had taken its sustenance away and it seemed as though it was about to go in search of a replacement food source.

The water funnel began to spiral faster and faster until the entire lake was caught in its throes and was drawn into its centre. At that moment a black mass shot into the air, getting larger and larger as it added more and more of the gloopy ebony lake to its form. Eventually a horned and spiny serpent stood in its place, reared up, its body coiled in the now empty lakebed.

Daniel stared dumbstruck at the creature towering above him. Aradia had been wrong, there was no heart hiding in the dark depths of the viscous lake, the whole thing was alive! This plan of escape suddenly seemed a whole lot more daunting than it previously had, but as he edged away from the beast, thoughts rushed through his mind; he knew that there was nothing else he could do.

He ran.

Ran like he always had done. Ran like he had from Bobby Brinkmeyer and his cronies. Ran out of fear. Ran because he was told he was too feeble to do anything else.

But here, in Ariest, he could do something. Here he was a mage. Here he was the son of a great warrior. Here he could be a hero too. All he had to do was have the courage to stop running.

Up ahead, beams of black light struck the ground over and over as more and more victims were sent to the Shade's pocket dimension to give it nourishment, to feed its hunger.

Trinity and the others were obviously doing their best to destroy the Shade, but Daniel knew it would be for nothing if he didn't do his part, because if he failed there would be no one to stop the creature from re-energising and continuing its battle with them.

Seeing the recently swallowed, dazed, and confused victims, and knowing what was in store for them, if they remained, bolstered Daniel's resolve. He was the son of Eric Mondragon and he needed to act like it. He had to try and stop the heart of the Shade, not only for himself but also for Aradia, for the people of Almedia, for Finn, for Trinity, for Timothy.

It now dawned on Daniel that he was their only chance, that the time for running had ended.

32

During her young life, Finn had had plenty of fun times, more than most to be fair; that much she could admit. The time she and Crellis 'borrowed' his grandmother's summoning ring and brought a Silver Lich to the village, or the time she and Jimbo snuck into Pamela Hoddentrot's kitchen when she was hosting a dinner party and added a little blue dye to her bluson-berry pie, and the time she won the Advance and Conquer annual tournament, stood out as some of the best. But the fun she was having now, in her uncle's automaton, at least rivalled, if not bettered all of those.

She was jumping and spinning, and punching and kicking, and grabbing and slamming any duplicate Shade that came near, and she did it all with a smile and a giggle.

'Your method of testing is somewhat more exuberant than that of Quinn Jesson, Finnuala Jesson,' Vincent stated.

'Well, I did say I was going to test the vekt out of you, Vincent, and if nothing else I am a woman of my word,' she replied proudly. 'You see, my uncle deals in theoretical testing, while I'm more partial to hands-on, real-world situation testing,' she grinned.

'Heavy handed with a tendency to break things, according to Quinn Jesson.'

'He said that?' Finn fumed. 'If that's the case I'd better not prove my uncle wrong!'

'I do not believe that will be necessary, Finnuala,' pleaded Vincent, fearing for his own safety, 'I am sure it was some sort of misunderstanding.'

'Is that so?' her words dripped with suspicion.

'Indeed! Besides, we must get back to our primary objective. Units one, two, and three have joined with Chief Seydou, Empress Xu Ping, and King Ewynn and are herding the remaining Shade into the centre of town as we speak.'

'Tristan's plan is working! The people will be out of the way and we'll be able to pick off those creatures with ease. Let's get in there and finish this off, Vincent!' Just as they were about to set off, Finn heard a familiar voice come from behind them.

'Well, well, well, what have we here? More trouble?' Trinity said as she gently landed on the city wall. She was just about to conjure up an attack when she heard Finn's voice from within the armoured suit.

'You're just in time for the endgame, Princess.'

'Where the hell did you get that suit? Never mind. Once the Shade is dealt with we can then figure out where Daniel is.'

'He's alive?'

'Somewhere...somehow...I felt him awaken his magic.'

'You felt him?' a downhearted Finn asked. It seemed to her that the friendship between Daniel and Trinity was more than either one of them cared to admit. But she was a fighter, always had been, and she wasn't about to give up, even if the odds *were* against her.

'Right, let's go, Fungal,' Trinity said before discovering that the Hobthrust laird had vanished once more. 'Damn you, you little...'

As Tristan rounded the corner, in the distance, he could see old Hyasda leaning heavily on her staff outside of her small and unassuming store. Although he felt that she could be a little harsh-tongued at times, and seemed to have a distinct dislike of Evelyn, Tristan was, all the same, very happy to see his guardian safe and sound.

He raised his hand to call her but his heart jumped when she was all of a sudden surrounded by several Shade. 'Hyasda!' he yelled as he charged in, fully prepared to cut down the shadows with Trinity's enchanted sword. However, as he neared, he expected to see the Shade feeding on her Essence; instead, it seemed that she was conversing with them, before they dispersed in all directions.

Confused by what he had witnessed, Tristan slowed to a walk. 'What's going on? Are you okay, Hyasda? I saw the Shade come for you.'

'And they found, to their chagrin, that I am far from the snivelling morsel like the other inhabitants of this city,' came her reply.

He had always suspected that the elderly woman was more powerful than she let on, but this was far more than he could have imagined. 'Perhaps you could banish the others the same way.'

'As powerful as I am,' she began, 'my body is no longer up to the task of continued use. Battles such as this are for the younger generation. Now help me inside and get back to saving the city. Put your skills to good use, my son.'

Tristan took her outstretched arm and slowly helped her into the store. Once Hyasda had slumped heavily into a chair in the back, Tristan was off heading back to the fray.

The aged alchemist waited a few moments and when she was sure that her godchild was gone, Hyasda stood up, unassisted by her staff, which floated magically beside her chair, and strode purposefully toward the back wall. She softly spoke several arcane words. Runes flashed on numerous bricks before they vanished, along with the stone block, to reveal her secret lab. She entered and the mystical entryway sealed shut behind her. Once more it looked like a normal wall, as if it hid no secrets and nothing was there.

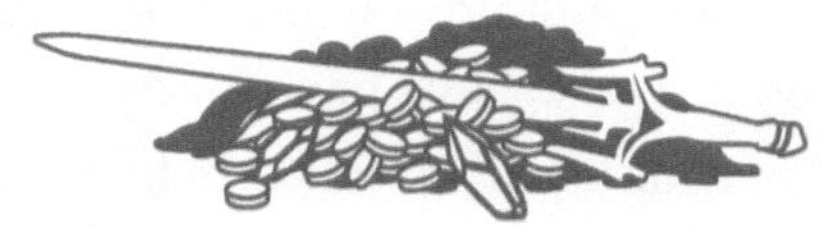

REAL MAGIC...IT OPENS your mind to new things, some wondrous, some dangerous...tension is a major barrier between us and magic...belief can be a powerful thing...extra responsibility.

The words Trinity spoke that fateful day in the library, when she had told him that magic did exist, resonated through Daniel's mind. It seemed so long ago when she gave her message of portent and since then, he had seen many wondrous things but this creature was definitely a tick in the dangerous column.

The Shade serpent struck out with several of its tentacles. One found its mark and latched onto a guard with its lamprey-like maw. Two more glued themselves to the hapless Almedian defender. He screamed and begged for help, desperately grasping at people, as he was hoisted into the air. Daniel and the recently ingested watched on in horror as the heart of the Shade fed on its victim. The sound of rushing wind could be heard as the poor man had his Essence and life drained away, slowly becoming a shrivelled husk, until all that was left was a luminous wraith, floating in the air.

After a moment of shock, panic came over the people. They ran this way and that in a vain attempt to escape, not knowing that there was no escaping a world controlled by the being they were trying to flee from.

'We have to do something, it's our responsibility,' another guard of Almedia said to Daniel. 'You're a student of Gydion, right? You were with those other adventurers, the ones fighting the Shade.'

Daniel suddenly woke up from his stupor at the mention of his friends. 'Yes, yes I am. Are they alright?'

'Yeah, I suppose. The battle has been going back and forth. We thought your pretty redhead friend had finished the beast off, but it rallied and almost killed her. It would have done if it weren't for Finn.'

Hearing about Trinity and Finn fighting the creature bolstered Daniel's courage, especially after seeing the garland still around his arm. 'This isn't our responsibility, it's mine. You keep those people together and out of the range of those tentacles. We have to cut off its food supply. If it's fighting out in Ariest, it won't have enough time to drain anyone directly, it'll be relying on its heart feeding on us and I'm not about to let that happen again. It's the responsibility of those that can to protect those that can't. The strong safeguard the weak.'

The guard nodded in admiration and wished Daniel good luck before he headed off to gather the festival revellers whom, although scared, couldn't fight the urge to stand and watch. For many of them, this would be as close as they had ever gotten to a mage casting spells in combat. Some questioned exactly how good could a trainee really be? Could they really leave their fate in the hands of a youngster? While others knew they had no choice, that he was their only real chance of survival.

If the onlookers' over-riding emotion was cautious excitement, Daniel's was pure dread. But that didn't change a thing; he knew what he had to do. He recalled the books he had read in the royal library of the Pichini Palace of Murias City, about how the Shade were defeated before. He thought about the few teachings Trinity and Aradia had shared, about accessing the Essence in his body. Finally, he called up the spells from the Book of Azul, made the necessary signs to cast an ice bolt...but nothing happened. He tried again, still nothing.

As Daniel readied himself for a third attempt, the Shade serpent attacked, lunging with its lamprey-like maw wide open. He dived out of the way, with mere inches to spare and as he got to his feet he wracked his brain. Why wasn't it working?

He ran to create some separation between himself and the creature, giving him vital seconds to come to the conclusion that Trinity's words rang true; tension was a major barrier. It had to be that, he surmised, but how could you not be tense in a situation like this?

Daniel suddenly had a lot of respect for magic users; juggling all the components to cast a spell was difficult enough but doing it whilst in control of your emotions was an added obstacle to overcome. And it sort of explained Gydion's 'greater than thou' attitude, thought Daniel; after all, having to suppress your emotions from time to time is bound to have some sort of adverse effect on you.

But that was something Daniel would have to ponder at a later date; right now he had people to save.

He breathed deeply and exhaled, just as Aradia, and Trinity before her, taught him. Each time he did, he felt his tension melting away, as his Essence began to flow freely, a feeling Daniel was beginning to like. The same sense of euphoria came over him, just as it had when he had done the exercise at college. He zoned in on the sensation. He was totally oblivious to the screams and shouts warning him of imminent danger.

The ebony creature attacked with its tentacle mouths itching to feast on Daniel's magical energy. Eight of the ten tentacles latched on to him hungrily, sensing the quantity and quality of what they were about to feed on.

Daniel was unperturbed by the assault, completely disinterested as if it were a gnat bothering a great jungle animal. The Shade tried to feed, but soon found that it had bitten off more than it could handle as, all of a sudden, Daniel's Essence erupted from his body and surrounded him like vibrant purple flame, and even his eyes took on the magical fiery effect.

'What is that?' someone asked.

'I don't know. I've never seen anything like it before.'

'His hands must be moving so fast we can't see him casting.'

'I'm not even sure he *is* casting.'

'He really *must* be the student of the Archmage.'

Several ice bolts thundered into the serpent Shade that had it reeling from the onslaught. Anything it tried was easily dealt with confidently by Daniel. Its energy was low, it needed food, it was battling on two fronts and it needed more Essence than it had drained from the guard. But this world belonged to the Shade; in this realm it was lord and master.

The black landscape began to undulate, more and more violently, throwing the Almedian people to the ground. At the first sign of the roiling, Daniel had encased his lower body in ice, which anchored his feet to the ground and made him completely unaffected and unimpressed by the Shade serpent's display of control.

A swirling ebony mass began to appear, out of nowhere, directly above the fallen citizens, and while they stared up at it, jet black rain drops began to fall from it.

At first people looked around in confusion, not sure what was going on, and even Daniel smiled smugly at the serpent, thinking that it had so little power left to make an effective attack. Then the first screams rang out. He turned to see that it wasn't rain that was falling on them but lamprey siphons, draining the Essence of all the people, and channelling it to the ebony creature.

A part of Daniel wanted to let it drain the citizens completely, so that he might gain some satisfaction from destroying the serpent, knowing that it was at full strength. But there was a voice, a sensation, a part of him that knew letting that happen would condemn them to death.

He thought for a few moments and then made his choice.

'Enough of this,' Daniel finally said. When he spoke, it seemed like it was many voices coming from all directions. 'You are no match. You are not worth my time and effort. There is nothing that you can do to me. Unfortunately for you, there is a lot I can do to you.'

Daniel created a swirling blue mass above the Shade, mimicking and mocking its own black one, for his was twice as large, and peppered the creature with giant spikes of ice.

Each one that struck pinned the Shade's heart to the ground and brought a roar of agony and defiance. It had survived hidden for years as part of a master plan, but now its death would end its participation in it, but the others would continue. With one final death cry, the serpent creature, the physical heart of the Shade, died.

33

The plan to corral the smaller Shade duplicates into the centre of town worked perfectly. Without the protectors of Almedia having to divert their attentions to protect the innocents, they could concentrate all their energies on wiping out the remaining Shades. However, bringing them together also made it easy for the Shade to reform, returning to its more powerful and resilient state.

'The plan remains the same! We hit it with everything we have until either it falls or we do!' After giving her rallying cry, Trinity weaved her magic and called a blizzard down, localised around the creature of the shadows.

The sleet and snow clung to it, and the frozen air weakened it further, but still it fought back. The Shade thrust several mandibles, fashioned into solid ebony spears, into the ground only to make them appear again from the shadows behind the city defenders.

'It's using the shadows as portals!' Tristan cried. 'Watch your back!' His warning came too late for some, as they were pierced violently by the vicious weapons, held in the air, before being dumped unceremoniously to the ground.

In an attempt to counter the Shade's use of the shadows around the group, Trinity, created the largest lumin ball she could and set it directly above them, eliminating all the darkness, or so she thought.

One of King Ewynn's horses all of a sudden whinnied and collapsed dead to the ground. Then a guard screamed and several more were heard. Each one cut short by the gurgling, frothing blood escaping from an open wound in their throat.

'Damn it!' Trinity exclaimed. 'The light is causing darkness under their chins. The bloody thing is using it to slit their throats! Everyone get back!' Try as they might, nobody could move. The bright light had created a shadow directly underneath them and now it held them fast. By illuminating the area, she had hoped that her spell would have had a positive affect against the Shade, but the creature seemed to be even more lethal and deadly since it became whole again.

Trinity knew that she should extinguish her light spell but, out of the blue, she suddenly had a strong feeling of indifference wash over her. The sound of wind rushing past her ears was evident, not that she cared much given her current blasé attitude. It didn't last long, however, as a glistening flashing blade suddenly flew by, severing the elongated neck of the Shade which was draining her Essence.

The young mage blinked her eyes, as if she had just woken from a deep sleep, to see her sword sticking into a nearby wooden post, gently vibrating from the force Tristan had thrown it with.

The severed appendage of the Shade, which had already reformed another head, snaked its way back down her body and returned to the shadow beneath a startled Trinity. *It must have targeted me because I have the highest amount of Essence here*, she surmised, as she dispelled her lumin ball. *Or perhaps it remembered that I command magic and that I came close to destroying it before, and I'll be sure to finish the job given a second chance.*

These thoughts and many others formed in Trinity's mind when, suddenly, the Shade let out a long, monotonous groan and became stock still before it began to change from ebony black through the grey scales, to a brilliant white.

All the remaining warriors looked on in puzzlement. Finn opened Vincent's hatch and jumped down. 'What's it doing?'

'No idea, but we'd better stay ready,' cautioned Trinity. 'Be careful, Tristan!'

The brash adventurer, having retrieved Trinity's enchanted sword, ventured closer to the discoloured Shade. Using the flat edge of the sword, he struck the creature several times in different places, each time getting a resounding clang. 'I think it's dead,' he concluded after his investigation.

'That's strange. I remember my father saying that the Shades which were killed during the war dissolved into nothingness.'

'Perhaps it's not dead then,' Tristan rephrased as he slowly stepped away and raised the schiavona, just in case.

A huge crack suddenly appeared on the Shade, leading to a multitude of others to web out and cover its entire surface. Then it imploded, sending dust and debris everywhere.

It took a few moments for the implications of the events to sink in. Bewilderment swiftly gave way to unbound joy as the guards cheered and danced.

'It's dead! The Shade is dead!'

People in the nearby homes heard the shouts of jubilation and tentatively opened doors and windows, just to make sure it was safe, before they ventured out into the streets. As more and more onlookers joined the throng, the news that the Shade had been dispatched spread like wildfire throughout the city.

Tristan was all set to lead the way to the nearest ale house and kick the doors down in order to get a celebratory drink. But Tristan hadn't noticed that some were far from in the mood to be celebrating.

Trinity looked shell-shocked as she glared wide-eyed at the remains of the Shade. 'What about-'

'Daniel,' Finn sighed forlornly.

Her moment of potentially having something with Daniel had been stolen from her. It was just like she always said; her and fate were eternal enemies. Providence had screwed her again. Just as she had with Finn's first real love, Crellis. He was a member of his tribe's royal family, but not the heir, meaning that he didn't have to tow the line, that he could live his life and have fun with Finn. But an accident changed all that. Quinn had said that duty to his people would always come first, and it had.

The loss that Trinity now felt was nothing like she had experienced before. She didn't really know why she should be so devastated. Sure, she liked him, they had become friends, but she had made friends before, friends that she had left when she and Gydion had been searching for Daniel and moved from place to place and there were others that she left behind when it was becoming too difficult to explain away her youthful looks, and Gydion forbade her from (or couldn't be bothered) casting a spell of illusion to give her the suitable appearance.

As the two women stared at the dead Shade and thought about what could have been, the space that was once occupied by the creature began to shimmer. A swirling white spot appeared there, growing larger and brighter with every moment, until it was large enough for something to step through.

'Something's happening!' Trinity yelled as she and Finn took up a ready stance. Tristan and the others turned back to see what the commotion was and knew that their drink would have to wait.

A purple haze could be seen in the void, a haze that got more vivid and vibrant as the being it surrounded got closer to exiting the rift.

'Daniel? Is that you?' Trinity had instantly recognised the aura but was wary all the same. This Essence flare was significantly more volatile than what she had seen him produce back at college. This one was almost alive and it was affecting the space around him. She could taste his magic in the air, a metallic, ozone taste, and she felt it make her skin tingle and heard it crackle in the air as he slowly walked closer.

Even the usually cocksure Finn was cautious as an imperious Daniel stood before her and Trinity. 'We thought you were a goner, Daniel, but I'm so happy to see you made it! What happened in there? Where did you go?' She got no reply to her questions and turned to her red-haired companion as if seeking some answers and guidance on how to proceed, but all Trinity could do was give a concerned shrug.

'Look, someone else is coming through!' said Tristan suddenly as the survivors of the Shade stepped through the rift.

As they saw their friends and families, shouts of joy rang out. One of the last to come through was little Tommy Sanderson. He desperately looked around for his mother and, upon seeing her, called to her. Emily Sanderson, who had been talking to her neighbour about the recent events, thought was hearing things at first, but when she turned and saw him running towards her, she became so choked that she could barely say his name. He jumped into her arms and they hugged tightly as the crowd around them clapped and cheered.

'Look over there, Mummy,' Tommy said as he pointed back to the void. 'I found Daddy!'

The wraith that had been close to Tommy came through the portal and slowly took on the ghostly form of Gavin Sanderson, Tommy's father. The other wraiths followed and each turned into apparitions of their former selves.

A hush descended upon the crowd as they saw faces they recognised. Friends and families that never had a chance to say goodbye to loved ones who had disappeared were now given a second chance. Emily Sanderson couldn't believe her eyes as she once again saw the visage of the man she loved, married, and started a family with.

Still carrying Tommy, she edged closer to her husband, who smiled back at her. His lips moved as if to speak, but no words could be heard. Over and over he seemed to repeat words, to express his feelings, until she said 'I love you' and he finally felt she had understood.

All of a sudden, the apparition of Gavin Sanderson began to gleam like an incandescent beacon. Brighter and brighter he became, until it hurt to gaze upon him then, without warning, he vanished.

One by one, as they received their final farewells, each incorporeal being likewise disappeared until they were all gone. The gathered citizens of Almedia looked at one another and a pleasant sense of warmth radiated between them. As the sensations receded, the survivors of the Shade were excitedly asked questions about what had happened. Trinity listened hard and took particular notice of what was said, but she wasn't the only one.

'That's enough of that,' Fungal said as he suddenly appeared next to Trinity. He took a deep drag of his cigar, puffed out his cheeks, and blew the sparkling smoke over the people that were retelling the events that had happened within the Shade. 'That should stop them from flapping their lips too much. D'ya realise how bad this coulda been? An untrained mage doing the things he did? There are some that would want to control a power like that.'

'Like who?' asked a puzzled Trinity, but before the Hobthrust laird could answer, Daniel spoke.

'You didn't tell me it would be like this, Trinity. To be one with magic. To be in all places at once. I have read the records and seen what was, what is, and what will be. This is nothing like I could have imagined...that magic is alive...'

All of a sudden Daniel started to have a seizure, violently shaking, until with a whoosh his Essence extinguished and he collapsed, only to be caught by Trinity and Finn.

A FEW DAYS HAD PASSED since the Battle at Beltane, as it was being called, and life in the mortal capital of Almedia was getting back to normal. Repairs had already begun on the damaged buildings caused by the Shade and Finn's overexuberance with Vincent. Although the spectre of the Shade had been lifted, many had felt its deadly touch and some lives would never be the same again, but they were thankful that they were given the opportunity to say their goodbyes.

Daniel sat up in his infirmary bed and listened as Trinity told him what had been going on since he passed out, told him that he had exhausted his Essence reserves, that she had been transferring her own Essence into him until his reservoirs started producing again, something, he said, he would always be thankful for.

'...And apparently, this is the first time there has never been a goddess or consort chosen.'

'So what does that mean? That they'll have a bad harvest?'

'Well, the council have decided that you have more than shown your worth, against the Shade, to be the consort.'

'But I wasn't the only man fighting out there.'

'But you *were* the only one that brought those people back. You fought the creature by yourself. These people think you're a hero now.' Trinity gestured to all the gifts that had been brought whilst he had been unconscious. 'Besides,' she continued with a smile and a chuckle, 'you're the only one that still had their garland.'

Daniel smiled back. 'I just wish I could remember more of what happened. I was making sure my Essence was topped up, just like you told me to, and that's it, until waking up here a few hours ago.'

'Forget about it. You're alive, that's the main thing.' She gently took hold of his hand, felt its warmth. 'We were worried about you,' Trinity began. She kept her eyes fixed on their hands but as she corrected herself, she raised her head and looked straight into his yellow eyes. '*I* was worried about you.'

Daniel visibly swallowed as he heard Trinity's words.

'But,' the flower-scented redhead leaned forward and held a kiss on his forehead for a few seconds, 'if you do anything like that again, I'll kick your ass myself, understand?' she said in a sweet voice.

'Ahem!' Doyenne Swanston cleared her throat as she entered the ward and saw Trinity leaning over her patient. 'There'll be none of that in my infirmary, young lady. Now, young man, I am here to check on your condition and see if you will be able to participate in the proceedings tonight.'

'What proceedings?' asked Daniel.

'The crowning of the goddess, of course! The scuffle with the Shade may have forced us to abandon the remaining two events of the Beltane Festival but with you having been named consort and having a garland, we just need to find out who its maker was and your goddess will be found!' she said excitedly.

That evening, the grounds of the palace were filled with as many people of the city as could be squeezed in. The throng were gathered in a semi-circle around the front of a hastily erected dais, and an excited buzz filled the crowd.

A fanfare sounded which heralded the arrival of the council of three. Empress Xu Ping led the way from the palace and up the dais. She came to a stop at a mark on the platform with Chief Seydou and King Ewynn flanking either side of her. For the next few moments they stood there smiling and waving at their subjects, soaking up the adulation rained upon them for their benevolent and beneficial reign. In time, the empress raised her arms and the masses fell silent.

'This Beltane Festival has been like no other before it,' the empress began. 'This year's festival will go down in history as one that was not finished; one that saw the Shade return; one that saw the passing of friends,' the crowd murmured their ascent, 'but also the one that brought us a new generation of hero.' Cheers and applause rang out. 'In the annals of history, we had the Archmage Gydion, Eric Mondragon, Grimgaard Thunderbeard. And Archdruid Tavisum.' Each name was greeted with more cheers. 'Today we have Trinity Evergreen, the daughter of Gydion, our very own Tristan Sturm, and

Finnuala Quinn.' Again the people cheered. 'These people fought for us and with us for no better reason than it was the right thing to do. But there is one more that needs to be addressed here.'

The crowd cheered and chanted Daniel's name.

'This young man,' the empress continued, 'was not born of this world, although he has the blood of one of our greatest heroes running through his veins and the courage and bravery he showed, standing alone against the Shade's inner being, proved that he is worthy to carry the mantle of his father's name. Daniel Mondragon, please step forward.'

As he heard his name called, Daniel took several deep breaths in an effort to calm his racing heartbeat. When he was ready, just as he was about to step through the palace doors, one of the guards thrust a piece of parchment in his face and asked for an autograph. It took him by surprise and that feeling only increased while the doors were opened and the roar of the crowd hit him as he signed his name.

He walked the same path that the council of three had and wondered if his father had taken these very steps on his way to a ceremony of his own. The chants of his name got louder and louder, and the closer he got to the dais and as he took the stairs up the platform, the cheers erupted.

Doyenne Swanston had instructed Daniel on the etiquette of meeting the three royals; bowing to each in turn, no physical contact unless initiated by them, nothing he didn't expect when meeting royalty.

'Daniel,' Empress Xu Ping began after the rapturous applause had died down. 'We, the council of three, would firstly like to apologise for the false accusation brought against you. You cleared your name by defeating the Shade and rescuing the boy you were accused of killing. You showed your integrity and true nature, and as such, it has been decided, that through your actions, you have more than proven yourself worthy to be the consort of any goddess.' The gathered audience roared in agreement. 'The Beltane Festival games are used to discover the next consort, but they are also used to find our next goddess. Our suitor has a garland, we have found who made it, and now it is time to unite them.'

Another fanfare rang out and once again the palace doors opened. As people caught glimpses of who their next goddess would be, there were hushed whispers of shock and surprise that spread through the crowd.

Daniel kept his gaze looking out over the gathering, just as the doyenne had told him to. He had to wait until she was on the platform before he could turn to her and place the garland on her head.

All this pomp and ritual was giving him a headache. Daniel was far from used to being the centre of attention and yet here he was standing next to royalty, in another world in front of a huge crowd being called a hero and about to crown his 'goddess.' If he had been told that any of this would have happened to him a few days ago, he would have laughed his head off.

He felt her presence next to him and he slowly turned around. Daniel had caught her fragrance on the gentle breeze, the same as the aroma that came off the garland, and when he saw who it belonged to, he was astonished to say the least.

'What's wrong with you?' Finn whispered as she checked the neckline of her dress. 'Is something on show that's not supposed to be?'

'No, nothing at all,' replied Daniel as he admired her new surprising look.

The blast goggles, which he thought were a permanent feature, were no longer on the top of Finn's head but hung loosely around her neck. The doyennes no doubt disapproved of them, not fitting in with the whole god-dess ensemble. Her short violet hair was parted and styled in a faux bob, and this was the first time he had seen her in any sort of makeup. The dress she wore was made from layers of gossamer chiffon fabric, each coloured a differ-ent shade of green. It was sleeveless with a deep V-neckline, a crossed lace-up back, and a thigh-high front split, which barely hid the strap of her holster; another lost battle for the doyennes. Each side of the split was long and led to a trail of leaves behind her which completed the gown, but also revealed the hat-trick of losses for the matrons as, instead of the elegant heeled open-toed shoes Daniel was expecting, Finn was wearing her usual boots with the turn-down collar. It was a mismatch of styles but it was a look which she pulled off because of her strong will and individuality.

'Well, if there's nothing wrong,' Finn replied, 'maybe you should close your mouth, stop gawping, and put that bloody thing on my head, so I can get out of this vekting thing!' she said in hushed tones as she continued to smile and wave to the crowd.

Their initial surprise at seeing Finn as the goddess had given way to hope. Hope that this might be the catalyst in getting her to change her sassy ways, stop stealing, rebel rousing, and hanging out with her gang of reprobates and actually become a lady. Little did they know, that there was as much chance of that happening as there was of getting Finn to stop her light-fingered gang from making their way through the crowd at that very moment.

After enjoying seeing the gun-toting, pipe-smoking, gambling, drinking bandit squirm in her formal dress for a while, Daniel stepped forward and placed the garland on Finn's head, at which point the crowd went wild.

'Kiss her!' someone yelled out.

Before a bashful Daniel could even do anything, Finn had grabbed him by the collar, pulled him towards her, and kissed him hard, literally taking his breath away. She released him and he staggered back as the audience laughed and clapped their approval.

'That must be difficult t'watch,' Fungal said to Trinity, once again appearing out of thin air.

'Why should it be?'

'Och, come on now. Why be coy? Ye know and I know exactly how ye feel about the wee lad. Or have ye switched ye interests to Tristan? He did have ye garland after all. The simple one I believe. The one Daniel had and dropped.'

'How did you-'

'The nose knows, lassie,' chuckled Fungal.

'It doesn't matter anyway. The goddess and consort don't always get married, right? It's just a symbol thing.'

'True enough, true enough, I cannae deny that. There's been two or three times they havenae married out of the hundreds of years this festival has been run,' laughed Fungal just before he vanished to avoid Trinity's kick.

Daniel held Finn's hand as they were paraded around the dais, receiving the adoration of the citizens of Almedia. All Daniel had ever wanted was to be accepted for who he was and not ostracised for looking different. He had never thought that he would have to take a journey to another realm to find that acceptance. But he found more than that. He found new friends, a strength he never knew he had, and an inner belief that was recognised and honoured by others. The position of consort to the goddess would last only a year but the title, champion of Almedia, would last a lifetime and beyond.

THE END

About the Author

Currently residing in London, England, D.G. Palmer writes in the Spec Fiction genre, using his imagination to create vivid worlds and captivating characters.

An avid reader and player of video games, in the past, he was part of table top roleplaying groups where he nurtured his storytelling by penning several story arcs.

Feel free to follow him on Facebook[1], Goodreads[2] and Instagram[3]. If you wish to receive updates about his latest books, event dates and other exclusive news, sign up to The World of D.G. Palmer[4] and enter his mind. He warns it can be a mess sometimes, so make sure you wipe your feet on the way out – you never know what you might take with you.

---

1. https://www.facebook.com/des.palmer.12

2. http://www.goodreads.com/dgpalmerindieauthor

3. https://www.instagram.com/dgpcreativesolutions/

4. http://www.dgpalmer.com

ACKNOWLEDGEMENTS

Although being an author can, at times, be seen as being a solitary venture, the truth is that behind every author is a team. I would like to take this opportunity to thank all those that helped me with this book.

Thank you to my editors, Danielle Wrates and Kerrie McLoughlin, I promise to give you less work next time. My beta readers Jelice Ramsey and Jen Henderson. Many thanks to Emma Andrews and the rest of the ARC team. And I can't forget George Long for the amazing cover.

Thank you to all my family, friends, and supporters and a final huge, big thank you to you, the reader. None of this would be possible without each of you.

A final word

Thank you for reading this book from the mind of D.G. Palmer!

If you enjoyed it, please take a moment to leave a review to help spread the word, increase its visibility and help it reach more readers.

Leave a note even if you didn't, after all, one person's trash is another person's bestseller!

And finally, don't forget to sign up to <u>The World of D.G. Palmer</u> to stay up to date with new releases and get exclusives!

Don't miss out!

Visit the website below and you can sign up to receive emails whenever D G Palmer publishes a new book. There's no charge and no obligation.

https://books2read.com/r/B-A-JGOH-OYHZ

BOOKS 2 READ

Connecting independent readers to independent writers.

Also by D G Palmer

The Chronicles of Daniel Welsh
Birth of The Mortokai

Standalone
The Choices Of Man

Watch for more at https://www.dgpalmer.com.

www.ingramcontent.com/pod-product-compliance
Lightning Source LLC
Chambersburg PA
CBHW032304070726
47590CB00015B/424

9 781838 038441